THE
LAST
TRAVELER

BOOK 1 IN THE LAST TRAVELER SERIES

MELISSA E. DAY

BQB

Virginia

The Last Traveler: Book 1 in *The Last Traveler series*
© 2023 Melissa E. Day. All rights reserved.

This is a work of fiction. All of the characters, names, incidents, organizations, and dialogue in this novel are either the products of the author's imagination or are used fictitiously.

Published in the United States by BQB Publishing
(an imprint of Boutique of Quality Books Publishing Company, Inc.)
www.bqbpublishing.com

978-1-952782-89-3 (p)
978-1-952782-90-9 (e)

Library of Congress Control Number: 2022952399

Book Design by Robin Krauss, www.bookformatters.com
Cover Design by Rebecca Lown, www.rebeccalowndesign.com
First editor: Andrea Vande Vorde
Second editor: Allison Itterly

This book is dedicated to:
Regan, for being there from the very beginning
and Joshua, for seeing me through to the end.

Content Warning

The Last Traveler is a contemporary YA Sci-Fi/Fantasy that explores an exciting new world and some complex social topics. Some of the content may not be suitable for certain readers. The story contains depictions of parental abuse and violence against a minor above the age of 15, mention of homophobia and homophobic slurs, the use of alcohol, and mention of violence against a fictional marginalized community. Readers who may be sensitive to any of these topics, please take note.

CHAPTER 1

Paxton Graves buried her feet in the moist sand and let the tide lap over them as she looked out to the horizon at the setting sun. The warm sea breeze sent her long black hair dancing in every direction. Her cool, gray eyes squinted in the sunlight to marvel at the tangerine sky. As she stood soaking in the tranquil silence, she was filled with unease. She reached down and grabbed a handful of the rust-colored sand, letting the grains fall through her fingertips.

Suddenly, the truth dawned on her. A rush of memories came flooding back. Memories of this same sunset on this same beach that she had seen a thousand times before. Except she hadn't actually been there at all.

"This isn't real," she whispered to reassure herself. "This isn't real!" she shouted at the sky.

Then, as if she'd angered the sea, the roaring waves grew louder and louder. Her confusion became complete terror as the ear-splitting roar of an engine filled her ears and the ground beneath her began to shake.

"No!" she screamed and covered her ears. Her vision blurred until she could no longer see that beautiful sunset.

Suddenly, she was falling. It was as if she had been sucked into a black hole. Her chest grew heavy, but her body was weightless as if she were only a whisper drifting through an infinite void. Then, in a split second, the impact of cold, hard tile against her face.

Her eyes flung open. It took a moment for her vision to focus on the face of her science teacher, Mr. Hornsby. His beady blue eyes stared intently down at her through the lenses of his thick glasses.

"Ms. Graves, if you please, next time you decide to use my class for nap time, could you be sure that you do not disrupt the rest of the class?"

Her classmates snickered all around her as she gathered herself from the floor and dusted off the back of her favorite slouchy black jeans.

"Yes, Mr. Hornsby."

"How gracious of you. And you will see me in the office after class."

"Ooh!" the rest of the class taunted in anticipation of the reproof to come.

"And unless the rest of you would like to join her, I suggest you wipe those grins off your faces and keep to your own business. Now, as I was—" Mr. Hornsby's lecture was promptly interrupted by the sound of the school bell reverberating from the intercom overhead. "Bollocks," he muttered under his breath. "We will continue this tomorrow. Hopefully without interruption."

Pax ignored his pointed jab and quickly shoved her notebook into her backpack before slipping out the door behind the throng of her classmates.

Eyes. That was all Pax could think about as she trudged down the long corridor of Golden Valley High. She could feel them on her back, watching her every step, as she descended among the crowd of teenagers swarming through the hall. She was used to the stares by now. The feeling of being watched had become second nature to her. In the pristine suburbia of Golden Valley, she was practically an alien. The girl whose mom had vanished without a trace. It was the biggest news in the little town for most of her childhood. She used to wish that one day everyone would wake up with no eyes so she wouldn't have to see the pity on their faces. But now she was sixteen, and the pity they once held turned to outright disdain. The poor, sad little girl whose mom vanished became the tall, lanky girl who wore her clothes two sizes too big and wouldn't look you in the eyes when you spoke to her.

In the town of shiny families who drove shiny cars and flashed fake porcelain smiles, she was always the freak. She wasn't an heiress or a future CEO. She was nothing to them, which was just fine with Pax. Aside from the two best friends she'd had since middle school, she didn't care much for the people of Golden Valley either. She had grown comfortable with being invisible.

But then the dreams came.

At first it was only at night, but this past year her dreams seemed to have taken on a life of their own. They would come at any time—in class, in the passenger seat of the car, in the middle of the school assembly—whenever they pleased and without warning. One moment she was awake, and the next she was sprawled out on the floor of her science class, screaming and covered in sweat, staring up at the faces of her peers whose expressions ranged from amused to outright horrified.

She could hear the snickers, the whispers, the jeers of her classmates as she made her way down the hall. She rolled her eyes as she shouldered past Gordy, a large basketball player.

"Hey! Looks like one of the aliens escaped from the spaceship," Gordy muttered to his friend as she slipped past.

Pax snorted. "Original," she said loud enough for him to hear. Then a hard tug at her scalp forced her head backward and she let out a gasp. She looked back to find Gordy had grabbed her long, messy ponytail with his meaty hands.

His face contorted into a dark smirk. Embarrassment and anger tinged her cheeks red as she met his eyes with disdain. Fear rose inside of her, but she mustered enough courage to grit her teeth and grumble, "Let go."

"Randy, did you hear something?" Gordy asked the freckled boy standing next to him with acne scars sprinkled on his cheeks, clad in a matching red Golden Valley jersey.

Randy guffawed. "No, I don't speak Martian. Do you, Gordy?"

Gordy shook his head. "I wonder if the human mask is glued on to her face. Let's find out." He tightened his grip on her hair and tugged.

Pax clenched her jaw, resisting the shriek of pain that climbed up her throat. He wanted a scene, to humiliate her, but Pax was sick of these games, and today she decided she wouldn't give him the satisfaction. When the dreams started to come more frequently and the teasing became relentless, she had always kept her head down and her mouth shut, trying to remain invisible. But she was tired and angry, and against her better nature, she growled, "Let go of me!" and stamped down hard on his foot with the heel of her lace-up black platform boots.

"Agh!" he yelped. The bustling hall grew silent as eyes from every direction zeroed in on the exchange. The boy loosened his grip on her hair and sent Pax tumbling to the sticky floor.

"What in the name of Satan's child is going on over here?" a voice called from behind. The crowd of bystanders parted as Mr. Hornsby came pushing through the crowd. He was a small man who stood with a hunch and wore old, wrinkled blazers that seemed to swallow him whole. In spite of his stature and quirky disposition, he had a commanding presence and a gruff British accent that, for whatever reason, seemed to make the otherwise feral students of Golden Valley respect him. He stood squarely in front of Pax, and his gray bushy eyebrows furrowed as he squinted at the two of them from behind his thick, black-rimmed glasses.

Pax's chest tightened as she picked herself up from the floor. She stammered but couldn't find the words to explain herself.

"Nothing," Gordy grumbled, and he smoothed his basket-ball jersey. "She just came up and stomped on my foot for no reason."

Her mouth dropped and the anger came flooding back in a rush. "What?"

"Hush, Ms. Graves." Mr. Hornsby put a hand up. "Did anyone else see what happened?" he called to the crowd.

"Yeah!" Randy piped up. "Gordy was out here minding his own business, then this girl pushed him, and when he said, 'Excuse me,' she came back and stomped on his foot."

Gordy nodded as he lifted his foot and massaged the toe of his shoe for effect.

"Why would Pax do that?" Mr. Hornsby questioned. He actually seemed dubious for a moment.

"I don't know, sir, she's a psycho. Maybe it's her time of the month or something!" Gordy offered, still massaging his toes.

Against her will, she heard herself fire back, "Of course. A woman couldn't have any other reason to be angry except when she's on her period." Her peers chuckled behind her.

"Enough, Ms. Graves!" Mr. Hornsby started. In frustration, he pushed a hand through the thin tuft of wiry white hair that sat at the top of his head, causing it to stick out in every direction. "I would write you a referral, but if I recall, you should already be on your way to the principal's office for your little outburst in fifth period."

The boys snickered from behind him. She shot them a piercing glare before saying, "Yes, sir."

"And don't forget about detention on Monday." Mr. Hornsby waved his hand toward the front office. "Off you go then."

"Yeah, go see Daddy," Jordy whispered.

"The rest of you, bugger off!" Mr. Hornsby shouted to the crowd as he waved his hands above his head, shooing the students in each direction.

Pax sighed in resignation, then turned on her heel to head in the opposite direction, leaving the hoops of laughter and taunting behind her.

CHAPTER 2

O nce Pax reached the office, her anger had subsided and was replaced with humiliation. Tears burned her eyes, but she shook it off quickly as she opened the door. She steeled herself for another meeting with Mrs. Schriber, the too-cheery guidance counselor. She loved to wear fifties-style cat eyeglasses and lots of polka dots. The administration never knew what to do with Pax's outbursts, so they deferred to Mrs. Schriber, whose approach typically involved a lot of positive affirmation and guided meditations. Her boots squeaked against the freshly mopped floors as she approached the secretary's desk.

Mrs. Wiles, the secretary, was a petite old woman with withered fingers and nails on the end that she always painted fire-engine red and kept long and filed to a fine point. Pax hated the sound of those pointy claws clicking against the keyboard. The woman barely looked up when Pax entered the room. She continued to click away as she mumbled, "Conference room. They're ready for you."

Pax paused. "They? I'm not going to see Mrs. Schriber?"

"She's there too," Mrs. Wiley responded as she shoveled a handful of potato chips into her mouth with one hand and continued to peck at the keyboard with the other.

"Well, then who—"

Mrs. Wiles cut her off with a heavy sigh and pulled her reading glasses off her face. "Look," she said between crunches of potato chips. "I'm not a teacher, which means I don't get paid to sit here and answer your questions all day." She jerked her thumb to point to the room behind her.

Pax stuffed her hands into her pockets and made her way to the conference room. When she rounded the corner and entered the doorway, she stopped dead in her tracks. There at the long mahogany table sat three of her least-favorite teachers: Mrs. Knox, the math teacher; Mr. Patrick, her history teacher; and of course Mrs. Schriber, the guidance counselor. Seated at the head of the table was Principal Victor Graves: her father.

"Ah, Ms. Graves! So glad you could join us!" Mrs. Schriber waved her over to the seat across from her.

She tried to obey, but her knees locked and her feet stayed glued to the floor. She rubbed her hands against her old jeans to wipe the sweat from her palms. "Hey," she said quietly.

"Please sit, Paxton," her father prompted again through his wide smile. Principal Graves was a polished man. He always wore a suit and slicked his dark brown hair back with an absurd amount of product, which made it so stiff it looked painted on his head. He spoke with an air of charm and oozed charisma that seemed to impress the parents but always felt cold and empty. Her father was a transplant to the Golden Valley community. Originally from Alabama, he moved to Ohio before she was born, working tirelessly to erase the stigma that their family was nothing but backwoods hicks. He enunciated every syllable, and always wore a big smile and an expensive suit, desperate to gain the favor of the Golden Valley elite. He had succeeded too, and was up for a seat on the school board this year, a fact that Pax was constantly reminded of when she screwed up. She glanced at him again, noting that his usual painted-on smile looked tight and forced.

"Paxton," he prompted again.

She hadn't realized she was still standing at the doorway, staring at them. "Sir?" she swallowed.

"Sit," he said firmly.

She nodded and moved so quickly that she stumbled over her feet, causing her to practically collapse into the rolling chair and collide with his. "Sorry," she mumbled.

He ran a hand over his hair and cleared his throat. Annoyance flashed across his face for a split second, but he quickly recovered. "Now, Pax, do you know why you are here?"

She shifted in her seat. "Because I fell asleep in class again?" she offered quietly.

"What was that?"

She looked into her father's penetrating glare. "I said . . . because I fell asleep."

"Your teachers called this meeting with me out of concern for you," he explained.

"Oh—"

Mr. Patrick spoke up from the corner of the room. "Your episodes are becoming a problem to the other students, Ms. Graves, and we are at a loss. That is why we decided to pull your father in on this one."

Shame and frustration burned in her stomach, slowly making its way through her body. *Episodes.* She inwardly rolled her eyes at the word the adults had come up with to refer to her dreams. Of course, Pax didn't know what to call them either, but "episodes" made it sound like she was having some kind of fit. This was not the first conference she had been called to about her episodes. They always ended the same way, with everyone agreeing that Pax was the problem and there was no solution.

"All right then, team . . . how can I help?" Her father flashed a grin that didn't quite meet his eyes.

The teachers shifted nervously in their seats, exchanging glances with one another, each silently begging someone to take the reins. Mrs. Schriber finally jumped in.

"Well, you know, Principal Graves, I have had several meetings with Pax myself, and we've tried lots of interventions and coping strategies, but nothing seems to be working. And I know . . . things have been hard since her mother—"

Principal Graves cut her off suddenly. "Yes, well, I am aware that has caused quite a strain on her, but that was a long time ago. Let's not rehash old issues. What can we do to move forward? I would love to hear some solutions."

Mrs. Schriber hesitated, less confident now. "I think it would be great for Pax to see a therapist. And perhaps she could be homeschooled for the rest of her junior year." Her voice came up at the end as if it were a question.

Pax's heart sank. She looked over at her father. He readjusted his red silk tie and smoothed down his shirt. Then he smiled as he fixed his eyes on her and his voice came out cool and even. It sent shivers down her spine. "That won't be necessary. Will it, Pax?"

Her heart clenched. She lifted the corner of her lips into a halfhearted smile. "No, I think I'm just . . . having a hard time."

"I'll take care of it," he offered as his hand clasped onto her shoulder.

Mrs. Schriber and the other teachers smiled in relief. "That is so good to hear."

The group droned on, but all Pax could hear was the soft echo of her father's voice: *I'll take care of it.* Her heartbeat sputtered and her breath quickened. She felt lightheaded, and the air suddenly felt thinner. She stood suddenly and snapped, "Are we done?" She hadn't meant to bark it at them, but she had to get out of there.

"Paxton," her father warned.

"Sorry." She took a deep breath

Her father's jaw tightened. "I suppose."

She nodded curtly. "Thank you. I'll see you at home," she managed to choke out as she spun on her heels and sped out of the main office. Her chest felt tight and heavy, and her breath was coming out in erratic bursts. School had ended about twenty minutes ago and the halls were now empty of students, a fact Pax was immediately thankful for as the flood of tears she had been holding back spilled over her cheeks. She slammed through the double doors at the school's entrance, ran down the concrete steps, and took a left away from the parking lot where her father's car was parked. She knew she would have to see him eventually, but when her mind replayed the last thing he had said—*I'll take care of it*—her whole body screamed at her to run. He needed time to cool off, and so did she. She leaned against the cold red brick at the corner of the school and inhaled a sharp breath, letting the air sting her lungs. She held it until her vision grew spotty, then exhaled heavily. She did this several more times, and when her panic subsided, she decided to take the long way home.

The wind blew harshly across her face, drying the tears streaming down her cheeks as she walked. She shivered. The sky was murky and gray, and the ground was still mushy from the last rain. It was the kind of day that she would often find herself wishing to be back in her dreams. Even though they always ended with her screaming in a heap on the floor, there was something about that beach. The way the emerald waters rolled onto the shoreline and stretched to kiss the horizon streaked with ribbons of orange and pink. But most of all, it felt so real.

Like her own private paradise away from her father, from her classmates, from Golden Valley. Sadly, the bliss only lasted for a second before it gave over to sheer terror. But she wished she could somehow find a way to live in that bliss forever. She had wanted to escape her life for as long as she could remember, or at least as long as her mother had been gone.

Pax remembered being five years old and waking up one morning to the sound of sirens outside their house. Her mom had gone missing in the night, but her car was still in the driveway, her clothes were still in her dresser, and no one had seen or heard from her. She remembered the look on her father's face. It was the only time in her life she had ever seen him afraid. The days and weeks following her mom's disappearance were agony. She spent most of her days staring out of windows, waiting for her mom to come walking up the driveway. Her father had given up so easily after the police declared her mother's disappearance a cold case. He locked every remnant of her memory away, and his humanity with it. Pax, however, remained hopeful even after days, and then weeks, and then months. But as the months turned into one year, and then five, her hope became suffocated by the burden of her grief. It had been nearly ten years now, and the hope she once held was snuffed out, now only a pile of ash without so much as an ember.

She used to daydream about her mom coming back and taking her somewhere where it would be just them and they could be happy. She got used to living in her daydreams before the dreams had ever started. Pax's grandmother used to tell her, "Girl, your feet are on the floor, but your head is in the sky." That was a nice way of putting it. For some reason, her life had never been able to hold her attention. Even on her best day, she was only half present.

She wandered slowly up and down the sidewalk of the Golden Valley suburbs, watching packs of women in different shades of Spandex leggings jog around the block, laughing together with their fluffy little dogs. She took her time, stopping to look at the multistory McMansions that lined each side of the street. By the time she came to a stop just outside her house, the sky was growing dark. The modest two-bedroom home sat just off the curb. It used to belong to Pax's grandmother, but she passed away two years after her mother's disappearance and left the home to Pax's father.

"Welcome home," Pax muttered sarcastically. It was all she could do to keep herself from going into a panic. She didn't know what was waiting for her on the other side of that door, but she knew she'd have to face it eventually. She set her lips in a straight line to keep her teeth from chattering. Her moist palm twisted the doorknob. As the door opened, nobody was there despite the pale light in the kitchen. It was eerily quiet. Maybe he wasn't home yet. Her father usually worked for an hour or so after the school day ended, and they didn't live far, so she would often decide to walk home. Today she had taken the long way and stayed out later than necessary in hopes that it would give him time to calm down before they saw each other again. She quietly shut the door and prepared to tiptoe through the kitchen.

"Did you think you could sneak past me?" his voice sounded from the living room..

Pax's head whipped over her shoulder. "No, sir," she said quietly. He was sitting in his recliner, a glass of bourbon in hand. His charming principal-of-the-year persona was long gone and replaced with the cold, hollow version of himself that he only showed to her. It was always so confusing to Pax how he could just turn it on and off like that. When she was younger, she used to think his evil twin had replaced him when he came home. But this was the real him. The charismatic leader was just a facade he put on to convince the rest of the world that he hadn't become an empty shell of a person after her mom skipped out on them all those years ago.

He took a long, slow sip from his glass. "That's good. You know you can't get anything past me."

She nodded.

He leaned back and took another sip. "Do you think it's fun embarrassing me? Hm?" he prompted.

"No, that's not—I don't know what's happening." They had never talked about her episodes in much detail. Her father preferred to ignore them and pretend they weren't happening, most of the time. But when they did talk about it, he approached the whole thing as if she was just a misbehaved child acting out for attention. Which usually meant punishment.

She frantically searched for an answer that would placate him. "I've been trying, Dad, I really don't know what to do—"

He stood from his chair and held up a hand, signaling for her to stop. He stalked forward until he was standing over her. "No. I'll tell you what you're going to do."

She nodded as he brought his face so close to hers that she could smell the liquor on his breath.

His tone came out in a soft cadence that chilled her bones. "You're going to stop these outbursts, or I will make sure you stop."

"Dad." She let out a breath in a shudder as a cry climbed up her throat. "I can't help it. I don't know how to stop it, I swear—" Her breath stopped short as her father's hand made contact with her cheek. A stinging shock surged down the left side of her face. She let out one hard gasp, then held her breath. She willed her tears to stop. She would not give him the satisfaction of seeing her cry. She steeled her jaw as he dug his hand into her bicep.

"I don't think you understood me. I said you *will* stop. Understood?"

She nodded. "Yes."

"Yes, what?" he growled.

"Yes, sir."

He released his grip and smiled. "That's my girl. You know, I really don't want to be this way. Things are just so much nicer when we can get along."

Pax hugged her arms and nodded.

He sighed. "Well, I'm going out for a while. Do your homework, all right?"

"Okay," she whispered.

He opened the front door, then stopped and turned to her once more. "Oh, and Paxton? Don't go anywhere."

Pax placed her hand over her cheek and leaned back against the wall. She let her tears flow down her cheeks. This wasn't the first time her father had lashed out at her in anger, but it never stopped surprising her how scary he could be when he was like that.

As a child, she often wondered what she'd done to make him so angry. Now she knew it had to have been one simple reason: she was her mother's child. The woman had abandoned him and left him with the burden of raising their child. She could see the resentment in his eyes every time he looked at her. She didn't see much of herself in her father. Truthfully, they didn't even look alike. Her dad was a handsome man. She had heard the other girls at school say so on numerous occasions when they giggled and whispered about him in the halls. His high cheek bones, sharp, square jawline, and sparkling blue eyes invited people in and made them want to trust him. Pax was tall, like him, but that was where the similarities ended. While he was all chiseled and angular, her features were soft and childlike. She had a round face, and wide, innocent eyes that sat too far apart for her liking, and were almost comically out of proportion with her little doll lips.

Pax's dad often told her she was just like her mother, especially when Pax had done something to make him upset. She didn't know if he said it just to hurt her, or because it was true.

Pax slowly slid down the wall to the floor and gathered her knees to her chest. She rested her head against her folded arms, and suddenly she was exhausted as if she hadn't slept in days. Her eyelids grew heavy, and her head bobbed up and down. She knew what was coming, but she was too tired to fight it. She let her muscles sink against the wall, and then she was falling.

CHAPTER 3

When Pax woke up, the room was dark. She must have slept longer than she thought. She sprang up from the floor, knowing her father would be home soon, and if she was anywhere around while he was drunk, she'd be in trouble.

It was unnaturally warm. It was late fall, and their house was always a bit drafty, so by the time the sun went down, she usually had to put on a sweater. Disoriented, she reached out to grasp the wall, but her hand found nothing but air. She became aware of the sound of waves lapping against the shore. She was on the beach again. She was dreaming. But it was always daytime on the beach when she dreamed of it in the past. This time, the beach was cast in the shadow of night.

Well, what now? She rose off the sand and looked around, trying to find some indicator of where she was in this dream world, but it was utterly pitch-black except for the stars. Where was the moon? She stumbled around in the ankle-deep sand that poured into her shoes.

So, I'm in a dream where it's completely dark and nothing happens? So much for my imagination.

Suddenly, she heard footsteps. She shut her eyes and whispered, "It's just a dream." The approaching footsteps sounded as if they'd come to an abrupt halt.

"Who's there?" Pax called nervously. She advanced in the direction she'd heard the footsteps. She could vaguely make out the shape of another body a few feet in front of her. It appeared to be completely frozen. She reached out to touch it. The person gasped and jumped backward in fear. Now confident in the fact that she was dreaming, Pax was no longer afraid.

"I'm not going to hurt you," she said.

"Who are you?" the voice inquired in a harsh whisper.

The longer this dream dragged on, the more curious it got. How could it be that the people in her dream world didn't recognize her? "I'm Pax," she responded.

"What are you doing here?" the voice said louder. She realized now that the voice belonged to a boy.

"I . . ." Pax stumbled for the words to explain herself. After all, how could she explain that this was just a figment of her subconscious imagination? "I . . . don't know. I just fell asleep at home, then I woke up here. Where is the moon?"

"Moon?" the boy inquired. Before Pax could explain, the boy interrupted, "Oh no, you're one of them." Panic rose in his voice.

"One of who?"

"You have to go now." He gripped her shoulders roughly. "You have to go back where you came from. They will kill you!"

Pax tried to shake herself from his grip, but he was strong. Then it was as if a heavy weight pressed down on her and she couldn't move. Her vision blurred into complete blackness, and then there it was—the terror.

The boy was still yelling her name. "Pax! Pax!"

She couldn't respond. She needed to get out of this dream. "Wake up!" she shouted at herself, but no voice came. She had to remove herself from this crushing weight.

"*Pax!*" the voice screamed again.

Suddenly, her strength came back with a jolt and her eyes shot open. She was back in her living room at home. Her heart rate accelerated and she went into a panic. *What just happened?*

"Pax!" someone shouted. She could still hear the boy's voice. No, this voice was more familiar. It wasn't the boy from her dream. It was her best friend Zeke. He was leaning over her, his dark brown eyes filled with panic.

"Pax, please tell me you're all right. Can you hear me?"

It took her a moment to find her voice to respond. "Zeke," she croaked.

He sighed in relief. "I came to see if you wanted to hang out, but when I knocked on the door no one answered. Then I saw you passed out on the floor, and I thought . . ."

"I'm okay," Pax replied, as she tried to pick herself up.

"Whoa, take it easy for a minute," he said softly, guiding her back to the floor.

Pax winced in pain as her head came back against the wall. It felt as if she had been run over by a train, but she was relieved to see Zeke. They'd become friends when he and his family moved next door six years ago. Pax was pretty good at keeping her father's anger problem a secret. She kept her head down and didn't say much, but it hadn't taken long for Zeke to figure out what was going on.

He wanted to report her father, but Pax begged him not to. She was too afraid of what would happen to her if everyone knew. Zeke knew that fear all too well. He had been out of the system for six years after being adopted by his foster mom, Abby. Before that, he was moved around from house to house, each foster parent worse than the last. He would never put another kid through that. Since that time, Zeke personally assigned himself as her big brother and protector.

"What happened this time?"

"It's a long story," she returned.

"Don't give me that."

She sighed in resignation. "Fine."

She explained to Zeke what happened in class earlier and about her dream. When she finished, Zeke sat quietly, going over the information in his head.

"So, you fell asleep in class and your dad slapped you in the face," he said humorlessly.

"You know I didn't just fall asleep."

"So, the dreams . . . they're getting worse?"

She nodded. "I don't know what it is. It just seems so real."

"How long have you been having this dream?"

"I don't know, since freshman year, I think? I don't remember the first time though. I've seen the beach before in my dreams. You know, like flashes of it or vague pictures in my head, but it's gotten worse with the fainting and stuff. Then today I—" Pax stopped short. It was the first time she'd met anyone in her dream, and she didn't know what to make of it. "It's just getting exhausting. That's all," she said.

"Yeah." He sighed and placed an arm around her shoulders as he settled next to her against the wall.

"There was a boy in my last dream." She found herself opening up to him in spite of herself. But then again, it had always been like that with Zeke. Pax had never had a guy friend before Zeke. As a matter of fact, she had spent most of her life trying to avoid boys, considering that the large majority of her experiences with them had been less than positive. But Zeke was different. He was warm and kind, and in spite of her efforts to close herself off to him, he kept coming around. He had broken her down, and Pax was eternally grateful for his persistence because she had never had a better friend.

"Oh, really? Anyone I would know?" Zeke teased.

She rolled her eyes. "No."

"Huh. Well, what did he look like?"

She shrugged. "It was too dark to tell. There was no moon in my dream. But when I asked the boy where the moon was, he freaked out and told me I had to leave. He actually grabbed my shoulders pretty hard . . ." Her voice trailed.

"What?" Zeke asked.

Pax quickly stripped off her school sweatshirt and lifted up the sleeves of her T-shirt underneath. Her shoulders were a little sore where the boy had grabbed her, so she thought he might have left a mark. When she realized how ridiculous that thought was, she sighed and plopped back against the wall.

"Pax, what just happened?"

"Nothing. My arms were sore, and I just thought . . ." She couldn't bring herself to say what she thought. "I was just being stupid."

"You're not being stupid. I think if all this was happening to me, I'd be pretty freaked out too. Your dad probably grabbed you too hard, huh?"

She nodded. "Yeah, that's probably it." Pax rested her head on his shoulder, taking in his comfort. She tried to shake off the eerie feeling that was rolling down her spine, but a million thoughts raced through her mind. She remembered the boy's words: *They'll kill you.* She could still feel his hands on her shoulders, gripping them as if he were holding on for fear of his life. Even though she decided to accept that it was just a very bizarre dream, just like all the others, in the back of her mind she knew it wasn't over yet.

"What time is it?" Pax asked.

"Uh, half-past six. Why?"

"Wow. I was out for about an hour before you came in."

"Are you okay? I mean, do you need to see a doctor or something?"

"No. I feel fine. I just—" Pax stopped short when she heard the wheels of her father's old Volvo pulling up to the curb. Pax and Zeke exchanged glances of mild panic. "Go out the back."

"Yep." He sprang to his feet and made his way to the back door. He turned to Pax. "If you need anything, come get me."

She smiled sadly and nodded. Footsteps approached the door. "Go."

Zeke gave her one last worried glance and quietly left just as the front door opened.

Pax grabbed her science book off the coffee table and sat on the couch, attempting to look busy. Out of the corner of her eye, she saw her father slightly stumble over the front step. He usually only drank at home, but sometimes when he'd had a particularly bad day, he would drive to a little hole-in-the-wall bar in the next town over where no one would recognize him.

He fumbled with his keys, but when he saw Pax on the couch, he stopped short. "Leanah?" he slurred.

She looked up at him in shock. Leanah was her mother's name. He must've been extremely drunk.

Before she even had a chance to respond, he straightened a little and cleared his throat. "I, um . . ." He shifted awkwardly. "I'm going to bed." Then he pushed past her without another word.

Pax couldn't help but feel sorry for her father, sometimes. The woman he loved had disappeared without warning of where she was going or why, and she'd left him with a kid whom he didn't care for. She wondered what her father was like before her mom left. She couldn't really remember. Was he cold and cruel back then too? Why else would her mom leave? An overwhelming sadness filled Pax's heart. Maybe her mom didn't want her either. She shook the thought from her mind for the moment. She had too many other things to worry about.

She was in desperate need of a shower. She trudged toward the bathroom at the end of the dark hallway, flipped on the lights, and quietly shut the door. As soon as her feet hit the tub, she jumped out. The water was still ice cold. She sighed in frustration. She resigned to a quick, cold rinse. She sprinted across the drafty hall to her room and immediately slipped on a pair of sweats and her mother's old gray sweatshirt before sinking into bed.

She mindlessly traced the aged lettering across the front of the sweatshirt that once read "Ohio State." Did her mom go to school there? She guessed so, but of course she didn't really know. Her father would certainly never tell her. But it didn't matter. It was the only thing she had left of her mother. The year after she left, Pax had dug it out of a pile of her mom's things her father left by the trash dump. The year they had given up all hope she would return. Sometimes Pax felt stupid clinging so tightly to this little memento of a woman who didn't care to come back for her.

But even though the memories of her mom had faded long ago, she knew she had cared for Pax. Her smile was always warm. She often sang songs to her in a language that Pax didn't recognize, but it always comforted her. She had a vague memory of her mom holding her one night, clinging her closely to her chest, rocking her back and forth, and humming.

"I wish I could take you away with me, baby," her mother had said.

A tear slipped down Pax's cheek, her heart aching with longing. Even after all these years, long after the memory of her mother's voice, her smell, and even her face had faded, the wanting never did.

CHAPTER 4

Pax sighed with relief at the sound of her father's car sputtering to life outside. Her body relaxed into the bed for a moment. Two years ago, when Pax started her freshman year at Golden Valley High, she and her father came to a mutual agreement that it would be best if she didn't arrive at school with him. She already caught so much crap for being the principal's daughter, and being seen walking in together was unbearable. Most days she either walked or had her friends pick her up.

She hadn't dreamed at all last night. It disappointed her. In the back of her mind, she wondered if she could get back into that dream beach, or whatever it was, so she could find the boy again. But now it all seemed so ridiculous. She shook the idea out of her head. Zeke was right. She had definitely been overreacting to the whole thing. She groaned and rolled sluggishly out of bed to dress for school.

She opened the drawer of her dresser and sighed at the state of it. Her clothes were crammed in haphazardly, and it was filled to the brim with old T-shirts and old jeans she had thrifted. She was struck with indecision for a moment, but then ultimately decided on her black oversized Andy Warhol tee that had the giant can of Campbell's soup printed on the front with tight black-and-white-striped long sleeves underneath for warmth. She donned her favorite pair of vintage wide-leg jeans she had scored from a yard sale. She scratched at the strip of white paint splattered across her left pant leg, no doubt left over from her last sculpture in art class.

Pax wasn't much for her regular school subjects. She struggled to keep up in almost every class, but she thrived in her art class. It was the place where she felt most at home, mostly because she could zone out and focus on whatever project she was working on. Her specialty was sculptures made of trash. She did her first trash sculpture in eighth grade when her school was doing a big push for on-campus recycling during "Green Week." She'd made a giant green sloth made out of Sprite bottles. She knew it was kind of a weird hobby, and it certainly didn't help her reputation to be known as the girl who collected other people's garbage, but she loved the idea of taking something that someone else had discarded and making it into something interesting. Plus, she had gotten to learn how to use power tools to put together some of her bigger pieces, which made her feel pretty badass. She straightened the little kitty-cat trinket she had made with copper wire that sat on top of her dresser. Just as she slipped on her old leather Docs, she heard knocking at her front door.

"Hey, Pax!" a voice sang from her doorway. Pax smiled and rolled her eyes. Ayana was always annoyingly perky, but Pax liked that about her.

Along with Zeke, Ayana had been her closest friend since middle school, but the reason why she had chosen to befriend Pax was absolutely beyond her. They were different in every sense of the word. Ayana was sunshine and warmth, always joking, always up for adventure. She had dragged Pax into more reckless choices than she could count, but even though Pax was a ball of perpetual anxiety and gloom, she appreciated their differences. They balanced each other out. Pax kept her from going completely off the rails with some impulsive plan, and she made Pax feel, well . . . normal.

"Get your perky little butt out here or I'll come in and drag it out!" Ayana yelled.

"I'm coming!" Pax called in mock annoyance as she grabbed her backpack and ran out to meet her.

Ayana flashed a bright smile that contrasted starkly with her go-to cherry-red lipstick. It was Ayana's signature thing. It didn't matter if they were going to school, a party, or hanging out at her house, she was never without it. Her caramel-colored bouncy hair curled in wild ringlets around her face, which highlighted her deep brown complexion. Pax felt a pang of insecurity but she quickly shook it away because if she expressed it, Ayana would come back with, "Pax, bad bitches like us don't compare ourselves because that's what the patriarchy wants us to do, and we won't give them the satisfaction."

"About time you made it out of bed. I was thinking I'd have to bust through the door," Ayana said.

"Yeah, yeah." Pax rolled her eyes.

Ayana followed her to the car. "So, what happened to you yesterday?"

Pax pursed her lips. "I don't really want to talk about it."

"I thought we were going to hang out after school. I waited for you for like an hour."

"Um, try fifteen minutes," Zeke's voice called from behind them.

Ayana spun around on her heels. "And how would you know? Weren't you at soccer practice? Are you stalking me?"

He scoffed as he opened the back passenger door and slung

his backpack in. "You'd like that, wouldn't you? No, I saw you peeling out of the parking lot just as I was coming on the field."

"A likely story," she fired back as they climbed into her white Jeep.

"Whatever, just admit you're a bad friend."

"Ugh! I would've waited longer, but I had to pee!"

Pax chuckled at their exchange. From the outside someone might think that Zeke and Ayana hated each other, and even though they had little in common aside from their love for Pax, they got along just fine. Bickering was their love language.

"Anyway," Ayana continued, "it's not like you waited for her either."

"No, but I did come over to check on her like a *good* friend would."

"Hey! No fair, you blew me off for him?"

"Um . . . not exactly." Pax shifted uncomfortably in her seat, and she and Zeke exchanged glances.

"What, were you guys hooking up or something?"

"No!" they both shouted simultaneously.

"I—I got called to the office again because I had another episode in science class," Pax mumbled.

"Oh," Ayana said.

"This time it was all the teachers and my dad. They told him I need 'professional' help."

"How did your dad react to that?"

"Oh, you know Vick," Zeke chimed in from behind her. "Smile and wave until no one is watching."

"Principal Dick strikes again," she muttered. "Wait, did he . . . did he hit you?"

Pax's stomach sank. She had done a really good job of hiding any repercussions of her father's outbursts for most of their friendship. He didn't hit her often. Most of the time, he approached her with an air of cold indifference, or at most, extreme disappointment. But on the off occasion that he was angry or stressed and had had a bit too much to drink, he could get aggressive. One day during freshman year, after a particularly rough performance review from the school board, he had thrown a book at her for forgetting to clean the dishes. It left her with a large bruise on her collarbone. She tried to hide it with her clothes, but Ayana noticed it right away when they were changing for gym class. She'd pulled her outside and practically forced the truth out of her.

Ayana gathered from Pax's silence that he had hit her. "I'm calling the police," she announced.

"Please don't," Pax groaned.

"Pax, how much longer are you going to keep this up? What are you protecting anyway? His reputation? Screw him," Ayana said, the fear evident in her eyes. "We have to report this."

"Listen, I know. It sucks. But if you call the cops, they will put me in foster care, and I only have two years left until I'm old enough to be on my own. I'd rather live on my terms than be at the mercy of more adults who don't care about me."

Ayana turned toward the back seat to Zeke. "And what about you? Are you cool with this?"

"Come on, of course I'm not. But I had a lot of different foster parents before Abby, remember? A lot of them are the same or worse than Pax's father. Sometimes they're good, but you just never know. It's Russian Roulette. And I'm not going to pull the trigger unless Pax wants to. That's her decision to make. If she wants to, I'll be the first to report it. But if not, at least she has us."

Pax unclenched her jaw and shot a grateful look to Zeke. He nodded and gave a half smile in return. She didn't know what she would've done without him the past few years.

Ayana sighed heavily. "Well, at least stay at my house tonight so you don't have to see him for a while."

"Weren't you supposed to go on a date with that senior tonight?"

"Who? Leila? She blew me off to get back with her ex-boyfriend." She rolled her eyes. "I was going to be free tonight anyway. So, it's settled. You're staying with me tonight," she determined without waiting for Pax to respond.

"I'll have to ask my dad."

"You know he'll say yes. He likes me," she said with an eye roll. It was true. Ayana had a kind of charm when it came to adults. All she had to do was smile and bat her eyes and they were mesmerized. Of course, when it came to Pax's father, it helped that Ayana's mom was the top donor to the school's drama department. He'd do anything to keep that money coming in.

"Sorry to hear about what's-her-face," Pax offered.

"Ugh, don't be. I'm so over being these girls' experiment, you know? Like, grow up and date me or stick with these varsity basketball bros who all have the same personality and the same five names. No offense, Zeke."

"None taken. I don't even play basketball." He laughed.

"Huh, I thought you did," she said as she pulled out of the driveway.

"You know I play soccer," he grumbled.

"Oh, same thing." She waved a hand carelessly as she sped toward the school.

He huffed. "Well, now I'm offended."

Ayana and Pax exchanged glances, then broke into laughter. Pax laughed harder than she should have, mostly just because it felt good to not think about anything else.

As soon as she was in Ayana's bedroom, Pax let her backpack drop to the floor and flopped onto the fluffy white duvet. Ayana already had music blasting from the Bluetooth speaker, and the string lights that framed her walls were pulsing on beat to the music.

"Welcome to Club Ayana," Pax yelled over the music.

Ayana threw her head back and laughed. "Don't you love the lights? I just set them up yesterday, and I'm obsessed."

"They're . . . something," she responded as she took Ayana's phone and switched the song.

"Ugh! Pax, no! Not Radiohead *again*!" Ayana snatched the phone out of Pax's hands.

"What? Why not?"

"They're so depressing, and the guy sings like he has bronchitis." She quickly switched it back to the happy pop music that was playing before.

Pax chuckled. "Fine. Who even is this?"

"No one you would know, Grandma," Ayana shot back at her.

"Hey! Radiohead is classic."

"Listen, I love a good nineties throwback as much as the next girl, but would it kill you to update your playlist a bit?"

"I think it would. My old ears just can't take it."

"All right, Ethel," Ayana teased.

"What?" Pax shouted in her best old lady voice and cupped a hand behind her ear.

Ayana giggled. "Hey, my mom won't be home until like ten tonight. Do you want to order some takeout or something?"

"Sure," Pax said without looking away from the blinking lights overhead. "Is she working on a big case right now?"

Ayana snorted. "Yeah, but that's not why she's going to be late. She's got a date tonight."

"You don't like the guy?"

"Never met him, but neither has she. It's a blind date. She signed up for a matchmaking service like some sad middle-aged Beverly-Hills divorcée."

"Your mom *is* a divorcée."

"I mean, yeah, but she's so loaded from becoming a partner at the firm that she has to pay my dad alimony. Not exactly the sad Beverly-Hills type," she said with admiration.

Pax felt a pang of jealousy over the relationship Ayana had with her mom. Sima worked a lot, but she loved Ayana. They would take lavish vacations together over the summer, just the two of them. They'd traipse around France or the Bahamas and shop, eat, and hang out like best friends. Ayana laughed and joked about her mom's drinking habits or the way she dressed in all black like "the reaper," but it was all lighthearted. She idolized her. Pax didn't see her often because she worked so much, but she could see why Ayana was obsessed with her.

The woman was self-made, wildly successful, and blindingly beautiful. She had the same gorgeous curls and warm brown skin as Ayana, but she was curvy all over and carried herself with the kind of confidence that commanded the room. She even made Pax's father nervous, a fact that Pax found very amusing in the interactions she had witnessed between them. Sima always talked to Pax and Ayana with a cool aloofness. Not that she was uncaring toward them, but it was as if she was above the stress and the drama of motherhood. She had resigned to let Ayana be who she was, and Ayana let her do the same. Pax wasn't so sure that it was always as easy-breezy as it seemed. She always thought Ayana wished for a little more from her mom, but if she did, she never said it to Pax. It probably seemed in poor taste to complain about her mom to someone who didn't have one.

"Pax," Ayana whistled, pulling her out of her daze. "Where'd you go?"

"Uh, I don't know," she lied, not wanting to admit she was thinking about how much she wished she had a mom like hers. Or any mom at all, for that matter. "What's up?"

"I was saying, do you want to go to Aaron's house tonight for the Smash Brothers tournament?"

Pax sat up and stared at her skeptically. "*You* want to play in a Smash tournament?"

"I might," she shot back playfully, then threw a pillow at Pax.

"Hmm. Are you sure this has nothing to do with the fact that a certain hot, pink-haired gamer will be at this tournament?"

"Nope. They have nothing to do with this." She paused. "Okay, so Jordin *might* have something to do with this."

"Didn't you guys break up last year because you didn't have anything in common?"

"Yeah, but . . . I don't know, Pax. It's slim pickings for a gay girl in suburban Ohio, okay? Prom is coming up and I'm getting a little antsy. Besides, I feel like I didn't really give Jordin a proper chance. So, we're gonna try again. Maybe we have more in common than I thought."

"You mean you're going to pretend to like Smash so it looks like you have more in common than you did before?"

Ayana bit her lip.

Pax snorted. "How progressive of you, Gloria Steinem."

"Hey, don't bring Gloria into this! Besides, she would totally be on my side. I'm not any less of a feminist by pretending to like something Jordin likes. I'm *compromising*. It's a sign of growth. You should be congratulating me for maturing in my romantic relationships. Besides, Jordin listened to me talk about astrology for forty-five minutes during lunch, so if they can pretend to care about my stuff, I can do the same."

"Look, I totally support you. I hope it works out this time," Pax reassured. "And yes, I'll go with you for emotional support . . . and for when you inevitably give up on trying to care about this tournament."

"Ugh, rude!" Ayana pushed her off the bed. Pax landed with a thud on the floor, laughing.

CHAPTER 5

Pax shifted uncomfortably in her seat on the leather couch in Aaron's basement, which had been converted into a huge entertainment area. There were four flat-screens located in different parts of the room. Aaron was using each one to broadcast a different tournament. There were crowds of people surrounding each screen, eyes glued, chatting intensely about the tournament in front of them. This was way beyond your normal nerds gathering to play video games. It looked more like a party than a tournament, a fact which made Pax deeply uncomfortable. Not that she didn't like parties, per se. She thought if she actually had friends, she might like them just fine. But Pax's only friend at this party had abandoned her an hour ago to sit on the arm of Jordin's gaming chair to cheer them on. Jordin seemed slightly annoyed at this point as they lightly nudged Ayana's hip, mid-gameplay, hoping she'd get the hint. She didn't. Pax pressed her lips together to stifle a laugh and contemplated whether she should go over there and let Ayana know.

"What's up, Unabomber? Why are you sitting over here by yourself?"

"Huh?" Pax turned as Zeke plopped down right beside her. "Oh, Zeke. Thank God."

"Seriously, Pax, you look like you'd be happier getting heart surgery than being at this party right now.

"Shut up." She dug an elbow into his ribcage.

He passed her a plastic cup. "Well, I'm here to save you anyway."

"No thanks." She pushed the cup away.

"It's water," he said, as if it had been obvious. "Drink."

Pax rolled her eyes. "Thanks, Dad," she said sarcastically as she took a sip.

"Well, somebody's gotta look out for you."

Pax was grateful for everything Zeke had done for her, but sometimes he could be overbearing. "Ayana said you weren't coming tonight."

"Yeah, well, Abby got off work a little earlier than she thought, so she gave me the night off from babysitting."

Zeke's mom was an ER nurse. She worked weird shifts sometimes, which meant Zeke had to watch his little sister, Maria, at night. Pax never understood how he was able to juggle so much at once: straight-A student, varsity soccer player, live-in babysitter, and not to mention, her personal lifesaver. He never seemed to mind though. Before Abby took them in, Zeke was practically raising Maria. His father was killed on deployment in the Iraq War after Maria was born. His mother never recovered from the loss, which led to her subsequent heroin addiction when Zeke was six. He and his sister were removed by social services, and had been split up in different homes for a few years. He took care of everyone around him without even realizing he was doing it. Pax felt guilty about him always looking out for her. It must have weighed on him. But he wouldn't stop, even if she begged him to, and truthfully, she needed his friendship. He understood her in ways that Ayana never could. He knew the pain of losing a parent, of having to raise yourself. They'd fought the same demons, but for some reason it seemed like Zeke had carried them a little better than she did.

"So, have you had any more weird dreams since I saw you last?" he jested, a smile playing at the corner of his full lips.

Pax shot daggers at him. "Nope," she replied tersely as she sipped her water.

"Come on." He playfully pushed her shoulder. "I was just messing. But seriously though, if your dream guy gets rough with you again, let me know. I'll kick his ass."

"Shut up!" Pax replied in half annoyance, half embarrassment as she pushed him roughly off the couch.

He cackled as he hit the floor with a thud, the remaining contents of his cup splashing as he did. Pax laughed as he scrambled to wipe up what had spilled onto the tile with a napkin that someone had discarded.

"See, that's what you get," she said as she stood over him, offering her hand.

He took it and pulled himself up. "Yeah, yeah . . ." he replied with a sideways smirk.

"Hey, Hernandez!" a sandy-haired boy called from across the room. "You got next!"

"Oh, uh—" Zeke ran a hand through his thick black hair, shifting uncomfortably. He shot a glance at Pax, clearly feeling the need to stay with her and keep her company.

Pax cut him off. "Go."

"Are you sure?"

She huffed. "Yes, I'm fine. Go punch someone or . . . whatever."

He nodded before jogging off to meet his friend. "Let's gooo!" he shouted, flexing his arms as he charged across the room.

Pax sighed and settled deeper into the couch, feeling her eyelids getting heavy. She checked the clock on the bookshelf in the corner of the room. Almost midnight. She looked around for Ayana, hoping she was ready to go home. She spotted her springy curls tangled up with a sleek pink bob on a loveseat in a dark corner of the room. It looked like she and Jordin had found something they both liked to do. Ayana wouldn't be ready to go anytime soon, and the idea of breaking up whatever was going on over there brought a wave of discomfort over Pax. So she slipped off her shoes and curled up against the cool brown leather of the sectional. As she stared up at the dark ceiling, her mind wandered again to her dream from the other day. Her body relaxed into the sofa as she wondered when the next time would be that she would end up on that shore.

———

The next thing Pax felt was warmth against her forehead. No, not warmth. Humid, sticky heat and sweat. Her eyelids fluttered, then quickly slammed shut again as the sting of sunlight pierced into them. She rolled to her side and slowly blinked again, allowing her eyes to adjust. She sat up and looked around, disoriented. Her hands were caked in thick rust-colored sand, and she rubbed her palms together, the grains falling to her bare feet. She looked out at the horizon. The sky cascaded from a soft peach into a nearly iridescent pink where it touched the surface of the pale green ocean. She was on the beach.

This was usually about the time where an earth-shattering rumble would wake her up screaming. But it never came. And the world around her felt so intensely real. The colors, the heat, the feel of the sand on her skin. It was as if she wasn't in a dream at all. *Strange.*

She turned her back to the shore and found a massive stone wall about fifty yards behind her, stretching for miles in each direction. She had never noticed it in her other dreams.

What the hell is that for? she wondered. She stared at the massive wall for a few moments until it dawned on her that if she were dreaming, she could do anything she wanted. After all, it was all in her head, right?

Pax contemplated for a moment. *If I could do anything right now, what would I want to do?* Then it dawned on her. She'd always wondered what it would be like to fly. She shook the sand off her body and positioned herself on the tips of her toes, extended her arms, and tried to jump, only to find that she was still firmly planted on the ground.

Maybe if I get a running start. She fixed her eyes ahead of her, rolled forward onto the balls of her feet, then took off in a hard sprint across the shore. She ran faster and faster, feeling the wind whipping through her long, black hair, then when she was ready, she leaped in the air. And for a single moment her body hurled weightlessly through the air, but a nanosecond later, she tumbled to the ground—hard. A sharp pain stabbed her ribs, knocking the breath out of her.

She groaned, feeling the full impact of her stupid choices hit her body. *I guess you can't do anything you want just because you're dreaming.* She lay there for a moment, trying to regain her breath, when she heard someone snickering from behind her.

Pax leaped quickly to her feet—too quickly, because almost as soon as she stood up, the world spun and her vision blurred. Her knees buckled, but instead of crumpling to the ground again, she felt an arm catch her. She looked up to see a pair of golden eyes staring down at her. They belonged to a boy who looked about her age. He had curly brown hair that hung down on either side of his face and stopped just below his jawline, highlighting the obnoxious smirk that curled at his lips. A heavy sheen of sweat glistened in his tawny complexion, and his simple beige tunic was smudged with grease and dirt.

"What are you doing?" his deep voice asked, barely

concealing his laughter. His accent was thick, but not one Pax could place even though it seemed oddly familiar to her. The way he rolled his r's off his tongue was very distinct. Was it Spanish? Or maybe Arabic? Then it dawned on her: this was the boy from her dream the other night, the one who had grabbed her. She decided not to say anything, considering his reaction the last time they spoke.

Pax looked at him blankly for a moment until she realized he was still waiting for her to respond. "Oh, I . . ." She had no idea how to explain that she was trying to fly without sounding crazy. But then she remembered she was in a dream, and it didn't matter if she looked crazy or not because this person was not real. "I was trying to fly," she said.

He stared at her, bewildered. "You were what?"

Her cheeks flushed, and she suddenly wasn't sure about telling him the truth. "I was . . . yeah."

"You were trying to fly? Like a bird?" he repeated slowly, clearly thinking she must be unhinged. "Why would you do that?"

Pax grew flustered. There were enough people in the real world telling her she was crazy. She didn't need this boy with his judgmental golden eyes treating her like this. This was her dream. She pulled her arm back from his grasp and straightened her posture, trying to salvage what was left of her dignity. "Yes, I was trying to fly because this"—she gestured wildly to their surroundings—"is a dream. It's not real. So, I figured, why not? But apparently, the laws of gravity are still in effect here."

The boy stared at her blankly. "Are you . . . all right? Is there somewhere I can take you? Do you live in the village?" He gestured at the wall behind them.

That explains the wall. "No, I'm not from here. I'm from Ohio, and that village over there isn't even real," Pax shot back in annoyance.

"Where is Ohio? Is that in Nomadesales?" He pointed to her oversized tee and baggy jeans she was still sporting from this morning. "Does everyone there dress so strangely, or did you choose to wear this?"

"That was rude," she mumbled under her breath. "You know what? Don't worry about it. I'm fine. I'm just gonna go . . ." she trailed off. She actually had no idea where she was going to go. Every time she had this dream, she had only gotten as far as the beach. Suddenly, the loud roar of a low-flying plane sounded from overhead.

The boy spat a curse, anxiety now replacing his smug expression. He held out a hand to her. "Come with me. Now! We must run."

Confused, Pax took hold of his rough, calloused hands and nearly stumbled as he wrenched her forward by her arm. The hot sand stung her feet as they tore across the terrain.

"Why are we running?"

The boy did not answer. He led her directly to the stone wall. It must have been fifteen feet high. There was no way they were climbing that. The boy knelt down and began to clear large pieces of rubble away from the base of the wall, revealing an opening just large enough to squeeze through if you slid on your stomach. The rumble of the plane grew closer.

The boy scrambled under the clearing, offered his hand, and pulled her through. He then dragged her away from the massive stone structure and practically pulled her arm out of its socket as they sprinted into the village on the other side of the wall. He led her into a nearby alley and pressed her firmly against the wall of a little red clay cottage. They stood in silence next to each other, their labored breathing the only sound in the air. They waited for several minutes until the roar of the plane faded away.

Pax was still holding the boy's hand. She awkwardly released hers from his grasp and looked away. The boy turned his back to her and made his way out of the shadows to peer around the front of the house. Not knowing what else to do, Pax followed him. He nodded to her, signaling it was safe to come out of hiding and lead her into the village. They walked along an unpaved path with little cottage-like homes stretching for miles on either side. The houses looked as if they had been hand-built with wood and large red clay bricks. The path was empty aside from a few children chasing after a ball in the opposite direction. Pax heaved a sigh of relief as they traveled farther down the dusty path. Toward what, Pax was unsure, but at least they weren't being chased anymore.

"So, um, what was that back there?" Pax called after the boy.

He turned to her. "You really don't know?"

She shook her head.

"That was the Guadaros. They work for the Terra Dignida."

She stared at him blankly.

"The Fellowship?" he prompted. "They are guards for them. How far is Ohio, anyway? I thought the Fellowship ruled everywhere."

"It's, uh, really far," Pax replied stupidly. She quickly changed the subject. "So, why were we running from them?"

"The Outlands are off-limits to anyone but the Travelers. If you are caught out there, they'll arrest you . . . or kill you."

"So, what were you doing out there?"

He shot her a sharp look. "I could ask you the same thing."

"Fair enough. Did you put that hole in the wall?" she said,

referring to the small crawlspace they had shoved themselves through.

"Yes," he said but didn't offer any further explanation.

She decided to drop the subject. "So, what's your name?"

"Arivhan. But most people call me Ari."

"Nice to meet you, Ari," she replied, offering her hand.

He stared down at it. "What are you doing?"

She blushed. "Oh, um . . . I was offering you my hand. You know, for you to shake it?"

"Why?"

"Well, that's what we do where I'm from when you first meet someone."

"Well, here, hands are for family and lovers. When we meet, we do this." He gave a slow, intentional bow of his head.

Pax raised an eyebrow. "But you took my hand earlier."

It was his turn to blush. "That—that was different. If I hadn't, you would have died. You should be thanking me."

"Whoa, I was just joking." She paused awkwardly. "You're right though. I'm sorry. Thank you for saving me." She bowed her head graciously, mimicking his gesture.

"So, what is your name?"

"Paxton, but everyone calls me Pax."

"Pax?" His dark eyes grew wide. "Pax," he whispered.

She realized her mistake as soon as she made it. She should have lied, but she wasn't thinking. "Why did you come back?" he said.

"I don't know. I don't even know how I got here. Why are you so afraid of me?"

"Afraid? Of you? I'm not afraid of you. I'm trying to *save* you. You are from the Otherlands, no?"

"The what?"

He huffed. "You are not from this world?"

"I . . . I suppose I'm not."

"So, you are a Traveler. The Fellowship will kill you if they find you here."

"I'm sorry, I'm a what?"

"A Traveler. It is what we call people with the gift."

"What gift?"

Ari placed his head in his hands and huffed in exasperation. "You can jump between this world and your own. Yes?"

"I . . . don't know. I mean, I just fell asleep and then I was here."

He stared at her blankly for a moment, then he paced anxiously and muttered under his breath in a language Pax didn't understand.

"You don't know how you travel?"

Pax shook her head.

Ari paced more frantically than before. Then, suddenly, he stopped with a look of determination. "You will come with me." He turned to sprint in the opposite direction. Pax stood for a moment, confused. He turned to her, exasperated, and shouted, "Come!" Pax quickly followed behind.

"So, can you at least tell me where we're going? Or where I am?" she shouted to Ari as they ran along the path behind the rows of homes.

"You are in the land of Terra."

Pax furrowed a brow. She wasn't the best at geography, but she had never heard of a country called Terra before. "That's on Earth, right?" She felt stupid asking the question.

"I do not know what that is," he replied.

Pax's mouth gaped. *I'm on another planet?* She forgot for a moment that this was all a dream. However real this alien planet felt, soon she would wake up and be back in Aaron's basement.

Ari continued, "This is the West Village of Rehama. Rehama is the only land in Terra that is independent from the Fellowship's rule."

"So, if you aren't ruled by the Fellowship, then who is in charge?"

"No one. And everyone. We believe each person in the village plays a role in our livelihood. We are taught to be responsible for each other, and to use our skills and wisdom to make life better for everyone. So, people step up and lead when they can and where it is needed."

"Huh," Pax said, digesting the information.

Ari finally stopped in front of one of the little cottages and climbed up the worn wooden steps. Pax tentatively followed him, unsure of what was going to happen when she walked through the door.

Ari stopped at the doorstep and turned to her. "Listen, you are my friend from another village, okay? I will do all of the talking and you just nod. Whatever you do, you must not let my sister know who you are or any of the things we discussed, *especially* not the water. Say nothing about being beyond the wall."

A wave of anxiety flooded over her, but because she would be stuck in this dream for a while, she simply gave a terse nod and followed the strange boy inside.

As she entered the threshold, the delicious smell of spiced meat wafted through the air. The space was small but homey. The walls were enforced with wood panels but were adorned with colorful tapestries. There was a small table with wooden chairs in one corner and two cozy pallets piled with woven blankets in the other. There was a peacefulness in the air that could only be found in a loving family home.

"Arivhan!" a voice called from the other side of the room by the fireplace. A small, thin woman with fierce eyes was staring at them. She stomped across the floor and slammed a platter of food onto the table as she shouted at Ari in a language Pax couldn't understand. The little woman stood in front of him with her hands on her hips. Even though she couldn't be much older than twenty-three, she carried herself like someone much older.

Ari's head tilted upward as he sighed in apparent exasperation and shot back at the woman with a frustrated response.

Pax crossed her arms and shifted uncomfortably from foot to foot as the two went back and forth with each other, gesturing wildly. It was clear that Ari was in trouble. Finally, he gestured toward Pax, and the woman's piercing eyes looked at her intently. Pax shrank deeper into the wall she stood against, regretting her decision to follow him in.

"Dinah, this is my friend Pax. Pax, this is Dinah, my sister."

Dinah's unreadable eyes lightened slightly as she approached Pax. "Pax? Welcome to our home. I'm sorry this stone-headed child did not give me more warning that you would be coming. I could have prepared you a place tonight." She smacked the back of Ari's head in half jest.

"Oh! Um . . ." Pax paused in discomfort. "That won't be necessary. I will be leaving before night."

"Ari says your mother was taken by the Fellowship and you have nowhere to go?"

"Uh," Pax shifted her gaze toward Ari, who was standing behind Dinah, nodding at her with exaggeration. "Yes," she replied, not wanting to give anything away. "But I promise I can find somewhere to go. I don't want to put anyone out."

"You will do no such thing. You will stay here with us until you can find somewhere. We know what it is like to have loved ones sacrificed for the Fellowship." She practically snarled out the words. Then she put her hands on Pax's shoulders. "I am so sorry about your mama. You have nothing to worry about. You are safe here." She looked sincerely into Pax's eyes as tears began to form in her own.

Pax's heart dropped into her stomach with guilt. It was clear that Ari and Dinah had suffered a lot of pain at the hands of the "Fellowship," whoever they were, and it made her feel terrible to lie to this woman who was so willing to take her in. In some ways, she reminded Pax of her own mother. Perhaps it was the wild black mane she had woven into a braid down her back, or the intense protectiveness she clearly held for her loved ones. Pax, at a loss, simply mumbled, "Thank you."

"Please, sit. Come eat," Dinah said, quickly ushering her to the table.

Pax sat quietly in one of the chairs and folded her hands across her lap, discomfort spreading throughout her body. She couldn't remember the last time she had a family meal. She watched Dinah gingerly pick up the meat she'd prepared with wooden tongs and place it on her plate, smiling at her in an offer of generosity. Pax was humbled by the gesture. The fact that this woman was willing to take her in and share her meal without any question or hesitation was almost too much for Pax to bear. She hesitantly picked up her fork and stabbed the strip of what appeared to be beef or lamb and bit off a piece. The flavor was like heaven in her mouth, and she excitedly stabbed another slice and shoveled it into her mouth. She was so caught up in her meal, she had failed to realize that Dinah and Ari were staring at her expectantly. She covered her mouthful as she chewed, feeling sheepish, though she didn't know why.

"If you don't mind, we are going to say thanks to the Great Mother for our meal," Ari prompted frantically, hinting for her to stop lest she give herself away.

"Oh!" Pax placed a hand over her mouth. "Yes, of course, I'm so sorry. It's just been so long since I've had a meal, I had . . . forgotten."

Dinah reached across the table and placed a hand over hers. "Of course, you have nothing to apologize for. You can have as much as you like. We will be quick with our thanks then, yes?"

Pax nodded, then looked at Ari, who bowed his head and peered up at her, clearly hinting to follow. She immediately followed suit.

Ari started in reverent prayer, "Mother of our universe, it is to you we give our dearest thanks for this meal. For you have birthed the food on our table, the love in our home, and the fabric of our world. For this, we are forever grateful. *Illyatsia.*" He bowed his head and used his fingers to draw a shape symbolizing infinity across his chest.

"*Illyatsia,*" Dinah echoed.

Pax attempted to do the same, clumsily trying to draw the same shape across her chest as she spoke. She cast a glance at Dinah, desperately praying that she hadn't noticed. She didn't seem to. Ari gestured for her to pick up her fork, and she did so gratefully. It had been so long since she had eaten, and the food in front of her tasted incredible.

"So, Pax," Dinah started, "Ari says you are from Nomad-esales, yes?"

Pax nodded, deciding it was safer to just agree, then quickly picked up another mouthful of food, hoping it would keep Dinah from asking her questions. It didn't.

"Which part?"

"Hmm?" Pax mumbled as she chewed.

"Which part of the eastern villages?"

"Uh, Nomadesales, like you said," she muttered quietly.

Dinah chuckled. "I suppose I would not know the place even if you told me."

Pax breathed a sigh of relief.

"Her family belonged to the Binos village," Ari chimed in.

"Ah, I have never been there. What's it like?"

"Oh . . ." Pax chewed vigorously, praying that the right answer would come to her. "It's, um . . . beautiful! So much natural beauty. All the trees. It's . . . it's lovely."

Ari buried his head in his hands. Clearly, that was the wrong answer. Suddenly, Pax wondered what she was doing here. She could have just turned around and walked away. Then she remembered she was stuck here for the time being, at least until she woke up, so she might as well play along.

"Strange. I've always heard that the Binos village was completely empty of natural surroundings since it is at the capitol's border. It is all buildings and factories, is it not?"

Pax scrambled. "Yes! Yes it is." She was so nervous she was practically shouting. "But . . . um, there are parks with some nature and trees in the distance. It's a beautiful view. Besides, it is my home, so I will always think it is the most beautiful place."

Dinah nodded sympathetically. "Of course. I've never heard of these 'parks,' though. We do not have those in Rehama. Perhaps after the Founder's Festival, we could spend some time there. It has been a while since we have been on a trip, has it not, Arivhan?"

Ari nodded, contributing absolutely no help to the conversation, yet somehow managing to look utterly frustrated and disappointed with Pax's performance.

There was a long pause. Pax decided to take advantage of the situation and steer the conversation away from her. "So, it's just you and Ari?"

"Yes, well, there used to be five of us, but our mother and father were killed in the uprising many years back, and then our sister, Nyla . . . she passed just a few years ago in a raid."

Pax's heart grew heavy for them. Dinah's eyes were filled with despair. The kind that only came from deep, terrible grief. Pax sensed that she blamed herself for her sister's death.

"So, it has been the two of us ever since. But we make it through . . . just as you will, Pax." There was warmth and care behind Dinah's smile, and the tightness in Pax's belly began to grow. The guilt was beginning to overpower her.

"Dinah," she started. "I . . . I'm sorry. Ari, I can't . . ."

Ari's head shot up from his plate and his eyes widened, pleading with her not to go on. But Pax's better judgment got hold of her. "I did lose my mom, but it was when I was little. I barely remember her."

Confusion crossed Dinah's face for a moment, then she shot a furious look at Ari. "Arivhan, who is she?"

Ari sat in silence, scrambling for an explanation. "Dinah, she was lost. She was going to die if I hadn't found her beyond the wall, and I—"

"*Beyond the wall?*" Dinah snapped. "How many times have I told you about this? You could die there, Ari! How could you do this again? *Who is she?*"

Ari cursed. "I couldn't very well let her die, could I?"

Pax interjected. "Don't be angry at him. Be angry at me. He was only trying to help. I just woke up on the beach, and I didn't know where I was or that it was dangerous. It just . . ."

"You are not from the East Village, are you?"

"No. I'm from . . . farther away."

"Where?" she demanded.

Pax sat silently, trying to come up with an answer. But the silence told it all.

Dinah's dark eyes widened in terror and fury. She stood from her chair and whipped her head toward Ari. "A Traveler? Of course. I should have known from that tunic."

Pax looked down at the Campbell's soup tee. It was a wonder she wasn't found out as soon as Dinah saw her.

"You brought her *here*? To our home? Are you trying to get us killed?"

"I was trying to help."

Dinah paced in a rage. "You have to go. *Now.*"

Pax rose out of her chair. "I'm so sorry. I didn't know what else to do." Her voice wavered. Suddenly, Dinah crossed the table to her and placed her hands on Pax's arms. "Do you not understand? You are one of *them*. You can't be here. You must find somewhere else to go!"

Ari began to protest from across the room, but suddenly her head filled with the sound of blaring sirens.

"I'm so sorry!" she shouted over the sirens in her head as Dinah pushed her toward the door. Her feet shuffled backward. Ari rushed toward her as she lost her footing, and then she suddenly she was falling backward as the darkness enveloped her.

CHAPTER 6

The leather couch was cool beneath her fingertips. She was back in the basement. But from what she could see in the harsh light glaring from the television screens, no one else was there. The drafty basement air hit her skin. She sat for a moment, grappling with the memory of her dream, then slowly lifted her arms to inspect her skin. Surely enough, there were still scrapes from where she had slid between the ground and the rock of the wall. Her clothes were covered in a layer of dirt, and her skin was still sheened with sweat from the humid air of the village. She wasn't sure what was real in that moment, but she knew for certain that her dreams were not just dreams.

She stood slowly, still disoriented, and cast her gaze to the small window at the far end of the room. Red and blue lights flashed against the glass from outside. She stumbled up the stairwell and ran to the front door. As she stepped outside, she squinted to adjust her eyes to the lights. A crowd of her classmates surrounded a cop car. What had happened while she was sleeping? Pax moved slowly toward the crowd and spotted Ayana speaking to a police officer between sobs as he jotted something down in a notepad. Zeke was talking frantically to someone on the phone. She pushed her way through the crowd toward her friends.

"Ayana?" she called.

Ayana's head shot upward, and her eyes widened. *"Pax!* What the hell?" She ran to her and gathered her into a crushing hug. "Are you okay?"

Zeke ran toward them. "Where were you?" he demanded.

"What are you talking about?" Pax asked, confused. "I was on the couch in the basement. I fell asleep."

"No, we looked all over the place for you!" Ayana said. "I called my mom, we called Zeke's mom. We went by your house. You were nowhere! We thought something happened to you! Where did you go?"

"I . . ." Pax stopped. She had no idea how to explain what was happening. She had fallen asleep on the couch and woke up on the couch. "I was on the couch."

The police officer looked at Ayana. "This is the girl?"

"Yes. This is her." She breathed deeply. "I'm sorry."

"Well, if there's nothing else, you all need to be getting home now."

"Yes, of course, Officer," Zeke replied.

The glares of her peers stung as they slowly began making their way to their cars. Her face heated with embarrassment at all the unwanted attention and disdain. She approached Zeke tentatively. "You didn't call my dad, did you?"

"Of course not. But I was close," Zeke said. "Seriously, Pax, you couldn't have given a notice or something? We've been looking for you for two hours."

"I swear I didn't go anywhere."

"Tell that to your clothes. You look like you've been dragged through the dirt," Ayana responded angrily.

"Okay, I promise we won't be mad," Zeke said. "We were just worried. We thought someone had kidnapped you or something. Just tell us where you went." He placed a comforting hand on her shoulder.

Pax stood in silence.

"Seriously, Pax?" Ayana shot a look at her. "I know you've

got a lot going on in your life, but if this is about, like, getting attention or something, you could do it differently. We want to be here for you."

Pax's teeth clenched. "Are you kidding? I swear, I'm fine. I just . . . went out," she finished weakly, unable to explain what she didn't understand herself.

Zeke shook his head, frustrated. "Okay, I need to go home."

"Zeke, I swear I wasn't trying to—" Pax began.

"Pax, just . . . don't," he said tiredly before walking toward his friend's car. After a pause, he turned back. "Do you want me to ask Austin to take you back with us?"

There were already four boys from her class crowded into the black SUV. She couldn't bear to face them. She shook her head. "I'm staying with Ayana," she responded, though she had no intention of going back with her. After all the embarrassment, she just wanted to be alone.

He nodded, then hopped into the back seat.

Pax shoulders sagged. Tears prickled her eyes.

"We should go home," Ayana said quietly.

"I think I'll just walk back to my place," Pax said softly.

"Um, no. I'm taking you back with me. I can't risk you running off again."

Pax took in a sharp breath. "Can you just drop me off at home then?"

"Yeah. I guess."

Pax slid into Ayana's car and slammed the door shut, mentally searching for an explanation for what had unfolded tonight. She and Ayana sat in uncomfortable silence as they drove down the empty street, both lost for words. Pax prayed she could get home without any further questions from her friend.

"Are you seriously not going to tell me what happened to you tonight? Because I'm looking at you, and you sure as hell weren't just sleeping on the couch."

"How would you know? You were too busy feeling up Jordin to have noticed where I was."

"Is *that* what this is about? Are you jealous that I wasn't giving you attention or something?"

"No. I'm just saying, if you weren't so desperate to get the attention of someone who is clearly not into you, then maybe we'd be back at your place just watching Netflix or something right now." Pax looked over at Ayana, instantly feeling guilty for the way that she'd responded. She could see the pain on her friend's face. "Ayana, hey, I'm sorry. I didn't mean—"

"No, you did. I'm sorry I blew you off." Tears were beginning to smudge her eyeliner.

"No, I didn't. I want you to be happy, okay? I'm not trying to monopolize all of your time. I know that my life is . . . a lot. And you're a really good friend."

"Look, I don't see you as a project or something, okay? We've been friends for five years. I love you, but I just want you to be honest with me. I thought we were closer than this."

"We are. I just . . . I don't know how to explain what happened tonight."

"Can you try?"

Pax searched her mind for where to begin, or if she even should. Then she said, "Okay, so do you remember when Zeke was making fun of me about the dream I had the other day?"

Ayana listened intently to Pax's story. Her eyes widened when Pax showed her the scrapes and bruises from her dream. When Pax finished, they sat in silence for what felt like eternity.

"So," Pax started, "I'm being honest when I say I was on the couch. But in between then and now, I have no idea what happened to me. I just know that, apparently, I must be able to ... time travel or teleport. I don't know. God, that feels so stupid to say out loud, but I don't know how else to explain it."

Ayana sighed. "Pax, I think you need help. Like, maybe see a therapist or something. I don't know. I care about you, and I hate to see you going off the rails like this, but there is clearly something going on."

Tears welled up in Pax's eyes. "Please believe me. I'm not crazy. Something is happening to me. You believe in astrology and crystals and all kinds of other crap. I'm just asking you to believe me right now."

Ayana pushed her foot on the brake until the car came to a stop. "We're here. I think you should get some sleep."

"Yeah, maybe you're right."

"I'll call you tomorrow, okay?"

Pax sniffed. "Okay." Her footsteps were heavy as she trudged toward her front door while Ayana's car pulled out of the driveway. She slumped against the door as the tears began to fall freely.

She wept quietly for a while, looking up at the stars. "Mom," she called softly. She hadn't done this in years, but when she was a child, Pax would talk to her mom when she needed her. And even though she knew her mother couldn't hear her, it would bring her comfort. She felt foolish doing it now, but she felt so alone she didn't know who else to turn to. "I wish you were here. You would know what to say, or how to help. I know it must've been horrible here with Dad, but why didn't you take me with you?"

Grief welled up inside her. She had spent years picking up all the pieces and putting them together on her own in whatever ways she could, but just then it was as if she had shattered, letting all of her grief and rage pour out of her as chest as racking sobs shook her body. "I hate you for leaving me," she called to the stars. "*I hate you.*"

Pax froze at the sound of footsteps crunching on leaves. But she relaxed at the sight of Zeke, who was barefoot with sleepy eyes and mussed hair. He looked like a little boy. Through puffy eyes, Pax searched for a sign of what he was thinking as he groggily stood there with his hands stuffed into the pockets of his flannel Hulk-themed pajama pants. He was unreadable. She grappled for something to say, but no words came. Then Zeke unzipped his hoodie, placed it around her shoulders, and settled beside her on the doorstep. Pax was suddenly overwhelmed by the compassion of her friend. She shattered again as Zeke enveloped her into a warm embrace, holding her securely to his chest as he rested his chin atop her head. She sobbed onto his T-shirt as he gently stroked her back. She couldn't say how long they had stayed that way.

"Are you going to be okay?" Zeke asked after her heaving sobs had settled.

She looked at him, seeing the exhaustion in his face, and nodded.

"Do you want me to help you inside?"

She gave him a small smile. "No, I'm good. I think I'm just gonna sit out here for a while. But I'm fine. Please, go back to bed."

He gave her a short nod as he climbed to his feet. "Try to get some sleep," he mumbled as he turned back to his house.

Finally feeling like she could breathe again, Pax took in a deep gulp of air. She was exhausted, but not knowing where she would end up when she closed her eyes made her afraid to even attempt sleep. She leaned her head back against the door and looked up at the sky, trying to make sense of what was happening to her. She knew she wasn't crazy or hallucinating.

Something was going on. She grappled with her thoughts for a moment. Her mind wandered back to the world she had encountered earlier that night. The vivid colors of the sand and water in this strange planet.

Planet.

Pax tried to wrap her mind around the fact that she had been on another planet and hadn't even known it, but everything there had looked so normal. She thought about Ari and Dinah, trying to recall if there was anything distinct or "alien" about their appearance. Aside from Ari's starkly golden eyes, she couldn't think of anything particularly out of the ordinary. She'd never given much thought to life on other planets, but she assumed that if there were aliens out there they would look like little green men, or maybe like the terrifying creature from the movie *Alien vs. Predator*, but Ari and Dinah looked as human as she did.

She remembered what Ari had called her earlier that evening. *Traveler*. Whatever she was, it was so common they had a name for it, which meant there were more people like her walking around in Ari's world. She tightened her lips and determined her course. She couldn't explain it, but she hoped she could find the answers she was seeking if she could just get back there. Ari had said it was dangerous for her to walk around openly as a Traveler. But she could go in disguise, find someone trustworthy to help her. It might be a long shot to get Ari to assist her, but he was all she had, so she had to try. But not right now. She would have to wait until no one would be looking for her for a while so she didn't have another fiasco on her hands. But she knew in her heart she had to get back. It was the only way. The sun was emerging over the trees now, and she settled in to watch the sunrise.

CHAPTER 7

As the sun peeked out over the horizon, Pax finally picked herself up off the stoop and decided to go inside. Just as her hand reached for the knob, the door swung open and Pax was face-to-face with her father, who was clad in a pair of mesh running shorts with his gym bag slung over his left shoulder. He went to the local club on Saturdays to play tennis and schmooze some of the school board members.

His features crumpled into a scowl. "Have you been out all night?" he grumbled.

She shook her head. "No, sir. I came back from Ayana's last night. I woke up early and decided to come out to watch the sunrise."

He narrowed his eyes at her for a moment, then nodded, accepting her explanation. "Best get inside. I'll be back later."

"Yes, sir." She stood as he trudged past her to his car, rubbing his hands over his face. He turned back to her with a brief nod of goodbye. She waited until he pulled out of the driveway before dashing into the house.

She closed the door to her room and paced the floor, unsure of her next move. She should at least clean up. She shuffled to the bathroom to shower and brush her teeth. Her reflection in the full-length mirror was evidence of what a miracle it was that her father hadn't given her the fourth degree about where she'd been. Her wide, gray eyes were puffy from crying, her hair was tangled, and her jeans and shoes were still covered in sand. She was a mess.

After her shower, she changed into clean clothes. She had the morning to herself. She wanted to go back to find Ari, but she should clean up the mess she'd made of last night before she made any plans to travel. She snatched Zeke's black hoodie off the chair where she had discarded it when she came inside, and headed out the door.

The brisk autumn air sank into Pax's skin as she made the short trek from her house to Zeke's. She wrapped her sweater more tightly around herself, shivering while she shuffled her feet at his doorstep for a moment, buying time as she thought of what to say to him. She could still see the disappointed look on his face from last night. She had to figure something out. She gave a timid knock at the front door. Soon, there was the sound of quick, little feet approaching.

"I got it!" a tiny voice called from inside. Pax immediately felt a smile pulling at her lips as the door swung open.

"Pax!" the voice squealed.

"Maria!" she cried as the girl launched herself into Pax's arms.

"It's been so long since you've come over! You have to come see my room. Zeke made me a tent!"

"He did? Well, I definitely need to see it!" Pax said as Maria tugged her into the house and slammed the door.

"Mama! Pax is here!" Maria called.

"Oh, good!" a warm voice replied from the kitchen. But before Pax could respond, she was being pulled into Maria's room.

"Look! Isn't it beautiful?"

Pax smiled at the makeshift tent in the corner of the room, assembled together with some old pink sheets and a few wooden rods. Tiny butterflies hung from thread inside the tent.

"It is pretty awesome."

"Yeah! Do you want to come inside?"

"Oh, maybe some other time. I—"

"How's it going, Pax?" Abby said as she stood in the doorway to Maria's room.

"Oh! Um, pretty good," she lied.

"Yeah? We were all pretty worried about you last night when I got that call. What happened?" Her caring brown eyes widened in concern.

"Yeah . . ." She searched her mind for an excuse. "I had gone for a walk in the woods near Aaron's house to get some air, and I guess I just got lost for a while. I'm so sorry I worried everyone." She passed the lie smoothly, mentally kicking herself for not thinking of it last night.

"Well, maybe stay out of the woods from now on. That's no place for a young girl, especially at night. I'm so glad you're safe," she said, wrapping Pax into a warm hug.

"Thanks, Abby." Pax leaned into her. She always smelled like vanilla and laundry detergent. It was a comforting smell. But then again, Abby was a comforting person. She had been a foster parent for years before she adopted Zeke and Maria. She was the kindest woman Pax had ever met, and there was no pretense with her. She didn't demand any sort of authority, which was why she asked everyone to call her Abby. Zeke and Maria didn't even have to call her "Mom" if they didn't want to.

"Well, listen. I have a shift in thirty minutes, but I made fresh pancakes and bacon and the leftovers are sitting on the stove if you want some. Please help yourself." She wrapped her hair into a tight bun.

"Oh, thanks. But I'm good."

"Yeah? When was the last time you ate?"

Pax hesitated, thinking.

"Right. Look, please just take some home with you if you can't stay. Maria hates bacon, and Zeke ate like seven pancakes already. And you're welcome to take the empty syrup bottle and egg cartons for your next masterpiece."

Pax smiled. Abby had always taken an interest in her art. "Thanks. Do you know where I can find Zeke?"

"Oh yeah. Sorry. He's in his room getting ready for practice. You probably have some time to catch him before his ride gets here."

"Okay, thanks."

"Sure thing, sweetie. I'll see ya. Maria, Mrs. Collins is going to be here in ten minutes. Be good," she called as she headed out the door.

"Okay," Maria's voice said from inside her tent.

Pax sighed heavily as she trudged to Zeke's room at the end of the hall, racking her brain for what to say. She paused awkwardly in his doorway at the sight of him with his back to her, shirtless. She stood in quiet fascination for the briefest moment, noting the muscles that rippled down his back. She had seen Zeke without a shirt once before, and it was shocking then too. She'd never say it out loud to anyone, not even herself, probably because she'd die of embarrassment, but her friend was hot. Of course, he knew it. Zeke had never struggled to find a date. As a matter of fact, he could probably have any girl he wanted, but he was too kind to play with people's hearts for the fun of it. She stared for just a moment too long because suddenly Zeke was turning toward her.

She swiftly angled her face away, staring at the wall as her cheeks burned bright red. "Sorry. I was just—"

"Don't worry about it," he said. Pax swore she saw a grin playing at his lips as he shrugged on a white long-sleeved athletic shirt that hugged his muscular chest. "What's up?"

Pax turned back to him and stared silently for a minute, trying to find her words again. "I just wanted to talk to you about what happened last night."

He sighed. "You don't have to apologize for that. You know I'm here for you."

"Oh, not that part. I was talking about the thing that happened at Aaron's."

"Oh. Okay. Well?" He looked at her expectantly.

"Look . . . I messed up. I'm sorry. I just took a walk in the woods for a minute and I got lost, but I didn't want to say anything because I was embarrassed."

He looked puzzled. "Well, why didn't you just tell me that? That seems a lot less embarrassing than trying to convince everyone that you vanished into thin air. I spent my ride home trying to tell the guys you weren't crazy, but honestly, Pax, I don't know. You seemed kind of . . . you know."

Pax felt her cheeks heat again. "I'm *not* crazy. I just—" she stopped. She really didn't want to get into this with him. She knew he'd never believe her in a million years. Zeke was a good guy, but he was also practical. Everything had a simple, logical explanation in his mind. There were no mysteries, no gray areas. Only facts.

"Pax, we've been best friends for like six years now. I know when you're lying, but the thing is, I just don't get why. You know I'm always on your side, and if something is going on, I want to know."

Now what? The lie had fallen flat but she didn't dare tell him the truth. But she didn't want to lose his friendship over this secret. It just wasn't worth it. Against her better judgment, she began to recount her story for the second time. Her heart rate began to elevate as he stared at her, listening intently, his face stone-cold and unreadable.

"Look, I know it sounds kind of out there, but it's the truth."

He stared at her for what felt like hours. "Pax, I don't understand why you're doing this."

Her shoulders slumped, instantly regretting her decision. "I'm not doing anything. I swear to you, this is what happened. And I don't know, maybe it's just dreams and I am losing my mind, but I don't have any other explanation."

He rubbed his fingers against his temples, distressed. "Look, Mom knows some people at the hospital. If I talk to her, maybe we can get you in to see someone."

She threw her hands up in exasperation. "This is impossible. Look, it was a mistake coming here. I'm sorry for wasting your time." A car honked from outside. "I think your ride's here."

He looked at her once more, frustration evident on his face. "Take care of yourself, okay? You look like you haven't slept." He shouldered on his backpack and walked past her.

She stood in his room for a moment, trying to process what just happened. That definitely did not go as she'd planned. She made her way back through the empty house. The babysitter had already come to get Maria. She stood in the dark living room. The car outside was still honking frantically.

"Jesus," she muttered to herself. Zeke was already outside, so why were they still blaring the horn? She opened the front door to find Ayana's white Jeep parked in Pax's driveway. She locked Zeke's front door, closed it behind her, and started toward the car. Ayana got out, clad in black sweats and a tight gray crop top, her hair tied up in a puff at the crown of her head.

"There you are! I've been out here for like twenty minutes. Get in!"

Pax trudged toward her friend, bracing herself for another confrontation. But Ayana didn't look mad. She looked frantic.

She impatiently waved her hand as she took a gulp from her Starbucks cup.

As soon as Pax got into the passenger seat, Ayana handed her a coffee. "Here."

"Oh. Um, thanks. What are we—"

"I didn't sleep last night. I have to tell you something."

"Okay. But first I want to apologize for—"

"No, no, I'm sorry. That's why I'm here. I think you were telling the truth."

Pax paused. She didn't know what she had been expecting, but it was definitely not this. "What?"

"After I dropped you off, I thought about what you said. And I realized that even if you are losing it, you're not a liar. So, I had to find out for myself what you were going on about."

A wave of relief and gratitude rushed over Pax. "Ayana, thank you so much. I didn't know what I was going to do if I had to sort this out by myself. I was worried I'd lose my friends over it too."

"Hey, you could never lose me. We've been through way too much together for me to back out now. Anyway." She reached into the back seat, one hand still on the wheel as she sped around the corner. "Here, look at this." She shoved a massive stack of documents toward her.

"What's all this?"

"Research," she said as if it had been obvious. "Do you remember when I did that project about conspiracy theories in Humanities class our freshman year?"

"Yeah . . ."

"Okay, so last night I pulled up all of my sources for that. Then I remembered this one article I read of this government experiment about people who could not time travel, but basically they would meditate using these sound frequencies, and they could move their consciousness into other dimensions."

"Okay, so . . ."

"So? That could be *you*. Maybe your consciousness is like . . . predisposed to that kind of thing so you can just do it in your sleep. I found this whole Reddit thread about people who have claimed to be able to do interdimensional travel when they're sleeping. The idea is that even though our bodies are asleep, our internal consciousness *isn't*, and that when we dream, we actually *are* traveling. But somehow your subconscious has evolved to the point where you can travel with your physical body too." She stared at Pax, breathless.

"You got this all from a Reddit thread?"

"I mean, not *all* of it, but most of it. Look, I know some of the stuff on there is totally made up, but I mean, if you're out here claiming to have disappeared into some other world, then who knows? So, if you really did just like go off last night or something and you are lying, then please tell me now because I'm already too invested in this."

"I promise I'm telling the truth."

"I need you to swear on our friendship."

Pax rolled her eyes. "Okay, I swear on our friendship that I'm telling the truth."

"Okay, good. So, I need you to start taking this seriously because I put a lot of time into this."

Pax smiled. "You're right. I'm sorry for being skeptical. I just . . . it was hard for me to accept the truth for myself at first, so it feels crazy to even consider conspiracy theories to try to find answers. And I'm sure there is a lot of lies out there, but if there's even a chance I can find out what's actually going on with me, it's worth a try."

"Thank you!" Ayana said in relief as they pulled into her driveway.

"So, what exactly are we going to do?"

"I don't know. Experiment, I guess?"

Pax didn't like the sound of that.

———

Once they had settled on Ayana's bed, she immediately spread out all the documents in front of her. The amount of information was overwhelming. Articles, government documents, Reddit threads, all color-coded, tabbed, and covered in high-lighted portions.

"Wow, you really did put a lot of work into this. Thank you."

"Of course! I *live* for this kind of stuff. You know that. Do you remember when I got super into simulation theory after we thought we saw that bird sitting still in the air?"

"Yeah, but that turned out to be a leftover Halloween decoration that was suspended from a fishing wire."

"That's not the point." Ayana waved the thought away. "Fake bird or not, I'm still not fully convinced that theory is a hoax. I mean, the evidence to support it is definitely there."

Pax chuckled. Ayana had always had a fascination for unexplainable phenomena and the supernatural. She had gone down this rabbit hole more than once in their years of friendship, and Pax usually had to talk her off the ledge. Now she was going down the rabbit hole with her.

Ayana handed her a bulk of papers. "This is a government document that was released in 2003. It's super dense, so I highlighted the most important stuff."

"The Gateway Experience?" Pax said.

Ayana nodded, taking another big gulp of her coffee. "So,

this is what I was telling you about. The idea that you can project your consciousness into other dimensions."

Pax skimmed the highlighted portions while Ayana looked on with anticipation. There was so much information that she wished she hadn't slept through science class. Her brain was spinning as she flipped through the pages. "So, this is legit?"

"I mean, it's real government research. This Dr. Monroe guy had like a whole institute where he studied this stuff. Look at the seal on the top. And they're claiming there were people who went through this Gateway process and were successfully able to travel outside of their body. It even talks about how we do it in our dreams. Does this sound like anything to you?"

Pax's mind swirled. "I don't know . . . maybe. I mean, I know I'm going somewhere when I'm sleeping. But for a while I would end up on this beach, and it felt so real, but obviously my body was still, you know, here." She gestured, indicating the entire dimension. "Maybe this is on the right track, but it still doesn't explain how my whole body just vanished while I slept. Or how I was able to experience this other world to the point that I was covered in dirt and bruises and scrapes. It wasn't just my consciousness that was there. It was me."

"Yeah." Ayana contemplated for a minute. "Okay, so check out this article about the multiverse theory and interdimensional portals."

Pax snorted at how ridiculous this all sounded. "This is so insane."

"Hey! No snide remarks. You're the one with the crisis happening. Do you want to figure out what's going on or not?"

Pax huffed. "Fine. Give me the thing." She read through the article. "I mean, the idea that there are multiple universes definitely would explain how I ended up in a different, very real physical world. It looked almost the same as ours, but it was hotter and the colors were more vivid, I guess."

"Okay, so you ended up on another *planet*. God, that's so cool. I'm jealous."

"Believe me, if I could figure out a way to trade places with you, I definitely would."

"Okay, but you don't find what's happening to you even the least bit exciting?"

"I don't know. I've been too busy being terrified."

They read for hours without stopping, engrossed in their research. They hadn't even noticed when Sima, Ayana's mom, was standing in the doorway.

"Wow, what's going on in here?" Sima asked.

Ayana and Pax both jumped. "Oh . . . it's for a project," Ayana offered.

"Cool, what's the topic?"

"Uh," Pax grappled for a response.

"Space travel," Ayana rescued her. "But . . . we're like super busy right now. So we're going to get back to it, if that's cool with you."

"Oh, sure, sure. I was just popping in to see if you girls were interested in ordering a pizza."

Pax's stomach grumbled at the thought. She hadn't eaten since yesterday. They had read right through lunch. "Yes, please."

"Definitely. Veggie with vegan cheese for me, please?" Ayana said.

"Sure thing. Don't work too hard," Sima said as she left the room.

Pax heaved a heavy sigh and put her head in her hands.

"You good?" Ayana asked.

"I'm just exhausted from all this. I feel like the deeper we go, the more confusing it gets. It's like, I'll find something that seems sort of right, and then the next thing I read contradicts the first, and I feel like we're no closer than we were when we started."

Ayana agreed. "But at least you know you're not alone and that other people have had similar experiences, if not the same one. We can take a break and try again later if you want."

"Actually, I was wondering . . . since you know now, if you could help me with something."

Ayana's eyes lit up. "Yeah?"

"Okay, when I was there, Ari—"

"The guy you met?"

"Yeah."

"His name is Ari? Sounds hot." Ayana cast a teasing glance.

"Can you please focus?"

"Sorry. Okay, so what about *Ari*?" She said his name seductively.

"He said they have a name for what I am, for people who travel there from other worlds. They call them 'Travelers.'"

"Travelers." Ayana tried the phrase out. "Cool."

"Yeah, but what I'm thinking is if they have a name for whatever I am, there must be more people like me in that other world. I think this research will only get me so far. I need to talk to someone who knows what's going on, but whoever that is, they'll be in that other world. So . . . I have to find a way to get back."

"Well, it shouldn't be that hard, right? I mean, you've gone there by accident like a dozen times."

"Yeah, but I can't always control when it happens or even if I can get there. Sometimes I go to sleep and it's just that. Sleep."

"Okay, so what do you need?"

"I need you to help me buy some time. I need to figure out how to get back there, and I need at least a day to, you know, not be 'here' without people getting freaked out and calling the police."

"Hmm." Ayana thought for a moment, then her face suddenly brightened. "Okay, so how about you and I have a girls' trip to my family's lake house next weekend?"

"Will there be anyone there?"

"Nope. It's mostly a summer spot. I mean, it's technically my dad's, but he won't care if we go, especially since he decided he was going to become a free spirit after the divorce. He's in LA or something right now 'finding himself.'" She wrinkled her nose.

"What's that supposed to mean?" Pax snorted.

"It means he's doing yoga and hooking up with women half his age. So he honestly won't even know we're there. I'll just tell my mom we're going up alone because we need some time away. She's buried in this huge deposition right now anyway, so she'll probably be glad to have some time to herself. The only thing we have to worry about is your dad."

"He's got an Educational Leaders conference in Chicago that weekend. I was going to need a place to go anyway. Obviously, we can't tell him the part about the lake house, but I think this could work."

"Perfect! What are you going to do if you 'travel' again in the meantime?"

Pax sat thoughtfully. "I don't know. Now that there's a risk that my body won't be in the same place it was when I went to sleep, this whole thing just got way more stressful. I guess I'll just have to try to stay awake."

"For a whole week? I've read about people who try to do that and they literally go insane. There's gotta be a way to get yourself back here if you do end up traveling to Terra. I mean, you've always come back, so how does that work?"

"Beats me. It's like one minute I'm there, then the next I'm being sucked back here." She hesitated, thinking. "Wait. That's not right. The only reason I was able to come back the last time is because I heard the police sirens outside Aaron's house. Even though I wasn't physically there, my consciousness was still tied to that location somehow, and the loud noise brought me back. I guess if I could recreate that scenario, it might keep me from floating off into the multiverse or something." Pax laughed halfheartedly at her own joke.

Ayana shot up out of the bed. "You need a kick."

"A what?"

"A kick. Okay, don't tell me you've never seen *Inception*."

Pax shrugged and shook her head.

"We really need to work on expanding your film repertoire."

Pax shot a biting look at her. Ayana was a bit of a snob when it came to her extensive knowledge of movies. She wanted to go to film school after she graduated and had seen practically everything.

"Don't worry. That's what I'm here for, babe. Okay, so there are these people who build dream worlds where they can travel, and they seem really realistic. They will be so deep into their dream that they need something big to wake them up. They call it a 'kick.' That's what you need."

"Okay, yeah, I guess that would make sense."

"You need an alarm. God, screw your dad for not buying you a phone. What was the reason for that again?"

Pax shrugged. "Clout, mostly. He says it's because experts say they're taking away our ability to communicate and develop healthy coping mechanisms. But it's really because he told other people he didn't believe in giving teenagers phones, and then he got invited to speak at a parenting conference and suddenly everyone thought he was Father of the Year."

Ayana laughed. "What an arrogant ass. Well, we have to get you an alarm. Actually . . ." She got up and shouted, "Mom!"

"What?" Sima's voice called from across the house.

"Do we still have Dad's stupid clock radio thing?"

"Uh, yeah, it's at the top of my closet."

Pax heard Sima bounding through the house before waddling through the doorway like a penguin. Pax giggled at her freshly painted toes and gray face mask that was now starting to bubble up. Her hair was wrapped in a silk headscarf to keep from getting caught in the goopy mess on her face.

"You look so hot right now," Ayana said.

"It's called 'self-care,' okay? Don't judge me." She pushed her daughter playfully. "Anyway, here." She shoved a big, hideous-looking alarm clock toward Ayana. It had a fake wood-grain exterior with a clunky dial switch. "What do you need this piece of garbage for?"

"Because . . ." Ayana paused.

It was Pax's turn to jump in. "I have trouble waking up in the mornings, and you know my dad won't let me get a phone."

Sima snorted. "Well, let me tell you, girl, that thing will do the job. It won't just wake you up—it'll wake your dad, your neighbors, your whole damn street. Ayana, I can't tell you how many times your dad and I got in a fight over that stupid alarm. I think he left it here just to spite me."

Ayana cackled. "Oh, he told me he did. He said he wanted you to have something to remember him by."

Sima cast an annoyed glance. "As if I could ever forget. I've got a court order to financially support his lavish lifestyle of music festivals and vacations to Cabo with a twenty-four-year-old named Jennifer."

Pax's eyes widened at the accusation. She wasn't used to adults sharing so much about their own drama. The familiarity between Ayana and her mom was almost too much sometimes.

"I'm sorry, Pax," Sima said, reading the expression on her face. "I shouldn't be airing out all my laundry for you to see."

Pax smiled. "Thanks for the clock."

"No, thank *you*," she said as she turned to leave. "Now I'm going to go wash my face. I feel like I'm molting." She scrunched up her nose as she picked at the dried goop on her cheek. "Have fun, girls."

"This ought to do it," Ayana said once her mom was out of earshot. She inspected the clock. "So, we've got a plan, we've got a kick. Now you just need to practice."

Pax furrowed her brow. "Practice what?"

"Traveling! You don't want to waste the whole weekend lying around the lake house because you're waiting for it to come to you. It's too risky. Plus, you've got to figure out if there's a way to control when you go and for how long. It would probably make this whole thing way less stressful if you weren't constantly worried you were going to disappear in the middle of Mrs. Tully's AP History class because you fell asleep."

"I see your point," Pax said. "But I have no idea how I would even begin to 'practice.'"

"I mean, I'm not the one with the superpowers, but I'd probably start with this stuff." Ayana handed her the documents on the Gateway Experience. "The article says it takes people months or even years to be able to travel at will, but you've already done it several times, so you've got a head start. I saw in the Gateway Experience documents that there are some kind of audio tapes available online. You are supposed to use them when you meditate. The sounds are supposed to elevate your brain frequencies so that your mind can move through different dimensions."

"Oh, is that all they do?" Pax teased.

Ayana ignored the jab. "But I wouldn't play with this until you understand it, so I think you should do a lot more studying before you give it a try."

"Ugh, but it's physics."

"So, ask for help. Zeke is taking physics this year, isn't he?"

"I don't think Zeke and I are on speaking terms right now. We got in a fight earlier. Or . . . I don't know. Not really a fight. I think he's just worried about me and thinks I'm unhinged."

"Oh, Pax, you told him?" Ayana said, and Pax nodded. "That was a terrible idea."

"I know, okay? But I just don't keep secrets from you guys. I even tried to lie to him, but he didn't buy it. I guess he thinks something is wrong with me now."

Ayana sighed. "Well, you're just going to have to prove to him that you're not crazy. But take it one thing at a time. Worry about the big stuff first. Besides, Zeke is a good guy and he cares about you. He won't stay mad forever."

"I hope you're right."

CHAPTER 8

The rest of the weekend passed slowly and painfully. Pax slept fitfully. Even with her "kick," she was still terrified of getting sucked into a dream from which she could never return. At one point on Sunday morning, she felt flickers of the beach, the heat, the sound of waves, but they were quickly and aggressively interrupted by the blaring gong of her new alarm. It resounded throughout the house, even managing to rouse her father.

"Turn that damn thing off!" he'd shouted.

There was no doubt that the gift from Ayana would be effective, or at least she hoped it would be if she became fully engrossed in her dream again.

She spent the remainder of her downtime trying to make sense of the research that was supposed to be helping her control her "abilities," or whatever they were. She wasn't even sure if the Gateway stuff was real or garbage, but it was all she had to go on at this point. Whenever she tried to read the article and wrap her mind around the conspiracy theories, it felt like her mind would implode. She hadn't taken physics yet, but even if she had, she wondered if it would even help her understand what this Dr. Monroe was talking about. She wouldn't get very far with this on her own. She'd have to ask someone for help. But she wasn't sure if the person she needed would be very forthcoming.

The news of her vanishing act, and her subsequent story of claiming to have no memory of leaving the party, had spread quickly through the student population over the course of the weekend. By the time she got to school on Monday morning, the whispers were all around her. She tried to lay low, but by the end of the day, someone had made a remark about it in almost every class. In the afternoon, she walked through the busy halls of her school, clutching the massive stack of papers against her chest, trying to protect them from the bustle around her. As she passed Zeke in the hall, she received little more than a perfunctory nod. She hesitantly smiled at him, still unsure of how to deal with the situation. They had never fought like this before, or at all. That was what she liked about her friendships: there was no drama. She hated knowing that she was the source of it, but at this point she didn't know how to fix it. She tried to shrug it off as she reached her locker to retrieve her science book.

"Excuse me, miss, but I have some questions about the space-time continuum," a voice said from behind her. Ayana snorted at her own joke.

"*Shh!* Can we not talk about that? Everyone thinks I'm weird enough as it is."

"Ugh, ignore them," Ayana said. "Your disappearance is the only gossip we have at this lame school right now. It'll pass."

"Easy for you to say. It's not you they're gossiping about." Pax shut her locker and started walking toward her last period.

Ayana put her arm around Pax. "Do you want them to be gossiping about me instead? Because I could definitely start something if you need me to."

Pax glared at her for a moment. "Please don't."

Ayana laughed. "Oh, come on. I was kidding! Sort of."

"Hey!" a voice boomed from up ahead. "I heard they had to call the cops on you at Aaron's party. They haven't taken you back to Mars yet?" Randy approached with a twisted grin spreading across his freckled face.

"Shut up, Randy!" Ayana shot at him.

"Make me, dyke!" he shot back.

"Wow, that's so original. I can really see that 1.9 GPA is working out well for you."

"Bitch," he hissed.

"You're damn right I am," Ayana said, shouldering past him. She strutted away with her head high.

Pax was always in awe of how well Ayana handled herself when people tried to mess with her. When she came out in the sixth grade, kids like Randy tried to give her hell for it. But nothing ever seemed to bother her. There was a group of girls who wrote the word *fag* on her locker in lipstick that year, and Ayana came back the next day and decorated the word with stickers of rainbows and hearts. She wore an insult like a badge of honor. She always told Pax, "When they call you a 'bitch,' what they really mean is that you're a woman who can't be controlled. Always take it like a compliment."

"Anyway," Ayana said now, brushing off the exchange with Randy like it never happened. "Do you want to come over after school today? I found those sound frequencies to help you . . . you know."

"I can't. I have detention with Mr. Hornsby after school."

"You fall asleep again?"

"Do you even have to ask?"

Ayana laughed. "All right, I'll see you later."

The class period crawled by at a glacial pace as Mr. Hornsby lectured about cellular mitosis, but Pax willed herself to stay focused, take notes, and even participate when he asked the class questions. She needed to be on his good side for her plan to work. She chuckled to herself as she watched Mr. Hornsby gesture wildly at the figures on the board. In regular conversation, he was pretty subdued, but when he talked about things that interested him, he would get a wild look in his eye and his deep British voice would jump almost a full octave as he passionately waved his hands about.

When the bell finally rang, she breathed a sigh of relief. Her classmates slowly filed out, but she settled into her desk and waited patiently for Mr. Hornsby to finish rifling through the papers on his desk.

"Right, Ms. Graves, I had almost forgotten. Well, here is your assignment. Read through this article on the reproduction process of earthworms and then write a paper about—"

"Actually, Mr. Hornsby, I was hoping I could get you to help explain something to me? Something science-related," she explained nervously.

"That's not usually how detention works, Ms. Graves." He waved her request away.

Pax persisted, determined. "I know, but I'm really stumped on this stuff, and I need it for this project I'm working on. It's about . . . space travel. Well, sort of. But I don't get the physics stuff, and I know you teach biology, but I was hoping maybe you—"

His eyes lit up. "I got my graduate degree in physics. I certainly could be of assistance. Okay, show me what you're working on."

Pax pulled out the papers she'd stowed away in her backpack and presented them to him nervously.

Mr. Hornsby studied the papers with a furrowed brow. "The Gateway Experience? Ms. Graves, this is not real science. This is nothing but superstition and conspiracy."

"I know, but that's what my project is about. I need to be

able to explain the science when I give my presentation, even if it's only hypothetical."

"Very well." He intently skimmed through the papers for a moment, grunting and snorting at the words. "What a load of bollocks," he chortled, tossing the sheets back onto her desk.

"I know, but I'm already kind of committed to this project, so do you think you could explain it to me anyway?"

He sighed heavily. "Very well. Let me start by saying this is a waste of your time, and the science here is half-cocked at best, and mixed in with a load of pseudo-spiritual nonsense. That being said, the basic idea is that the world that we live in is not a physical world at all, but a holograph of sorts that is made up of different frequencies, and these frequencies operate at such similar rates that to the human eye the differences between them are indiscernible, thus creating the illusion of reality."

"So, like *The Matrix* or something?"

He rolled his eyes. "Yes, a bit like that. But instead of the whole red-pill-blue-pill concept, you can force yourself out through meditation using a series of sound frequencies meant to interrupt your normal brain frequencies."

"Okay, but I still don't get how that pushes you into a different reality. People meditate all the time."

"You seem to be operating under the assumption that this load of horse manure is actually achievable and not the incoherent bumbling of an old hippie who experimented with too much LSD. It doesn't have to be applicable because it is not real."

"Right. But let's just say, for humor's sake, that this was real and people were actually able to achieve this. Aside from the logistics of how to get there, why would it even work?"

He sat back in his desk for a moment, crossing his arms over his chest. "You realize this is an insult to my doctorate degree, don't you? All right then." He looked around for a moment, and then grabbed a stack of paper and scribbled a stick figure on the first sheet with a marker. "This is you," he said, holding up the paper. "Your world exists within the confines of this single sheet of paper. You were born on it, and you will die on it. You know no other universe besides this white void on this single two-dimensional sheet." He flipped the sheet backward and forward.

"Okay . . ."

"But behind your sheet of paper, there are hundreds of other sheets of white paper. Even though you cannot see or experience them, they are there. Even though your body cannot leave this paper, Dr. Monroe claims that with the right amount of 'pressure' achieved through the disruption of your brain frequencies, your mind, or your spirit—whatever you want to call it—can transfer through the other layers." He pressed the red permanent marker into the center of the stick figure, and the ink bled through the papers beneath it. "Make sense?"

"I suppose." She paused, unsure of how to approach her next question. "Okay, so what if, hypothetically, someone was able to transport their entire body to these other sheets. Like, not just their consciousness, but the whole stick person?"

"Ah, see, now we're talking about science." A grin spread across his face. "Unfortunately, you are broaching on a question that even the greatest minds in the world have yet to answer."

"But do you think it's possible there are different worlds out there and we can transport ourselves to them?" Pax asked.

"I don't know. Now, are you asking if I believe there are other places out there in the great expanse of space with inhabitants and civilizations that we can encounter? I'd say that is highly probable. The likelihood that all life in the universe is limited to this tiny ball of water floating around in this single galaxy is incredibly slim, and if it is the case, vastly disappointing to the scientific community. When you say 'transport your body' though, we are talking about something entirely different. Someone would have to figure out a way to move matter by sheer force of mental energy." He waved his hands in the air.

"So, that part is not possible?"

"Well, based on what I know of the universe, the mere thought is highly illogical. Then again, it was only a hundred years ago that the idea of a sun-centered universe was highly illogical. Or a spherical Earth, for that matter."

"So . . ."

"What I'm saying, Ms. Graves, is that the only way to truly find the answer to these burning questions is through continuous pursuit and experimentation." He glanced at the clock above his door. "I believe we are now three minutes past your obligated time." He rose from his chair.

Pax shoved all the papers into her backpack and headed toward the door, lost in thought.

"Paxton?"

She pivoted on her heel. "Hmm?"

Mr. Hornsby shifted, looking uncomfortable for a moment. "It's . . . nice to see you care about something. Keep it up." He gave her an awkward thumbs-up.

She felt herself trying not to outwardly cringe.

"Too much?"

She laughed. "A bit."

He chuckled. "Right, well, see you tomorrow."

Pax spent the walk home mulling over Mr. Hornsby's words. It seemed that, at best, she had a half-baked theory about what was happening to her, but there were still so many holes in the reasoning. She certainly had never meditated or intentionally sought out ways to "spirit travel," or whatever it was. She often wished she could blink her eyes and be somewhere else, away from her father, but she never thought it could actually happen. But she had to keep digging, if for no other reason than to figure out how to keep herself from pulling a Houdini out in public. But more importantly, maybe this other place could help her find some missing pieces about herself. Everyone around her seemed so sure of who they were. But she was always two steps behind them, floundering, desperately trying to find a grasp on reality but hopelessly drowning, half alive. If there were answers on the other side of the universe somewhere, she had to find them.

When she arrived home, she made sure to tread as lightly as possible so her father would have no reason to pay attention to her. He was seated at his office space in the corner of the kitchen, buried underneath paperwork. He barely noticed Pax was there. She quietly set to work, assembling a makeshift dinner for the two of them out of the variety of packaged food items that were stashed away in the kitchen. She heated up a hodgepodge of burger patties, instant mashed potatoes and frozen gravy, and some boxed macaroni. She fixed up a plate, then quietly set a tray on the edge of the desk next to her father and freshened his glass of bourbon.

Her father looked over at the plate and muttered an awkward "thanks" as he took the tray.

"I'm headed to my room to do some homework, then I'm going to bed." She hoped that would be sufficient enough for him to not disturb her.

He grunted an acknowledgment as he shoved a spoonful of mashed potatoes into his mouth.

Pax heaved a sigh of relief as she locked her bedroom door

behind her. She paced anxiously for a moment. She needed to prepare for her next experiment. She showered and then rifled through her drawers to find something appropriate to wear. She settled on a pair of beige flowy drawstring pants and a simple white tee with some leather strap sandals. She approved of her reflection. The clothes were comfortable and inconspicuous enough that she wouldn't stand out. She compulsively straightened up her room and checked the alarm clock three times before she sighed in defeat. She needed to stop procrastinating. She walked over to the clunky old laptop that sat on her desk and fired it up. After what seemed like forever, the search engine screen finally came to life. She began to type, but then quickly shifted course and decided to check her email in one last ditch effort to delay the inevitable. But at the top of her inbox was an email from Ayana titled, "Here ya gooooo!" The message read, "Bon voyage!" followed by a million emoji and a URL link.

Pax took a deep breath and clicked the link. It led to a series of mp3 recordings preceded by directions:

1. Find a comfortable position. This can be lying down or sitting.

2. Make sure your eyes are closed for the entirety of the experience. It is imperative that your external surroundings are undisturbed.

3. Release all tension and stress from your body, empty your mind, and focus only on the sound and the pictures that come to view in your consciousness. Happy travels!"

Pax snorted. Even with her own knowledge and experiences, the thought of meditating to achieve "spiritual enlightenment" felt so ridiculous. She contemplated closing the page and watching Netflix for a while, but then she remembered what Mr. Hornsby said about "continuous experimentation and pursuit." She sighed as she moved the laptop over to her bedside table and plugged a pair of earbuds into the side.

She spread her body out across the mattress, remembering to keep her shoes on just in case, then slowly placed the buds into her ears and clicked the first mp3 link. Her brows furrowed as a low, continuous beeping noise filled her ears. The sound was unnerving, but she gritted her teeth and decided to give it a fair shot. She nestled further into the pillows, closed her eyes, and waited. She focused her mind on trying to see "images in her subconscious," as the instructions said, but the only images that came were the little static colors that always formed when she closed her eyes. She huffed and turned to check the time. It had only been five minutes. She sighed. This was going to be a long night.

She clicked through a few more audio files, each time sitting and waiting for something to happen. But nothing came. By ten o'clock, Pax was annoyed, exhausted, and feeling completely stupid. She decided that Mr. Hornsby was right, and this stuff was absolutely a load of garbage. She slammed her laptop shut, kicked off her shoes, and went to sleep.

─────

"Crap," Pax exclaimed as she looked down at her bare feet in the sand. "Should've kept my shoes on." She looked up at the sky. The sun's position told her it was sometime in the afternoon. It seemed like this world was on an alternate time schedule to her own.

This thought was interrupted by the sound of a plane approaching her, and it was flying low. Pax whipped her head around toward the wall and searched for the hole in the concrete Ari had led her to last time, but it was too far from view. She hurled her body into a full sprint, her bare feet tingling from the hot sand. If she was going to make it without getting caught, she had to get to the other side of the wall. When she reached the wall, she got on her hands and knees, desperately groping for the vulnerable spot in the rock but to no avail. She crawled further to the left, praying she was headed in the right direction. But the sound of the plane's engine grew closer.

"Where is it?" she cried as she frantically scooped sand away at the base of the stone wall in search of the opening. Suddenly, she fell onto her hands and knees as she heard the sound of gunshots firing close by, bouncing off the solid rock. She could be mere inches from death. Her only protection was the rock and mounds of sand she was wedged between.

About five yards ahead of her, a stake was nestled into the sand and tied with a strip of worn red fabric. It had to have been Ari marking the hole in the wall for her. If she moved, she might be struck by the bullets shooting from the plane overhead that were dangerously close to encroaching upon her. But if she didn't move, she would most certainly die.

She ground her teeth together and nestled herself as tightly as she could against the wall, then crawled on her arms alongside it. The plane looped back around and fired bullets just a few feet in front of her. Her heart slammed through her chest as adrenaline pulsed through her, thrusting her forward until she finally reached the flag. Tears of relief pricked at her eyes at the sight of a mound of rocks piled high against the wall. Last time, Ari had moved rocks away from the hole to escape from the helicopter. She kicked out her foot and knocked the pile of rocks out of the way to reveal the hole Ari had dug at the base of the wall. A bullet ricocheted off the wall just inches from where she forced her body through. With one final shove, she was safely on the other side. She sprinted forward until she was hidden within the shadows between two cottages, safely out of sight.

Her legs gave out and she slumped down against the cottage wall. Her breath fought its way out of her lungs in forceful huffs. She buried her face in her hands and gave way to tears of horror and relief that flooded her eyes. She didn't even have time to slow her breath when the scratch of an intercom system sounded from overhead.

A shrill voice echoed from speakers she could not see: "Please stand by for an important message from the Fellowship. Please stand by for an important message from the Fellowship."

Then a different, more commanding female voice, took its place: "Attention citizens, this is your general speaking. At approximately eighteen hours past, an unauthorized person was spotted on the forbidden land just outside the West Village. They have since breached the wall. This person is considered to be an enemy of the Fellowship and is therefore extremely dangerous. The suspect appears to be female, dark-haired, and is wearing a white tunic. If you have any information about their whereabouts or spot any person of this description behaving in a suspicious manner, please report it to the guard immediately."

Horror struck her as people shuffled out of their homes and looked around. She didn't know where to go, but she knew she couldn't stay here. She rose to her feet and fled from her hiding place to run further down the row of houses, keeping her back glued to the wall. Ari's house was at the very end of the road. Even though she didn't know what would happen when she got there, it was her only shot at survival. These people, whoever they were, were out to kill her. And if she were captured, they most certainly would. She sidestepped more quickly, pausing at the sounds of footsteps and voices. If she started running, she would be heard and captured immediately, so she went low and slow, desperately trying to escape unnoticed.

Just ahead, a figure sprinted toward her. Her heart sank. She froze against the wall like an animal caught in a trap. Her only option was to fight. She clenched her fists into tight balls, her blood coursing through her veins. The only way she might get out is if she surprised her attacker. As the figure grew closer, she sprang forward without a second thought and advanced on the figure at full speed. It was only when she was close enough to see his face that she realized it was Ari. But by then it was too late. She had already flung her body forward and pounced on top of him. They both went hurdling to the ground and landed with a painful impact.

Ari cursed, then moaned as he brought a hand to the back of his head. "What in the Holy Mother do you think you are doing?" he choked between breaths. She had knocked the wind out of him.

"I'm so sorry. I thought you were trying to attack me."

"What? You just attacked *me*."

"I didn't know it was you. I'm sorry, let me help." She rose to her feet too quickly and stumbled forward, landing on top of him again.

"Agh!" he exclaimed at the impact. "No, please. I've got it." He slowly got to his knees and then made his way to his feet. When he gained his footing, he extended a hand to Pax. He had a taunting look on his face.

She huffed as he pulled her to her feet. "Why were you running?"

"I knew it was you as soon as I heard the announcement. I was coming to find you to get you to safety. Now, come!" he said, as if suddenly remembering his mission.

They crept quietly behind the houses until they reached his

home at the end of the road. Ari paused and turned to face Pax, examining her. "Wait right here," he said, then hurried away.

Pax was panicked, praying he wasn't going to leave her here. Every minute she was out in the open was another minute she was at risk of getting caught. Ari returned shortly with a brown sack slung over his shoulder. He tossed it to her.

"Here, take this."

"What is—"

"Clothes," he answered before she could finish asking. "They described what you were wearing in the announcement. If anyone sees you coming into my house dressed like that, they will know I am hiding you."

"Right. Thanks."

"I will keep watch. Change quickly." He turned to face the other direction, giving Pax privacy.

She stood awkwardly for a moment, wishing she didn't have to disrobe out in the open within extremely close proximity to a boy she barely knew. But she had no other choice. She reached inside the bag and donned the soft blue dress that had been inside. The material was thin and hugged her at the top, then softly billowed down to the bottom of her calves. The hem was embroidered with a hand-stitched pattern. It was a bit too short, but it would do. She reached into the bag again and pulled out a pair of worn leather shoes that came to a slight point at the toes. They were old but sturdy, and they fit like a glove. She cleared her throat to signal to Ari that she was dressed.

He turned and let his gaze slide across her in approval. Pax shifted uncomfortably at the attention. "Sorry if the dress is small," he said. "It belongs to Dinah."

"Won't she notice if—"

"She is a seamstress. She has dozens. She is working late

this week making clothing for the festival at the capitol. She's been sleeping at the factory a lot."

"Oh. Okay."

"So, you are a bit taller than her, but I think if you move quickly, no one will really notice."

"What do you mean?"

"You have black hair, like Dinah. I think we can pass you for her, so long as you do not talk to anyone and keep your face hidden. Do you know how to braid?"

"To what?"

"Braid. Your hair? So you'll look like her."

"Oh, uh . . . no. No one ever taught me."

Ari huffed in frustration. He placed himself inches from her face and hurriedly gathered her hair until it spilled in front of her right shoulder.

Pax took a step backward. "What are you doing?"

"Hold still," Ari ordered. "I'm trying to get the strands even." He was intently focused as he skillfully weaved the pieces into a long braid.

Pax blushed, feeling deep discomfort at the unexpected intimacy of the act. "How did you learn to braid?"

"Dinah taught me. After Mom was killed, we both took care of our youngest sister, Nyla. I did her hair most mornings."

"If you don't mind me asking, what happened to your parents?"

Ari's brow furrowed, and Pax wondered for a moment if she shouldn't have asked.

"I don't know all the details. I was little when it all happened, but people in the village have told me stories about my parents and how they fought to keep our land when the Fellowship attacked. Our papa died first. We had Mom for two more years, but then she died too."

"Oh, I'm so sorry," she sighed heavily. Though she could empathize with the loss, she couldn't imagine living through what Ari had lived through. He shifted uncomfortably as the emotion began to show in his eyes. Pax decided to change the subject. "So, um, your eyes . . . they're gold." Pax realized how stupid that sounded, but she was so uncomfortable with him standing this close to her, she was having trouble forming complete sentences.

He smirked. "Was that a question?"

"I mean, that's not common where I'm from."

"Yes, well, it is here. My father had eyes like mine. He used to say it was how you could spot a true Terran from a Traveler. But that is not really true, since Travelers mate with Terrans all the time."

"Oh." She wasn't sure what else to say.

"Done," he announced as he finished tying a leather strap to secure the braid. "Okay, so remember: walk quickly, do not look at anyone, do not talk to anyone. Just keep going until you get inside the house."

Pax nodded with determination as she followed him out. They rounded the corner with purpose, trying to swiftly get inside, but not so quickly to arouse suspicion. Even with her gaze casting downward, Pax could tell there were at least a dozen people outside speaking in frantic tones. Ari and Pax hurried up the old wooden steps, and he opened the door and ushered her in. As soon as the door closed, they each heaved a sigh of relief and sank down into a kitchen chair.

Pax's muscles burned, finally feeling the full impact of the chase hitting her body now that the adrenaline was wearing off. She slumped forward, letting her forehead rest on the table.

"Is it the same each time?"

She lifted her head. "What?"

"Do you always end up here when you travel?"

"Yes."

"Why?"

"I wish I knew. It's not exactly something I have control over."

"I see."

"So, I'm not exactly sure how much time I have until I go back." She struggled for the words.

"Well, I hope it will be soon."

Pax glared at him.

"Not that I mind, but you know, just so that you are not found."

They sat in silence for a moment, both unsure of what to say. They had never really sat and had a conversation before. The few interactions they did have mostly consisted of Ari saving her against his own will. They weren't exactly friends. She was more like a disease he couldn't seem to get rid of. At least, that was how Pax assumed he felt. Then she remembered something. "Did you leave that marker by the wall for me?"

Ari looked down and nodded sheepishly. "I just thought you should be able to find the opening so you didn't die out there."

"You knew I'd come back?"

"No, I just . . . thought maybe you would."

"Well, I owe you. I really would have died today if I hadn't seen it. So, thank you."

"Have you ever tried to travel anywhere else?" he asked, quickly changing the subject.

Pax shook her head. "I didn't even know I could travel until recently."

"Is it not something you are born with?"

"I don't know. Actually, that's why I wanted to come back. To find answers. There are others like me here, aren't there?"

Ari nodded. "Most people in the Fellowship and many in the city have the gift, but I have never met one before you."

Pax furrowed her brow. "Wait, so if there are people in the Fellowship who can travel, then why do they want to kill me?"

He shrugged. "Power, if I had to guess. That is a question for someone with far more knowledge than me."

"Do you know someone?"

"What do you mean?"

"Someone who would know, I mean."

He thought for a moment. "Perhaps . . . but we cannot go to him today. We should probably wait until there are not people trying to kill you."

"Right." She laughed humorlessly.

A knock at the door caused them both to jump. A man's voice called from outside. Pax looked at Ari, panicked.

"Go lie down over there." Ari pointed to one of the pallets in the corner of the room. "Be sure that he cannot see your face. Say nothing."

Pax nodded and settled herself down on the blanket as Ari went to the door.

"Ari," a deep voice greeted him.

"Shulem! How are you?" he responded, trying to sound casual.

"Well, my friend. I came to warn you and your sister. The Guadaros are coming to search the village for the fugitive," Shulem replied.

"Oh."

"Dinah, are you all right, dear one?" the man called after her. Pax froze, then slowly nodded without turning around.

"Oh yes. She is just not well today."

"Well, perhaps I could help. You know I am a practiced healer."

Pax clenched, feeling panic wash over her as she heard the footsteps approach.

"Oh, that will not be necessary," Ari said, then lowered his voice. "It is just her woman's time, sir."

"Ah," the man said. "Well, er, yes. Feel better then! And remember, friend, when the Guadaros come, be safe and respond calmly."

"Of course. Thank you for the warning. The Mother be with you, friend."

"And with you," the man responded gravely and left.

Pax shot upward in a panic when Ari closed the door. "The guards are coming? What am I going to do? Should I run?"

"No! If they are coming to search, there will be hordes of them, and they will be armed. You cannot outrun them. There is no doubt they have doubled their patrol of the Outlands as well."

Pax's chest tightened and her breathing became shallow.

Ari stood in front of her and placed his hands on her shoulders, his golden eyes meeting hers. "Listen to me, Pax. I need you to trust me. There is a space underneath the floor where we store food. You can hide there. I will hold them as long as I can, but you must try to get home."

Her heart stopped. She was giving over to a panic attack, hysterics building in her chest as her breath came out in heaving sobs. "I—I can't. I don't know how to do that. I've never—"

Ari moved his hands from her shoulders up to the sides of her face and brought his forehead to meet hers. "Shh." He lowered his voice to a whisper. "Quiet your head. These thoughts will not help you now. Don't ask yourself how you will do this, just decide that you will. It is your only chance. Can you do this?" His gaze bore into her soul, radiating calm and confidence.

Pax bit her lip, looking up at him, and whispered, "Yes."

He nodded, then kneeled on the ground in front of her. He wiggled a piece of the floorboard loose and wrenched it upward. It was barely large enough to fit through, but Pax squeezed herself in, shoving carefully wrapped bits of food to the side so she could lay flat.

"Listen, Pax," Ari called from above. "I will do my best to get out to mark the spot again, but if I cannot, the hole is directly in line with where the sun sets in the horizon. Find it, then come find me."

"But what if I don't—"

He shook his head. "You will."

Loud banging and shouting came from the homes on either side of them. Ari turned toward the door, then looked down at her one more time. "Remember, do not make a sound. I will see you again, Pax," he vowed, as if trying to instill confidence in her.

Pax nodded as he slid the floorboards back into place. Despite his confident demeanor, Ari's footsteps paced above her. Her anxiety spiked again, but she shook her head. She had to focus. She closed her eyes and exhaled.

"Come on," she whispered. "Wake up, wake up, wake up." She sighed, knowing she was still in Ari's crawlspace. She squeezed her eyes tightly together, tensing every muscle in her body as she commanded herself, "Go home!" Still, she felt nothing.

Suddenly, a rapid banging sounded from the door overhead. A scream gathered in Pax's throat. Someone gruffly demanded to open the door. Ari's calm footsteps strode toward the door.

"Good evening," was his muffled greeting.

"Move," a booming voice commanded.

"As you say, sir."

"Have you seen any suspicious figures here?" another voice questioned as multiple footsteps stormed about the small space.

Pax's chest heaved in panic. This was it. This would be her end if she couldn't find a way to leave. She searched her brain for something, anything to help her. But all that was coming to her mind was a lullaby her mom used to sing to her. Maybe it was because she knew she was going to die, but in that moment she let that memory take over. A sense of calmness flooded through her body, slowing her heartbeat. In her mind's eye, she saw her mom—young and beautiful, her raven hair falling in long tendrils down her back. Her soft, warm skin. Her arms wrapped around Pax as she laid her little head against her mother's chest. The vibration of her mother's voice as she hummed. As the footsteps sounded just above her now, Pax was enveloped in the warmth of the memory of her mother. Her vision filled with a warm light. Just as the floorboard creaked above her, something inside of Pax made her whisper:

"Home."

CHAPTER 9

Pax thought she must have set a record for how quickly she had showered and gotten dressed the next morning. When she realized she had successfully traveled back home, she stayed up for hours trying to wrap her mind around it all. She hadn't even realized she had fallen back to sleep until the blaring of that obnoxious alarm had jolted her awake. Realizing she was still in Dinah's dress, now dirty, she raced to get ready. However, her thoughts were so preoccupied with the events of last night, and trying to find more suitable clothing, that she had forgotten to blow-dry her hair. It was still damp when she flung herself into the passenger seat of Ayana's car.

"You look clean," Ayana offered.

Pax huffed. "Don't start. I had a really long night."

Ayana's eyes lit up. "So you did it? You actually went to Terra?"

Pax smiled. "Yes. Well, not on purpose, exactly. The whole meditation thing was a load of crap. But I ended up there when I went to sleep anyway, and when I got there I almost *died*."

"You *what*?"

"Yeah. I was running, and there was this plane, and I couldn't find the opening to the wall, and then they just started *shooting* and—"

Both girls froze at the sound of the door to the back seat popping open.

"Don't stop on my account," Zeke mumbled grumpily,

clearly not thrilled to be with them. His ride must have bailed this morning.

"Oh, we were just talking about a TV show we've both been watching. It's not important," Ayana lied.

Zeke grunted with disinterest as he closed the door. "We should go."

"Right," Ayana said as she pulled out of the driveway. The ride to school was silent.

Pax spent the school day lost in thought. She kept thinking about her final moments in Terra, replaying them in her mind, trying to find the secret ingredient that magically transported her home. It was the first time she had ever traveled back by her own will. If she could figure out how she got home, she could use the same technique in reverse. She jotted down a list of her thoughts and feelings right before she traveled back: *deep breaths, staying calm, memory of Mom, home.*

She repeated the steps in her head in art class, trying to figure out what the secret was as she worked on her latest sculpture: the figure of Argus, the many-eyed giant in Greek mythology, made from the scraps of metal from discarded desks that she had soldered together. Perhaps these steps were like a formula of some sort. A naive part of her hoped that somehow it was her mom who had saved her, that maybe she was watching over her or something. She immediately shook that thought away. Her mother was gone and had no part in her life. She set to work on drilling eyes of varying sizes she had fashioned from skateboard wheels, aluminum cans, and old tennis balls into the metal skull of the beast.

"Mrs. Peterson?" a voice echoed from the intercom in the corner of the room, bringing the class to attention. "Please send Paxton Graves to the office."

"Ooh," the class taunted.

Pax rolled her eyes, and Mrs. Peterson, who was elbow-deep in a modeling clay sculpture, gestured her head toward the door.

Pax's pulse quickened as she set down the drill and trudged toward the door to the office. She didn't know why she was called, but prior experience taught her it was never a good thing. She stopped abruptly at the sight of Mrs. Schriber's short, curvy frame leaning against the door with a warm smile on her face. Pax eyed her dubiously, taking in her black-and-white polka dot dress and cherry-red shoes that were color-coordinated with her belt and glasses.

"This way, Ms. Graves!" Mrs. Schriber chirped, waving her over. "How are you doing today?"

"Um, good, I guess?" Pax retorted. "I'm sorry, can you tell me why I'm here?"

Mrs. Schriber good-humoredly smacked her forehead against her palm. "Of course! You know me, I'd forget my own name if it wasn't on the door there." She snorted at her joke. "I just wanted to pull you in today to have a little chat."

Pax knew from experience that a "little chat" with Mrs. Schriber was most definitely not a casual check-in. She settled into the squeaky chair on the opposite side of the counselor's desk. Much to her chagrin, the counselor decided to sit in the chair directly beside her, angling it only slightly away. Pax cringed inwardly.

"Now, Pax, I have been hearing some things through the grapevine. You know, aside from the usual. Would you like to tell me about that?"

Her voice went flat. "Nope. I'm fine."

"Now, I know it can seem scary to open up when you've got real stuff going on, but it can be really cathartic to just get it all out," she reassured.

Pax's jaw clenched. This was Mrs. Schriber's go-to move. Pax cut right to the point. "What exactly have you heard?"

"Oh, you know how kids talk. I heard about your little disappearance last week. Did something happen?"

"I like to walk in the woods. Sometimes I get lost," Pax responded, annoyed.

"I see . . ." Mrs. Schriber jotted a note on a slip of paper angled just far enough away that Pax couldn't read it. "And when you go on these walks, are you trying to run away?"

Pax rolled her eyes. "No, I'm just clearing my head."

"You know, Pax," she started hesitantly, "some of this behavior you are exhibiting feels like it might be a cry for help. The disappearing, the sleeping in class . . ."

Pax cut her off. "No. Look, I'm fine. You know, I'm just dealing with a lot of stuff."

She nodded. "The episodes?"

Pax looked down and nodded sadly, sniffling for extra effect. The truth was, she hadn't fallen asleep in class and woken up from a screaming fit since the night she disappeared from the party, but she knew Mrs. Schriber wouldn't let her go unless she felt like they had made some kind of emotional breakthrough. So she decided that blaming it on the nightmare episodes was easier than diving into her family drama. "You know what it's been like."

"Of course, dear."

"Listen, I don't know who made that report, but you know people at this school like to spread rumors because they're bored. I'm sorry they pulled you into it."

"No, dear. I believe the reports were made out of genuine concern."

Pax snorted. "I highly doubt it. Who even reported it?"

"Well, I can't tell you that, dear. But I can assure you they are trying to look out for you."

Pax's eyes widened in disbelief. There was only one person who would have possibly reported her for any reason that wasn't a joke. She felt her cheeks heat with rage. "Are we done here?"

"Well, I suppose. But listen, Pax, if you ever find yourself in any kind of danger, or if you just need to talk, please know that I am here. I can help you if you'll let me."

Pax nodded and stood to leave without a word. The bell buzzed overhead as she turned the corner and weaved through the hallway that was filling with students. She tore herself through the double doors leading to the courtyard where the students ate lunch and paused to scan the crowd. She finally zeroed in on him, standing with a couple of his soccer friends, laughing as he slid his backpack off his shoulders.

Pax didn't pause for a moment. Rage propelled her forward.

"Zeke!" she shouted across the courtyard. Heads turned all around them, focusing in on the drama that was sure to unfold. Zeke turned in her direction, but he hardly had time to process it until Pax was right in front of him. She slammed her hands into his chest, causing him to stumble backward.

"What are you doing?" he asked.

"You reported me to the guidance counselor?" she shouted without caring who heard.

People gathered all around them, snickering at the accusation. Aware of the crowd forming, Zeke took Pax by the wrist. "Not here," he said in a low voice.

Pax looked around at the taunting faces. In normal circumstances, she would never draw this much attention to herself, but she was so angry she couldn't think straight. She looked at him and nodded, allowing him to lead her to a more private corner of the courtyard.

"What exactly were you thinking?" she demanded when they were out of earshot.

He lifted his arms in exasperation. "I don't know, Pax. I just . . . something is wrong with you, and I can't help. And after what I overheard in the car this morning, it's clear that Ayana is encouraging it. But I won't let you go off the rails without doing everything that I can to—"

"But I never asked you to do that, Zeke. I don't need you swooping around trying to save me all the time."

"Of course you do," he shot back. "You're a mess, Pax!"

She stood with her mouth hanging open in disbelief. In all their years of friendship, Zeke had always been understanding, kind, and level-headed to a fault. His words seared into her skin.

Zeke looked almost as shocked as Pax, the weight of his words now crashing around him. "Hey, wait. That's not what I meant. I meant you're—"

"I'm what?" Her voice wavered as tears spilled down her cheeks. "Messed up? Guess what, Zeke. I didn't need you to tell me that. But it's great to know what you really think of me."

He reached out a hand to grab hers. "No, that's not—"

"Oh, yes it is. I'm just some sad, poor little girl who you always have to pull back together when her life falls apart. Well, I guess it'll be a relief for you to know you don't have to do that anymore."

Pax spun on her heels and sprinted toward the double doors with tears streaming down her cheeks. Zeke called after her, trying to catch up, but she wove in and out of the crowds, losing him as she entered the hall.

"Paxton," an icy, smooth voice called from behind her.

She froze, slowly turned around, and found herself face-to-face with her father.

"What is going on?" he bit out in a low tone, careful not to draw the attention of the teenagers shuffling through the hall.

"I—" she started.

"Why am I hearing from Mrs. Schriber that you went missing on Friday night?" His tone was smooth and controlled, but his eyes burned with anger.

"Dad, I can explain," she choked out in between sobs.

"Paxton." He moved closer and smiled tightly, careful not to let his frustration slip out. "You're making a scene."

"Pax!" Ayana shouted from behind her. Then she grabbed Pax and pulled her into a crushing embrace.

Pax began to weep the moment she felt her friend's arms around her shoulders.

Ayana turned to face Pax's father. "If you write us an excuse, I can take her home, Principal Graves," she offered in a sickly-sweet tone.

Her father smiled brightly. "That is very kind of you, Ayana. Yes, of course. I'll notify your teachers." Before he turned to leave, he leaned toward Pax. "We'll discuss this later."

Pax's blood ran cold at the subtle threat, but she shook it off. She would worry about that later. She turned to Ayana. "How did you—"

"I saw the whole thing," she replied. "Come on, I can't leave you crying in the hallway."

"Thanks," she sniffled.

"Of course. Now, come on. We're ordering a hundred sushi rolls and eating them in your bed."

An hour later, Pax and Ayana were sprawled out across opposite ends of her mattress, groaning in misery. "Do you want my last roll?" Pax offered.

"Ugh. God, no. If I ate any more, I'd probably explode." Ayana unzipped the fly of her jeans.

"Do you mind if I take the unopened chopsticks? I think I could use them for a project."

Ayana handed them to her. "Weirdo." She chuckled. "So, how are you feeling?"

"Like I might vomit, actually."

Ayana laughed. "That's not what I meant."

"Yeah, I know what you meant." Pax sighed. "A little shocked, I guess. But mostly ashamed."

Ayana sat up, confused. "What do you have to be ashamed about?"

"I don't know. Just the fact that I had a huge blow-up with my best friend. At school. In front of everyone. It's so . . ."

"High school?" Ayana offered.

Pax groaned and put a pillow over her face.

"Okay, but to be fair, what Zeke did was pretty messed up. I would've reacted the same way. I mean, the fact that he went and snitched on you? I thought he was better than that."

"Yeah. I don't know. In a way, I guess I see where he was coming from."

"You're too good of a friend. We're mad at him, remember?"

Pax laughed. "I'm definitely still pissed, but if it was the other way around and Zeke was acting sketchy and not talking to me about it, I'd probably flip too."

"Sure, but I don't know, Pax . . ." Ayana started, casting a wary glance toward her.

"What?"

"Don't murder me for saying this, but your relationship with Zeke is a little . . ."

"What?"

"Codependent?"

Pax shot a piercing glare at her.

"Don't look at me like that! I've been going to therapy for like three years now since my parents got divorced. I know what I'm talking about."

Pax snorted. "Okay, but going to therapy doesn't exactly give you a PhD."

"I know, but I only say this because I love both of you. Please remember that before you come at me, okay? And I'm not trying to judge you. God knows I've got my own weird, toxic drama. I get why it's like this between you guys. For a long time, Zeke was all you had. Your mom is gone and your dad is . . . your dad, and Zeke has been the only constant for you. And I know you probably feel like it's one-sided, but I know for a fact that you've been the same for him."

"Are we nearing the point here?" Pax said, annoyed by how right her friend was.

"Yes. What I'm saying is some time apart might be good for you guys. I think a little space might help you both realize what's really going on here."

"Which is . . . ?"

"Come on. You can't seriously not see it, right?" Ayana laughed.

Pax shook her head and shrugged.

Ayana sighed and placed a hand on Pax's shoulder. "Pax, that sweet, dumb little boy is in love with you."

Pax's mouth gaped at that accusation. Blood rushed to her cheeks before she could stop it, and nervous laughter escaped her lips. "You're not serious?" She cast a wary glance at her friend, who only nodded in return. "Shut up! That's so far from true." She shrugged Ayana's hand from her shoulder.

"Are you kidding? The way he checks up on you and takes care of you?"

"He does that to everyone!"

"Um, he's never done that for me. And if he tried to do those things for his soccer bros, I'd be questioning his sexuality."

"I think he just . . . I don't know. Feels sorry for me or something." Her palms began to sweat. "He is *not* in love with me."

"Look, you can keep shrugging it off if you want to. All I'm saying is that dude has been pining for you for as long as I've known you guys, and if this thing is gonna work, you both need to figure out what you want."

"What if I don't want anything to 'work'?" Pax shot back.

"That's fine too, but you'd better tell him that. Romantic feelings aside, I know you care for him, which means it would be super messed up for you to keep dragging him along just because it feels comfortable for you. That's not fair to him."

Pax sighed. "You're making valid points, but I'm not convinced you're right. He and I have been best friends for six years now. He's had all this time. I think he would've said something by now."

"Fair, and in a perfect world, maybe he would've fessed up years ago. But you know, he might be scared of losing the friendship."

"This is so stupid," Pax groaned, collapsing backward in exasperation.

"I agree. Hetero relationships are so stupid. You guys live for the drama. I blame romantic comedies. See, gay girls didn't have that representation growing up, so there were no weird expectations or guidelines for us. We just made up our own rules. If you were both lesbians, you'd probably already be dating, coparenting a cat, and planning to move in together after graduation."

"This is not helpful at all."

Ayana laughed. "I'm just saying, this doesn't have to be stressful, okay? Just take some time to figure out what you want, then when you're ready, tell him."

"You act like that's the easiest thing in the world."

"I know it's not as straightforward as that, but what else are you going to do? Ignore those feelings forever until the whole thing inevitably implodes?"

"Maybe." Pax felt overwhelmed. She couldn't imagine not being friends with Zeke.

"I give it five days before he comes crawling back," Ayana said. "You've been friends for a long time. One fight isn't going to ruin that."

Pax sighed. "I hope not. I've got other things to worry about right now."

Ayana narrowed her eyes, spotting Dinah's dress draped across the back of Pax's chair. "Where's this from?" she asked, rubbing her fingers across the stitching at the hem.

"Oh. I kind of stole it," she admitted sheepishly.

Ayana's eyes lit up. "You? Steal?"

"Well, I mean, technically Ari let me borrow it. It's his sister's, but she wasn't there, and I was still wearing it when I traveled back."

"I see. So, this Ari guy seems to be very willing to risk his life for you."

Pax scoffed, picking up the suggestive tone. "Don't get your hopes up. Ari barely tolerates my existence."

"Whatever you say. Speaking of Ari though, care to catch me up on the whole saga?"

Pax recounted her story with as much detail as she could remember: the planes, Ari marking the wall, pretending to be Dinah, the way she got out. Ayana clung to every word, absorbing every detail. When Pax finished, Ayana slumped backward as if she had been the one who experienced it all.

"Holy crap," she whispered in disbelief. "So you straight up could have died."

Pax nodded, still in shock herself. "Twice."

"So, if you die there, does that mean . . ."

"I think so. I mean, anytime I've gotten a cut or bruise in Terra, it always follows me back here. I don't think this is like virtual reality or something. This is the real deal."

"Are you sure you should be doing this?"

"I thought you wanted me to figure all of this out."

"Yeah, but that was before you became a fugitive of the law, alone in an entirely different planet where you could literally get killed and I'd never actually know what happened. You know what I mean?"

"Yeah, I get it. But what other choice do I have? Until I learn to control it, I'm going to keep traveling whether I want to or not. I think I have to go back, if for no other reason than to learn how to stop it from happening against my will, if that's even possible."

"Yeah. It just feels like this got so much more intense."

"Oh, believe me, I know. It was never exactly a game to me, but now that I'm being hunted, I feel like I'm just living in a constant state of paranoia." Pax fiddled with the hem of her shirt. "We've got three days until our trip, so for now I'm just going to try to stay alive. And away from Terra, if I can help it."

"Do you think you're any closer to figuring out how to control it?"

"Sort of. The Gateway stuff was garbage, but I was able to

get back by some miracle. I just don't know if what I did to get back home can also get me there or keep me here. And I think my episodes during class had something to do with the traveling because they've just stopped. I don't know what the connection is yet."

"Well, you're closer to an answer than you were before," Ayana offered.

Pax blushed at her next question. "Hey . . . do you think you could teach me how to braid my hair?"

Ayana raised a brow.

"It'll help me when I travel."

"Anything for the cause, comrade!" She gave Pax a military-like salute.

Pax laughed.

Suddenly, a car pulled into the driveway outside.

"That's my cue to leave, I guess." Ayana gathered her bag. "Are you going to be okay with him?" Her eyes were wide with concern.

"Yeah. I'll be fine." Pax swallowed the lump in her throat.

"You sure? Because I could wait outside."

"No, I promise it'll be okay," she lied. The truth was, she had no idea what was going to happen when her dad walked through that door. She had embarrassed him today, and in his book, that was an unforgivable crime.

"I'll talk to you tomorrow, okay?" Ayana said, looking back at Pax.

Pax nodded and forced a smile. When Ayana left the room, she flopped backward onto her bed and listened intently to the sound of her father's footsteps crunching the gravel outside, then the rattle of the doorknob, a brief exchange between him and Ayana, then the click of the door. She waited for the inevitable sound of his footsteps approaching her room, but they never came. When she woke the next morning, her father was already gone.

CHAPTER 10

T he rest of the week crawled by, leaving Pax to sit in the muddled stew of chaos that was her life. She hadn't heard from her father since their exchange in the hall. She came home before him and stayed in her room until she heard his bedroom door shutting. They hardly even saw each other. It was more unsettling than a confrontation, but she didn't dare approach him. Maybe he was so stressed about the conference coming up that he forgot. Whatever the reason, she wasn't about to bring it up.

That situation alone would be enough to drive anyone over the edge, but she still had other things to worry about. She flipped back and forth between stressing about her dad, to stressing about her fight with Zeke, to stressing about traveling. Or not traveling. Every night when she went to sleep, anxiety overtook her. Would she find herself in danger when she woke up? That was enough to keep her staring at the ceiling for hours, rehashing all the events from the week. The thought of Zeke made her tear up. She couldn't even begin to think about her conversation with Ayana. The possibility of her relationship with Zeke changing was too much to bear. But she knew Ayana was right. If he really did have feelings for her, she needed to sort through her own feelings. But it was complicated. Was she attracted to Zeke? Of course. She couldn't think of a single person with eyes who wouldn't be. But she had pushed the possibility of anything more than friendship so deep inside that she struggled to even entertain it. The thought of their friendship being something more made her heart jittery. She shook the thought away. How could she go there without knowing the truth? Besides, she had to survive this week before she could even think about it.

The possibility of finding herself back in Terra made her chest clench and her heartbeat pound in her ears. She was utterly defenseless against her own ability aside from some half-baked system she'd accidentally discovered to help her travel back. Every night when she was on the verge of dozing, she would chant quietly, "Stay home, stay home, stay home." She prayed it would be enough to keep her safe. Whether it actually helped or was just pure luck, she managed to wake up each morning from a dreamless sleep. But just in case, she would sleep in Dinah's dress and shoes each night.

When Friday finally arrived, Pax didn't know if she should be terrified or relieved. As she readied for school, she packed nothing but a few toiletries and Dinah's clothes. Before leaving, she wrote a little note to her father reminding him that she would be studying at Ayana's house for the weekend while he was away just in case he decided to care. That was the one plus side of him not speaking to her this week: she didn't have to worry about him calling to check in.

She spent the day deep in thought, planning what she would do once she got to Terra. But truthfully, she didn't know if she would even survive. A lump formed in her throat, but she quickly shook it away. It was her only option if she wanted to learn how to control when she traveled.

When the final bell rang, Pax rushed to the student parking lot. Ayana was already in the driver's seat, blaring her music so loud everyone in the parking lot turned to stare.

"Road trip! Road trip!" she chanted with excitement, pumping her fists over her head.

Pax hurried toward the car, trying to minimize the public display of embarrassment.

"Where you headed?" someone asked.

Pax stopped short. It was Zeke. She turned to face him but couldn't make herself meet his gaze. "Uh, me and Ayana are going to her dad's lake house for the weekend. You know, just to get away for a bit."

He nodded. "Oh. Well, I was hoping maybe we could talk?"

Her eyes met his for a moment, noting the quiet desperation behind those deep green pools. Even though the thought of their argument still made her angry, her heart wrenched at the sight of him now.

Ayana honked behind them in agitation. Pax flipped her head toward her, then back to Zeke. "We'll be gone until Sunday. So, when I get back?"

Zeke's shoulders sagged. Pax turned to walk toward Ayana's car. "Pax?" he called. She turned once again to face him. His face was sullen. "Enjoy your trip!" he said, trying to sound upbeat. She smiled and headed toward the vehicle.

When she closed the passenger door, Ayana was looking at her with an expression that said, *I told you so.* Pax shot a glare at her. "Don't."

Ayana laughed. "God, I hate it when I'm right," she said as they spun out of the parking lot.

———

The hour drive passed relatively quickly as Pax listened to Ayana chatter on about inconsequential things: girls, TV shows, drama from school. She tried to smile and focus on her friend, but her thoughts kept drifting toward the weekend. Pax was not the kind of person who didn't have a plan. She wasn't particularly brave or spontaneous. Her life had been too chaotic for that. Knowing what was coming comforted her. It was safe. But now she had no plan except to get back to Terra. What would she do when she got there? Would she even make it out alive? The thought unnerved her. A shiver rolled up her spine.

A tap on her shoulder made her jump.

"We're here," Ayana said gently.

"Oh," Pax said.

Inside the cabin, she stopped short. The sight astonished her. This was not a little cabin on the lake. This was a luxury home. She took in the wide-open space brightened by white walls and huge windows overlooking the lake. She counted six bedrooms from what she could see of the open upper floor. The banister overlooked the main room.

"This is your vacation house?" Pax said in awe.

"Well, it's my dad's. He had it redone after my grandma died. I haven't been here since."

Pax let out a breath. She was reminded of just how different Ayana's life was from hers. How did they even become best friends?

"So, want to order some food before you . . . ?" Ayana slowly raised her arms in some kind of ascending gesture.

Pax laughed. "Is that how you think it works? I just levitate into the sky?"

Ayana crossed her arms. "Well, I don't know! I've never seen anyone time travel before."

"It's more like space travel, but I get what you're saying. Food would be good."

Thirty minutes later, Pax and Ayana sat cross-legged on the large white sectional devouring their own boxes of pizza slice by slice. When Pax had had her fill, she leaned back onto the cushion and exhaled, content.

"So, what's the plan?" Ayana asked, her mouth still full.

Pax's palms moistened as she remembered why they were actually here. "Well, I guess I'll get ready and find somewhere quiet to, you know . . . try. Will you be okay out here alone?"

Ayana laughed. "Are you kidding? I'm going to sit in the hot tub and watch Netflix on the back deck for the next couple of days. I'm on vacation right now."

"Fair enough."

"What about you?"

"Well, I don't really know. I hope I'll be okay. I'll try to get off the beach and find Ari as soon as possible. Then I'll go from there."

Ayana gathered Pax's hands into her own and squeezed. "I know you have to do this, but please be careful. Do whatever you need to get home. I'll never forgive myself if you . . ." Her voice trailed off.

Pax squeezed her hand in return. "I'll be fine," she promised, even though they both knew it was a promise she couldn't keep.

Ayana led her upstairs to a room with a large bed in the middle. She flopped down on it as Pax changed into the clothes she had tucked into her backpack.

"Do you, I don't know, need anything?" Ayana asked.

"Actually, could you set up the alarm at some point? It's in my bag."

"Sure thing. When?"

"I don't know. Maybe four in the afternoon on Sunday? My plan is to try to make my way back before then. But just in case, you know?"

"Right." Her friend nodded gravely. "Well, if you need anything, I'll be just outside." She moved to the door, then glanced back, unsure.

"Go. I'll be fine." Pax forced a smile.

Ayana strode toward her once more and gathered her into a tight embrace before leaving the room.

Pax watched her leave, her heart sinking, knowing the hug was meant to be a goodbye. Her breathing quickened and her chest constricted, but she forced herself to be calm. She couldn't travel if she was anxious. Or at least, she guessed that much based on past experience. She settled back onto the soft mattress, wishing she could just fall asleep on it instead. She focused on all the places the mattress was touching her, calming her mind and making herself present. Instinctively, she spread out her arms and legs until she was in a starfish position. She recalled the memory of her mother that had brought her back home and closed her eyes, struggling to fix on the image. Then she imagined her mother's hair, her eyes, the sound of her voice humming. Her fingers tingled lightly. The last time she had done this, she had whispered, "Home." But now she was home. She struggled for a moment and dumbly muttered, "Terra," hoping these would be the magic words to transport her. Cool air brushed over her skin, creating goosebumps on her arms. She lay there for a moment in total stillness, then opened her eyes.

She was still atop the impossibly large bed in the lake house.

She huffed, then summoned the image again, muttering, "Terra." She tried this again and again to no avail. Frustration was building within her. What was the missing piece to this puzzle? Was it really just dumb luck that she had traveled back? She flipped over to look at the clock on the bedside table. Two hours had passed. She sighed, then slowly got to her feet, opened the door, and made her way downstairs. Ayana was sprawled out on the big white couch, flipping through movies on the TV screen, a bottle of Coke in hand.

Pax sat down beside her.

Ayana glanced over, unsurprised to see her, then offered her the bottle. "Want to watch something?"

Pax contemplated this. Then she accepted the bottle and took a long swig. She grimaced as the cold liquid touched her tongue. "Whatever."

CHAPTER 11

The sunlight that assaulted her senses made Pax grimace. Disoriented, she sat forward, her head spinning. She scrambled to her feet and swiped the sand off her dress, wincing at the sun in the soft pink horizon. There was no time to waste. She raised an arm to point at the sun, then carefully pivoted on her heel, lowering her arm until it was parallel with the wall. She wasn't sure if she had done that correctly, but she didn't have time to think about it. She needed to get on the other side of the wall as soon as possible. She sprinted toward the wall as fast as her body would allow, grateful for remembering to wear Dinah's shoes before she went to sleep. But of course, Pax remembered, she hadn't really been asleep.

Moments ago, she was reclining on the couch next to a sleeping Ayana. She was also on the brink of sleep but was not quite there when she found her mind wandering to Terra. The memory of Ari braiding her hair. His dark curls messily framing his face. His piercing golden-brown eyes as they focused on weaving her hair into a braid down to her shoulder. His full mouth twisting into a crooked half smile as he mocked her. As the image came vividly to her mind, the air cooled again, and her fingers and toes tingled. Uncomfortable as it made her, she fixated more on the memory until her body became weightless. She whispered, "Terra."

Pax didn't have time to congratulate herself on her success. She fixed her gaze on the wall, trying to locate the small red marker waving in the warm breeze. She studied the wall but could not find it. Panic set in as the sound of a plane approached from a distance. She whipped back around to face the horizon. She knew she was in the right spot, but there was no marker for her.

She didn't have time to waste. She ran straight ahead, dropped to her knees, and began to dig. Then she sighed in relief when she located the rocks that concealed the opening in the wall. She set them aside, slid herself underneath, and replaced them. She pressed herself against the shady side of the wall for a moment as the plane passed overhead. Her stomach churned, heat rose through her body to her cheeks, and a tingling sensation crawled up her throat. She dropped to her knees and vomited out the contents of her stomach, cursing her decision to scarf down a whole pizza earlier that night.

She got to her feet and paused to let the lightheadedness pass, then rushed in the direction of Ari's house. Were people still looking for her? She didn't have time to find out. She crept through the row of little cottages, making her way to the one at the very end.

She glued herself to the side of Ari's home. A woman's voice was coming from the deck, sounding frustrated. It was Dinah. Pax pinned herself closer to the wall. The last exchange she had with Dinah was less than pleasant. Something told her she would not be pleased to see her again. She hid in the shadows, eavesdropping on the exchange between Dinah and a voice that must have been Ari's.

"I will probably be at the factory again tonight, so try to clean up around here." Dinah sounded annoyed as she shut the door behind her.

Pax waited until Dinah was out of sight before tiptoeing toward the door but stopped short. Should she just knock? Suddenly, the door squeaked open, and she instinctively scurried back to the shadows, but it was Ari. She quietly approached him.

"Ari," she whispered. But he was walking in the opposite direction. Not wanting to run after him and cause a scene, she hissed a little louder, "Ari!"

He swung around at the sound of his name, confused, but then saw her. After looking around, he hurried toward her.

"Are you trying to get killed?" he whispered.

This gave her the answer she needed. She was still very much a fugitive here. "Sorry," she whispered. "I didn't know how else to—"

"Inside," he cut her off and rushed her toward the door.

Once the door was shut behind them, Ari's shoulders relaxed, and he pulled out a chair for her. "Sit."

Pax accommodated him, unsure of what to do now that she was here.

"Did you make it without being seen?" he asked.

"I think so."

"Good. I'm sorry I couldn't mark the spot for you. They've had eyes on me ever since—well, you know." He gestured toward her.

"Right." She nodded. "Well, your instructions helped. Thanks."

He offered her a half smile. "Yes. Well, we couldn't have you get caught."

"So, they've been watching you? Why?"

"They found my behavior suspicious during the search."

"Oh." Pax's brow furrowed. "I'm sorry, I didn't mean to get you into trouble."

He waved the apology away. "Even if you hadn't been here, I promise it would be no different. They look for reasons to torture us."

"Why?"

He shrugged. "Power. They don't have to worry about an uprising if they continue to eliminate our numbers. Keep us starving, sick, in prison."

"Oh," Pax breathed, feeling inexplicably angry for him. He quickly changed the subject. "So, when you were last here, we spoke of finding answers for you. I spoke to the man you need to see. He is expecting us."

Pax smiled. "Thank you! When should we go?" She stood.

He put a hand on her shoulder and lowered her back down. "Not now. I am expected at the dock. It will look suspicious if I don't show up."

"The dock?"

"It's where I work. I dock the cargo boats and unload shipments."

It hadn't occurred to her that he would have a job. Of course, it hadn't really occurred to her that he had a life at all outside of their encounters. All this time, she had thought of him as a character in her dreams. How stupid and selfish. Of course he would have a job and a family, friends, maybe even a girlfriend—he wasn't just some dream figure to provide guidance and keep her out of trouble. His face was contorted in concentration as he struggled to tie back the mop of curls from his face with a leather strap. This was a real person. Terra was a real place. The reality sank in for the first time.

Ari was rushing around the little house now, trying to put on a pair of leather boots when he looked in her direction. "You will stay here," he commanded as he finished dressing. Then he stood over her. "You must not leave this house. Most of the people in this village are good people. Even if they suspected something, they would not tell. But the Fellowship has eyes everywhere. You must not be seen or heard. Do you think you can handle that?" he asked with a sarcastic smirk, lightening his tone.

"Yes," she bit back.

He nodded, satisfied, then headed out the door, calling, "There is bread and some dried meat on the shelf if you want it."

"Thanks," she replied as he closed the door behind him.

Pax looked around, unsettled with the knowledge that she was alone in the house of a near stranger. She rubbed her palms together, stood from the chair, and explored the room. She stopped in front of a long table and shelf in the small kitchen and quickly found the bread carefully wrapped in soft mesh cloth. It was still warm. Dinah had probably baked it this morning before she left. Her chest tightened for a moment at the thought of the small, fiery woman. Her piercing glare, her hardened, weary features contorted into a mixture of panic and hatred. Pax quickly shook the memory away and prayed she would not have to face Dinah's wrath again. She tore off a piece of the bread and put it to her lips. It tasted heavenly. She tore off another piece and continued her way around the room.

A set of shelves hung on the wall beside the hearth. Pax eyed them curiously, noting the little knickknacks on top. She ran her fingertips across the small wooden animal figurines and clay pottery that was still rough in some places. They were handmade. There was a charcoal drawing of a woman who must have been Ari's mother. The woman looked kind with eyes that had the faintest glint of a smile in them. Next to the drawing were a pair of small leather shoes and a worn silk ribbon. Pax felt a hard tug at her heart. They must have belonged to the little sister Ari had mentioned the first time they met. Pax thought of Maria, Zeke's little sister. Maria was the closest thing to a little sister she had, and she couldn't imagine losing her. Each of these items must have been mementos of their family.

Like the sweatshirt Pax kept of her mother's, these were the last remnants of those who Ari and Dinah had lost. She stepped away from the shelf out of respect and seated herself on the pallet that she knew to be Ari's.

She couldn't explain why, but she found herself welling up with grief over Ari's family. She had never met them, but the thought of a loved one being stripped away in the most savage way possible was too much for Pax to bear. Anger bubbled up in the pits of her stomach and her fists clenched at the horrific injustice they had suffered.

Pax's eyes grew heavy as the hours ticked by. It must have been well into the early morning hours back home, and her body begged for sleep. But if she fell asleep, she couldn't guarantee she would wake up back here and she needed to stay. This could be her only chance to stay long enough to get the answers she had been seeking. She couldn't waste it no matter how tired she was.

A high-pitched scream made her entire body shoot up from Ari's cot. Despite her best efforts, she had dozed off at some point and now she was staring up at a red-faced Dinah. She wished she had traveled back home in her sleep.

"What are you doing here?" Dinah roared, her eyes squinting down at her. Before she could answer, Dinah grabbed a handful of the fabric gathered at Pax's ankles. "And you are wearing my dress! Thief! Give me one reason why I should not call the Guadaros!" she spat at her.

Pax shrank back. She desperately wished to disappear through the floor rather than face the full force of this woman's rage. She opened her mouth to speak, but her tongue went dry.

Suddenly, Ari's voice broke the tense silence between them. "Dinah, I can explain . . ." he started calmly, his hands up as if placating a feral animal.

"You can explain?" her voice boomed as she whirled around to face him.

He advanced forward and put a finger to her lips. "If you stop making a scene, then yes, I can explain. But if you keep screaming like this, I won't have a chance because the Guadaros will come storming through the door and we will all be dead. Is that what you want?"

The flames were still leaping through her eyes as she seethed, "Explain."

"I found Pax beyond the wall many days back," he started but was quickly cut off by Dinah's snarl.

"You've been sneaking behind the wall?"

"Yes, but I have good reason."

"There is no reason good enough for you to die for," she hissed.

Ari's head dropped to his hands in exasperation. Suddenly, Ari and Dinah were speaking in their native language in hushed tones. Whatever they were saying, it was clear Ari did not want Pax to know. She sat back nervously as she watched them communicate for a while before Dinah crossed the room, facing the opposite wall. Ari approached her and gently touched his sister's shoulders.

"I have to do this, Dinah. It is my duty to keep her safe," he said so low that Pax wasn't sure she was supposed to have heard.

Dinah's voice sounded broken. "And what of your duty to your family?"

Ari gently turned Dinah to face him and put his forehead to hers, like he had once done to Pax, and said something to her in a low, reassuring tone. It was the first time she had seen any kind of true affection between them, though she had always known it was there. Dinah's loyalty to Ari and desire to keep him safe was what fueled her. And Pax knew she would die for him if she needed to. She was moved by the connection between them, so much so that she was taken off guard when Dinah suddenly advanced toward her. Pax rose, awkwardly smoothing Dinah's dress over her hips. Dinah sized her up for a long moment, and Pax squirmed under the intense glare.

Dinah spoke in a threatening low growl. "I want to make one thing clear: I do not trust you, *Traveler*." She spat out the name like it was a slur. "But for whatever reason, Ari does. So, I need your word. I want you to swear by the Great Mother that you will do everything you can to keep my brother safe from harm, even if that means risking yourself."

Ari started from behind them. "Dinah . . ."

"No," Dinah said firmly. "She must swear it to me." Her dark coal eyes bored into Pax.

Pax's heart stuttered. She swallowed the lump in her throat, returned Dinah's intense gaze, and nodded. "I swear it . . . by the Great Mother," she added. Though she felt no connection to the belief in whatever god she had sworn by, she felt the gravity of her declaration in her bones. And it was true. For whatever reason, Ari was risking everything to help her. And should it come to it, she would do the same.

Dinah's small, weathered hand reached out and rested at the center of Pax's chest. Pax was confused for a moment, but then Dinah motioned for her to put her hand on Dinah's chest. Pax quickly followed and nodded.

"It is sworn," Dinah said, gesturing Pax to repeat after her.

"It is sworn," Pax said.

Dinah stepped away, grabbing her bag from the floor, and then a hunk of bread and meat from the kitchen shelf.

Ari and Pax watched her as she started for the door, then turned to Ari with a look of desperation. "Please," she begged.

"Don't do anything stupid." Ari nodded. And with one more glare at Pax, Dinah turned and left.

Ari approached Pax, and at the same time they said, "I'm sorry."

"What? Why?" Ari responded to Pax's apology.

"I just didn't know she would be home. I didn't mean to cause problems with your sister."

Ari snorted. "You will learn that there are always problems with my sister. I am sorry. I had not known she would be coming home to get food. But you don't have to worry about her."

Pax raised an eyebrow. "Are you sure about that? Because she doesn't exactly seem thrilled that I'm still here."

"Oh, she is not. She hates you."

"Thanks. That's very reassuring."

"Do not take it personally. It is not about you."

"I figured. Is it because I'm . . . like them?"

Ari nodded. "She will not be the last person you will encounter here who will hate you because of who you represent. You need to be ready for that. It does not make them bad people. They have very good reasons for their distrust."

"I know. I've made my peace with my place here. Being not well-liked is something I'm very familiar with. You don't have to worry about me."

Ari smiled at her admission. "And you do not have to worry about Dinah, or any of the others really. As much as they might hate you, they hate the Fellowship and the Guadaros more. You will be safe here. In time, you will earn their trust. Maybe," he added. "But we cannot worry about that just now. We must go."

Pax felt whiplash from the sudden change of pace. "Go? Where?"

"To meet the man who can help," he responded as if it were the most obvious thing in the world.

"Right." Nerves of excitement swelled in her chest at the thought of finally getting answers to the questions that had plagued her for so long.

Ari stood in front of her and lowered his voice. "When we enter the village, keep your head down. If the Mother blesses us, people will believe you are Dinah and we will go unnoticed. If we do get stopped, you are my cousin from another village and you are deaf."

Pax cocked her head.

"If you speak, your strange accent will give you away immediately."

Pax scowled at him. "Very nice."

"Sorry, but it is just the way you say things sometimes. 'I am fruum Aw-hi-oo,'" he mimicked.

She pushed him. "That is not how I talk!"

He cackled. "'Ware is da moooon?'"

"Okay, I get it," she responded in annoyance, though a smile crept across her face. "I hope this isn't insulting, but how is it that you know English?"

Ari perked up. "You mean Traveler's Speak? We learn it as children in our studies."

Pax was even more confused. "But why? It seems like everyone here has a native language that you all understand."

"Terrish is the language of our people, but Traveler's Speak is the language of the Fellowship. It is the language we must use for business, for trade, for everything outside of our own family and community gatherings. But tonight, you will not hear any of your language. The Watch exclusively uses Terrish during meetings to not be deciphered by those who cannot be trusted."

Pax huffed in frustration. Ari had a bad habit of not

explaining himself and expecting her to understand what he meant. "Who is the Watch?"

"I am," he said proudly.

"You?"

"Well, I am one of them. There are hundreds of us throughout Terra, and our numbers are growing every day. That is where you will find answers, but for now, we must go!" Ari took her elbow and guided her out of the house. "Remember," he said over his shoulder, "no speaking, and keep your head down."

Pax nodded, her anxiety climbing at the sight of the busy streets. But she kept her eyes fixed on the dirt path, the red dust gathering around her feet, staining her bare ankles. People were already calling greetings to them in familiarity. Each time, Ari would return with a casual greeting and usher them away.

As they made their way down the narrow path of the village, the aroma of evening meals wafted through the streets. Women stood laughing on their doorsteps as children ran all around them. This was the first time Pax actually experienced the village and she couldn't even look around. But even without looking, she could feel the warmth emanating from each home. This was a tight-knit community. She didn't know whether the bond was out of necessity or choice, but she could sense the loyalty each person had to the other, from the sounds of the chatter as she passed down the road, from the way everyone knew Ari's name and asked after them with genuine concern. Her heart swelled with a sense of longing. Her thoughts went to her little trio back home. She and Ayana and Zeke always had each other's backs. She thought about her last encounter with Zeke. The sadness in his eyes. The disappointment. She regretted not staying to talk to him, wishing she could explain, wishing he would understand. She shook her head and reminded herself to stay present.

It seemed as though they walked for miles. When the commotion of the village streets came to an end, Pax tentatively lifted her head and scanned the land ahead. No one was around, so she craned her neck around further. The sight before her almost took her breath away: high, sloping sand dunes stretched for miles and kissed the tawny horizon. She found where the wall met with the emerald ocean. She was awestruck by the sight of onyx mountains in the far distance.

"Wow," she whispered.

"That's the Madares Isles," Ari said.

"The mountain?"

"Yes, well, the island that the mountain is on. The mountain is called *De Entrana Dea*, "the Mouth of God." It is nearly a full day's boat trip out, but it is so big it seems much closer."

"Have you ever been there?"

He snorted. "I could not afford the money to buy a two-minute's passage upon those boats. It is a respite for Travelers, mostly."

"Oh." She was saddened by that, wishing she could know more about the island. It seemed unfair that Ari had never been able to visit it even though it was practically in his backyard.

After what must have been an hour, they finally approached a building. Though it was larger than the little homes that lined the streets, it was unassuming and sturdy. It was made of large carved stone, and vines with small orange flowers had grown all the way up one side of the wall. The building looked as if it had been there for centuries. She reached out to touch a stem of one of the flowers.

"Stop!" Ari warned.

Pax jumped back. "What?"

"Those are Testalos flowers. They are sacred healing plants. We use them to treat ailments, but they must only be handled by healers."

"Oh, sorry," she muttered, stepping away from the wall.

Ari held the door open for her and led her into a room lit by the glow of ornate lanterns lined on a pathway leading through the room. Pax took in the large, intricate tapestries that hung from each wall. Each one presented a series of pictures that were surrounded by loopy brush-script lettering she couldn't decipher. She followed the glow of the lanterns to the front of the room where an altar stood, alight with incense burning in a circle around a carved statue of a naked pregnant woman. The stone woman's features were gentle but firm, fixed forward as her hands cradled her swollen belly. Her long hair hung in waves that stretched all the way past her feet, and rested within it were tiny carved creatures. A laurel encircled her head, and above it was a banner that read, *Honohre Da Granda Mahdara.*

"Honor the Great Mother," he said. "This is the Mother's Temple. It is our sacred place."

"It's beautiful," Pax said in wonder. "The Mother is who you worship?"

"Well, I suppose you could call it that. It is more that we give gratitude to her. Our ancestors have passed down the story of the Great Mother, who was the creator of our world. The tapestries tell her story." He gestured to them.

"What is the story?"

"She was the daughter of a very cruel god who kept her captive all her life. But she longed to know love, so she left his kingdom and went searching across galaxies and universes until one day she met the son of a god, her father's rival. It is said they ran away together to a galaxy where they could never be found, and she became pregnant. During that time, they were so happy. She was overjoyed to have found the love that she had never experienced before. And it was from that love that our world was born. But then their fathers found them and began a war over who would have power over this new world. And to protect her, the goddess's lover stood between their fathers and took the weight of their wrath. He died, but his sacrifice made her pregnant again with a different kind of love. And from her grief, she birthed things into the world like pain, and sorrow, and death."

"That's heartbreaking," Pax replied.

Ari nodded. "Yes, but it was the lover's sacrifice that made those things possible. It reminds us that while death always gives way to life, evil gives way to good."

"Wow. That's so . . . hopeful," Pax answered.

"Yes, we try to always remember that hope. That is why our foremothers formed the Watch, because we have always believed we can change things for the better. And speaking of this, we should get to the meeting." He smirked. "This way."

He led her past the altar to a small, dark hallway leading to a dead end. But once they reached the wall, Ari didn't turn around. Instead, he pushed against the stone. Pax's brow furrowed. But with a click, Ari slid the wall backward, leading to a hall extending well past it.

Ari turned to her. "This passage was built when I was a child, during the rebellion," he whispered. "It was meant to be a place for women and children to hide so they would not be captured. As far as we know, the Guadaros have never found it."

"Cool," she replied as she squinted through the darkness.

"Up ahead there will be a drop. It is a staircase that leads to an underground room," he explained.

He slipped an arm around hers to guide her. She looked over

at him in the darkness as they stepped downward. How was he able to see in the pitch-black? Just as she finished that thought, a warm glow outlining a doorway appeared up ahead. She wondered how many times Ari had made this trip. She didn't know what "the Watch" was, but it must have had something to do with the Fellowship. From the way Ari talked about them, it seemed his people had no love for their government. How could they have anything but disdain for them? They were treated as outsiders in their own country, gunned down in their homes, taken from their families, stripped of their rights. It seemed only natural that the people would want to rebel. At that thought, Pax froze. What exactly was she about to walk into? After hearing about the Fellowship, she had nothing but support for Ari's cause, whatever it may be. But she wasn't ready to be an accomplice to some kind of revolution. She inhaled sharply as Ari knocked rhythmically on the door.

The door swung open, and Pax squinted as her eyes adjusted from darkness to the warm candlelit room. As her vision settled, she found herself in a stone room lined with wooden benches. The ceilings were high for being underground. How had they managed to build this? A scan of the room revealed about thirty men and women who cast looks at her ranging from curiosity to outright disdain. She nearly lost her nerve and bolted out the way she came, but she ground in her heels as Ari leaned in to whisper, "Take a seat here. And don't say anything."

Pax nodded stiffly and settled into one of the harsh wooden benches. The woman next to her scooted away from her. Pax crossed her arms tightly, trying to make herself so small she would turn invisible. Finally, all eyes shifted back toward the man who was standing at the front on a wooden stool to be seen over the crowd. He had thick brown hair woven into a braid that fell down his back. His temples were sprinkled with gray. He was large, wrapped in bands of muscle, and his jaw seemed permanently set in a scowl.

Ari offered her a reassuring smile. She tried to return it, but it came out more like a grimace. Ari snorted quietly, and she scowled back at him, which only made him chuckle. The man on the other side of Ari cleared his throat and the pair quickly focused on the front of the room, though a smile was still playing on Ari's lips. Pax had to set her mouth in a hard line to keep from laughing. Then the man at the front of the room stomped one foot on the ground repeatedly and shouted in Terrish.

Pax looked around. Whatever he'd said was very well received. People were clapping, or nodding, or muttering agreements. The man continued like this for a long time. Pax tried to focus, but she couldn't make out a single word the man was saying and her mind wandered. It wasn't until she heard Ari's name from the mouth of the harsh-sounding man that she snapped back to attention.

Ari rose from his seat and communicated with the man and the crowd. Pax froze when his hands gestured toward her. The crowd looked at her once again, distrust apparent on every face. Her cheeks were aflame. She wanted to sink through the floor. The man at the front exchanged a few words with Ari that sounded angry or maybe worried. Or perhaps Pax was imagining it. She couldn't stand being involved in the plans of a secret club without her consent. She fixed her eyes on a crack in the floor to keep her face controlled.

"Pax?" the man grumbled her name. She lifted her head, though she couldn't quite meet the man's eyes.

"Yes . . . that's me," she said timidly.

"Arivhan says you are a Traveler and he found you on the forbidden shore. You are the one they have been looking for. Yes?"

They were waiting for her response, but she was so nervous all she could do was nod.

He nodded in return. "We will speak further soon. But I can assure you that you are safe with us. Any enemy of the Fellowship is a friend of ours."

But despite the man's words, Pax knew it was not entirely true. At least, not yet. Shortly after the uncomfortable exchange, the man dismissed the crowd and everyone rose from their seats.

"Okay," Ari said, springing to his feet. "Let's go meet Zohn."

Pax swallowed hard, then followed him to the front of the room toward the man who had been leading the meeting for the past hour. He was surrounded by a crowd of people that seemed to be in the midst of an intense conversation. He was so intimidating she wasn't sure how she would find the nerve to ask him questions. But just before they reached him, Ari pulled her to the side. "That is Shahad. He is busy tonight, but we will speak with him tomorrow."

"Oh," she responded. The man looked at her and nodded in her direction before returning to his conversation.

Before she could ask more questions, Ari turned and faced her toward a small old man. Her eyes swept over the man as Ari introduced them. His olive skin was wrinkled and spotty, and he offered a gnarled hand to her. She shook it absently, staring at the man's eyes—or rather, the place where his eye should be. One eye was gray and filmy, but the other was only an empty socket covered by his eyelid. The puckered, purple skin told her the wound was old, but this was not a loss because of surgery or sickness. This was an act of violence.

"I know it looks like I can't see, but I can tell you are staring," he croaked at her.

Pax blushed. "Oh, I'm so sorry, sir. I—"

He laughed. "It was a joke, child. Your curiosity is natural. This right here," he said, pointing toward his sunken eye socket, "was a gift from my old commander in the Fellowship."

Pax looked at him in shock. "You worked for the Fellowship?"

"Oh, yes. For many years, in fact. But that is a story for another time. Let's talk about you, young Traveler." He gingerly rose to his feet on shaky legs when Ari caught him. "Thank you, son." He patted Ari's arm. "Come!" He waved his slender hand to Pax.

She followed behind them, unsure of where they were going. She looked at the limping old man before her. Who was he? He was certainly different from others she had met in the village. His accent didn't sound like the others she had heard in Terra. Terrans pronounced everything with long, dragging vowel sounds and soft syllables that blended all their words together musically. Despite his fragile voice that had grown raspy with age, Zohn spoke with hard syllables and short, staccato-like words. It was almost like an accent Pax would hear back home. Not necessarily in Ohio, but maybe in a big city on the East Coast or something.

They reached another doorway at the back of the room that led to another hall. It seemed there was an entire underground system beneath this temple. The walls glowed with candlelight as they walked past room after room. Living quarters, Pax gathered, at the sight of small bed pallets like the one in Ari's home, little warming stoves, round tables, and chests.

They finally came to a stop. The little man pushed open the door to a room on the right and led them inside, using the candle he held to light the little lamps in the room. The room was like the rest, but it was larger, and the back wall housed a wide shelf lined with dozens of leather-bound volumes.

"What is all this?" she asked, stroking the bindings.

"This is our history." He gestured a hand toward them.

"Zohn is our record keeper," Ari explained. "He documents important events, stories, the name of every citizen in our village, and he keeps it all down here."

"The Fellowship would destroy all of this if they could," Zohn continued. "So, some time ago, I moved the whole operation underground."

"But what would they want with stories and family histories? Why would they care?"

He looked at her for a moment, and Pax almost felt stupid for asking. "Well, because our stories are who we are, my dear. They make up the collective identity of a people. How long have you been in Terra, child?"

"Not long," she admitted.

"Yes, and I'm sure you have spent much of that time in hiding."

She nodded.

"Well, should you choose to continue to visit, you will find a sense of interconnectedness, at least within the villages. The people here understand and value the way our history weaves us together, like the tapestries on the walls out there. It unifies them. Strengthens them. That strength is a threat to the power of the Fellowship. They know if they can wipe out the stories, the history, they can destroy that bond. It might not happen overnight, or even in one generation, but as the years pass, the stories will fade and so will the culture and the bond. Suddenly, there is no Terra. There is only the Fellowship. That is what they want."

Pax understood. She remembered the warmth as she walked through the village, and the sense of longing to be a part of something like that. Ari had said the Fellowship wanted power over the villagers.

"So, what exactly is the Fellowship? Ari says they are Travelers like me?"

Zohn gave a slow nod. "And like me."

Her eyes widened. "You are a Traveler?"

He chuckled. "Yes, dear."

"So, does that mean you're from Earth?"

He shook his head. "No, I was born here. My mother was from one of the villages in Rehama, but my father was a Traveler. So, I am half-bred. Of course, there were many in the Fellowship who had much more unsavory names for what I am."

"Can a lot of people who were born here travel?"

"Oh, yes. But the Fellowship likes to keep that sort of thing within their own bloodlines. When someone like me comes along, it tends to be frowned upon. Of course, when I was born, it was a crime. But then that made it more exciting for young Travelers, so there was an explosion of mixed blood back in my time. They found it was much more effective to make it a social issue than a legal one. People will stand up to unjust rulers, but they are much less likely to stand up to their peers, their parents, or their communities. So, they simply let people do what they do, create social etiquette that renders the Travelers a superior race."

"Disgusting," Ari spat.

"Exactly," he chuckled.

"But I still don't understand," Pax said. "Where did they come from? How did they gain power?"

"The same place as you, child. Or at least the first Travelers were," Zohn said. "I served as the Fellowship's record keeper for many years, and they tell their history as if it was a feat of human excellence. They tout themselves as exemplary creatures. Nearly godlike." He sounded disgusted by their arrogance. "The story goes that there was a brilliant American scientist by the name of John Dickinson who had become fascinated with the marriage between science and the supernatural. He believed there were infinite universes waiting to be discovered, and that one could evolve oneself to where they could travel by the sheer will of one's mind. Of course, the Fellowship elitists won't tell you that Dickinson had encountered a shaman through a mutual friend. The shaman had graciously served as a guide to him in something they called 'spirit travel,' in which he was guided through a ceremony to allow his mind to travel to different worlds. None of Dickinson's discoveries would have been possible without the shaman."

Ari scoffed. "Of course."

"But I don't understand how they figured out how to transport their bodies," Pax said.

"Well, I'm getting to that part. In his research, Dickinson discovered that while everyone can spirit travel in some form or another, there was a very special genetic mutation that allowed some to use their mind's connection to a separate reality to physically break their body down to a molecular level and follow their spirit into another realm."

Pax's mind was spinning. "I don't understand."

Zohn contemplated for a minute. "Have you ever seen a dandelion?"

She nodded.

"Now, dandelions have hundreds of little seed pods connected to their stem, but they can blow about with a strong enough wind. Your mind is the wind. It is creating the force that tells your body to follow. Not all flower petals are so loosely connected to their stems in this way. That is only in the DNA of a dandelion." He leaned in closer to her. "There is something in you and me that makes our bodies more tethered to the wind than it does to the ground. And it does not matter what the

Fellowship does or doesn't do, that is a gift. Don't let them make you ashamed of that. We are not them."

She smiled. "Okay, so this scientist discovered that some people are like dandelions and he's one of them?"

"Unfortunately," he sighed. "See, it was during his research that he discovered his ability to travel. And behold, the man found himself lying on a beach with sand the color of a sunset and emerald water as far as the eye could see."

"Terra," she concluded.

"Exactly. Now, it started innocently enough. He would travel back and forth, and he began testing on other subjects and found that a handful of others could travel with him."

"So, does everyone who can travel end up in the same place?"

"Well, not exactly. There is still a great deal of science to traveling that is yet to be discovered, and how and where we end up in the universe is one of them. But the best we can understand is that our minds travel through fixed points."

"What does that mean?"

"The first time Dickinson traveled, it was purely by chance that he ended up in Terra. But his travel set a pathway of sorts for other Travelers to get from point A to point B. For example, if someone across the world had traveled, they might have set a fixed point in a different universe, and it is very possible that they have. There might be fixed points all across the galaxy, but we haven't quite figured out how to access them."

"Why can't we go to other points?"

"Our brains take the path of least resistance when it comes to making connections. The same is true for traveling. Our mind says, 'travel,' and it takes the easiest route. Though the Fellowship has been working for years to break this pattern, none have yet been successful to my knowledge."

"I guess that makes sense. Okay, so where were we?"

"The scientist ended up in Terra with a group of other Travelers," Ari prompted.

"Well, eventually Dickinson and his team encountered the locals," Zohn said. "Of course, at the time there was no wall separating the beach and the village, so Terrans were often on the beach bathing and washing clothes until they saw the men appear out of thin air. They thought the men were gods because of their divine power, and they opened their homes to them. They had feasts in their honor and offered them gifts."

"I'm sensing this is where everything started."

"You would be correct. Dickinson was a greedy man. He craved the power that was being offered to him in Terra. He had no interest in sharing the land. He wanted to take it for himself. He wanted to create what he called a 'New America.' So, he spent five years traveling back and forth, learning about the culture of the Terrans, their language, their beliefs, and he leveraged his relationship with locals to help him map the land. Meanwhile, in America, he was locating dozens of others with special abilities and training them to master their traveling. He had them train in combat. He told them the Terrans were demons and cannibals, that they would kill them and eat their flesh in their ritual sacrifices."

Pax glanced over at Ari, whose fists were clenched so tightly his knuckles became white. "He set them up for an ambush," she concluded.

Zohn nodded gravely. "Terrans didn't have the weaponry that your people had at the time, so they came in and wiped out entire villages: men, women, and children. They took command of the central region of Terra and drove the rest of the Terrans to the outer lands. They brought in enough people to start a colony. They dominated the land, forced Terrans to build them an empire . . . and here we are."

Pax furrowed a brow. "I don't understand. How is Rehama still standing today if the Travelers took over everything?"

Zohn smiled. "They have tried many times to overtake the villages in Rehama, as they have done with Nomadesales and the Madares Isles, but the Watch has been a fixture in our land since the Travelers' arrival in Terra. Our foremothers and fathers have fought to preserve Rehama and pushed back against the Fellowship more than once, the last time being nearly a decade ago. The Rehaman rebellion was successful in driving out the Fellowship's forces and forming an uneasy treaty with New America that we still hold to this day, but it came at a heavy price. Thousands were killed, leaving many of the children of our villages orphaned." He looked to Ari, whose gaze was cast to the ground.

Pax let out a long and heavy sigh. "I am so sorry."

"It was not your doing, child. Dickinson was an evil man driven by his own ambition. He saw the chance to seize power and he took it. But you can understand why many in our village would be hesitant to accept you."

"Yes. I don't have any interest in being associated with the Fellowship, but why exactly are they trying to hunt me down if they know I'm like them? I mean, do they know I'm a Traveler, or do they think I'm a native who crossed the wall?"

"Oh, they know who you are. That wall was built to keep other Travelers out. The patrol was set to kill others on site."

"But why?"

"To maintain control, of course. They are smart people. They know that if they could come in and take over, others could do the same. That is a threat to their power. It is honestly a miracle that you have made it this far. No others have succeeded. I have documented the deaths and burials of many like you."

"How many?"

"Hundreds over the years. You may very well be the last Traveler to survive the journey from Earth to Terra."

"Wow." Pax let that sink in. "How has it been a secret for so long? I mean, don't people from back home try to find the missing Travelers?"

"I'm sure, but how would they know where to look? The Fellowship did a very thorough job of wiping the evidence of Dickinson's research from your planet. There are agents in the Fellowship whose job it is to go back and monitor the research about it, and to manipulate the evidence to where it is only whispers and half truths passed over as conspiracy. So, often these people are killed and simply assumed dead."

Suddenly, a thought dawned on her. "You say that traveling is a genetic ability?"

"Yes."

"Does that mean it can be passed down? Like from a parent to a child?"

"Oh yes, that is why the Fellowship is so determined to keep their bloodlines pure."

"So, that means my ability was given to me by one of my parents?"

"Most likely. Have either of your parents ever mentioned anything?"

She sat stunned for a moment, as if she had been struck by lightning. "No, I'm pretty sure it's not my dad. But my mom disappeared when I was six." Her breathing quickened. "If she traveled here like I did and ended up on the shore with the patrol, does that mean she . . ." Her voice trailed off. She couldn't bear to speak what she now knew to be the truth. Her mother was a Traveler. When she disappeared all those years ago, she was probably shot dead on the shore, just as they had done to every Traveler before her. Her heart shattered.

The old man placed a hand on her shoulder. "I cannot say for certain. But I know that no Travelers who are not native to this land have survived past the shoreline. I am so sorry, child."

Tears filled her eyes. Pax had considered the possibility for years that her mother had died, but being confronted with the truth was like losing the last hope that she would ever see her again. She heaved heavy, chest-racking sobs as she buried her head in her hands. She felt a pair of warm hands squeezing her shoulders as Ari came to stand behind her. The two men sat comforting her as she wept.

"I'm sorry," she whimpered. "I just . . . all these years I didn't know for sure if she was, you know."

"Do not apologize," Ari said fiercely. "This is a great loss. It deserves to be felt."

The old man nodded. "Yes, there is not a person in Terra who has not experienced a loss like this at the hands of the Fellowship. We share in your grief, dear." The man clutched her hand with all his strength.

She felt the honor in his gesture, knowing it was one that was only meant for loved ones. "Thank you," she said through her tears.

"Perhaps we should go home," Ari said.

Pax looked up, her face swollen from crying. "But I have to learn how to travel back. I never learned. I need you to help me." She looked at the old man with pleading eyes.

"Of course, but it can wait," he said gently. "Your friend is right. You need rest now."

She nodded.

"When do you plan to return?"

Pax had to think for a moment. It was likely Saturday morning back home now. "Tomorrow? Probably before noon."

He nodded. "Then I will be expecting you in the morning."

She smiled at him through her tears. "Thank you so much."

He smiled softly in return. "Of course. You are one of our own now."

She bowed her head, humbled by his words. Then she stood slowly, allowing Ari to guide her out.

CHAPTER 13

Pax stood in the corner of Ari's home, hugging herself tightly. The evening chill had set in, and Ari was preparing a fire in the small hearth. She barely knew how she got back here. She'd spent the entire walk in a daze, replaying the conversation with Zohn in her head, recalling images of her mother, allowing grief to rise and fall within her like tides upon a shore.

Pax had known this process all too well, the way grief could overcome you one moment and then numbness the next—then made you boil over with rage, then utterly break and empty you all in the matter of minutes. Grief could build whole worlds inside of a person—a place they could descend into and live for years in the cold comfort of broken memories. On the outside, people like Pax seemed fine, if not maybe a little unfocused and heady, but inside she could see herself curled up at the base of a monument a hundred stories high that she had erected on behalf of her loss—the loss of her mother, the loss of her old self, the loss of the years of her life that she had spent hidden away, existing in old memories and a future never to come. For a time, she thought she was beginning to find her place again in the world outside of her loss. She was dreaming more, smiling more, and there were even some days that her pain felt like only a whisper inside her. But today, the pain came roaring back and clutched at her with warm, welcoming hands to pull her back down into her city of grief. She was sitting in it now, staring blankly at the flickering flames in front of her.

Ari cleared his throat. "We should eat. I will prepare us something."

Pax nodded absently as he pulled things from cupboards and assembled a meal. Suddenly, the hunger hit. It had been hours since she had eaten. She had been so caught up in the excitement of being here and finding answers that she had neglected to take care of her needs at all. She wrinkled her nose in disapproval at herself. A layer of dirt had accumulated on her legs, and the air had the slight scent of body odor. And among those, a more urgent and pressing need. She looked up at Ari for a moment, slightly uncomfortable.

"Ari?"

He lifted his head to her in response.

"Do you have a bathroom?"

He looked at her, puzzled for a moment. "We have a large basin. If you wish to bathe, we will have to boil water," he said with slight discomfort in his voice.

Pax shook her head, though a bath sounded like heaven right about then. "No, I mean, do you have a place where you . . . you know." She shifted on her feet, not wanting to meet his gaze.

"Oh!" he said, finally gathering her meaning. "Yes, of course. The waste room is around the back of the house."

She furrowed her brow. "Your bathroom is outside?"

He cocked his head. "Yes, it's a separate room. Do you mean yours isn't?"

She shook her head.

"So, you are saying that you relieve yourself inside your home? The same place you eat and sleep? What do you do about the smells?" He seemed to be in disbelief and slightly disgusted.

Pax blushed at the forwardness of his question but couldn't

help but feel amused. When he put it that way, it made a lot of sense to have an outside room. Of course, it did make "going" a bit more inconvenient, she noted, realizing the urgency of her need. "Can you just show me, please?"

He smirked in amusement and directed her toward the door.

When she returned to the house, Ari had a plate set out on the table for her and had already begun to devour the food in front of him. He dipped large chunks of bread into some kind of sauce and seemed to swallow his bites whole. He gestured for her to sit, and she obeyed. They ate in companionable silence for a while, and Pax was surprised by how nice it felt. Ari hadn't offered to comfort her or give condolences about her situation, which, in a way, was its own kind of comfort. Often, when people were faced with the pain of others, they were so desperate to make themselves useful that it became overbearing. Pax thought about the way Ayana and even Zeke acted when she was upset, trying to make her forget about it, or make her feel better, or fix it somehow. Their efforts, while always noble, were exhausting. With Ari, there was no pretense. He seemed to have no desire to "fix" it, or even make her feel better. He just let her be. And Pax realized it was only because he had experienced a great loss of his own, even more than she had, that he was comfortable sitting with her in her pain. People who were unaccustomed to feeling pain were so unsettled by it that they would do anything to make it go away. It was only people like Ari, who had known pain so great it was unimaginable to most, who could rest in it, let it stay its course, then move forward. Pax looked over at him in silent appreciation as he continued to lap up the rest of his meal.

When Ari had finished, he lounged back in his chair in contentment and looked over at Pax. "Have you had enough?" he asked.

Pax nodded, scraping the last bite of food from her plate and popping it into her mouth. "Yes, thank you," she said.

They sat quietly, staring at the fire. Pax recounted the events of the day. Her arrival, her confrontation with Dinah, then she paused. "Ari?"

"Hmm?" He perked up, looking as if he were about to fall asleep in his chair.

"What did you mean when you told Dinah it was your duty to look out for me?"

He paused, seeming hesitant to share for a moment. "Well, it's sort of my job, I guess?"

She looked at him, a question in her eyes. "What do you mean, 'it's your job'?"

"So, the meeting we went to tonight, for the Watch. We all have roles that we play for the cause. This is mine."

"And what exactly is the cause?"

"Taking down the Fellowship," he said, as if it was obvious.

So, it is a kind of rebellion, Pax realized. "Okay, how exactly does that involve me?"

"I don't know yet. I just know that when I came to the Watch and told them about you, they told me it was my job to man the coastlines in case you came back and try to keep you safe."

Pax stared in disbelief. "So, the Watch . . . they want something from me?"

Ari shrugged. "Perhaps. But know that if they do, it would never be forced upon you."

She felt offense building in her. "So, what? I'm just some kind of task on your to-do list? This whole time you were just doing your job?" She couldn't explain why she felt betrayed. Ari had made no pretense about them being friends, and he certainly acted like she was a chore to him.

He tapped his fingers on the table. "No. At least, not at first.

When I first encountered you on the beach, I had not been a part of the Watch. That was purely by chance."

"What were you doing out there?"

"Truthfully, I was just curious. The Fellowship tells us nothing about the Outlands aside from that they are forbidden and we would be killed if we violated the law. I just wanted to see what they were hiding. Imagine my disappointment when I just found a beach. Then there you were."

"Okay, so then what?"

"Well, nothing for a while. I realized the danger I had put myself in by doing what I had done, so I went about my life, trying to forget for a while . . ."

"And obviously that didn't work out."

He smirked. "What can I say? I am a rebel. I started sneaking back to the beach from time to time just to see if I could find anything. And a few weeks later, I found you again. I wasn't fully convinced the first time we had met that you were real or were just another villager who snuck out. Our interaction was so brief, I even thought I might've dreamed it. Then when I saw you disappear into the air the day Dinah found out, well, I suppose I was convinced."

"What was that like? Watching me travel. I've been curious."

"Terrifying. It was like watching boiling water become vapor. You were, and then you simply weren't. I thought Dinah's head was going to burst, she was so shocked." He laughed.

Pax stared at him with wide eyes. "Wow. Okay. So, I disappeared and then . . ."

"Then I went looking for answers. I had never met a Traveler who wasn't from inside the Fellowship. Even the ones who live in Terra almost never interact with us. They stay in their place, and we stay in ours. But I knew I couldn't go to just anyone. If word got back to the Guadaros that there was a boy from the village talking about a stray Traveler, it would be bad for both of us. I had heard some men down at the dock talking about going to the Watch meeting. I had known about the Watch for a while. They recruit from within the village from time to time, but I had never been approached. So I went, met Shahad, the man from the meeting tonight. He is on the Watch's counsel. I told him about you. Next thing I know, I'm being initiated and given a post."

She nodded, absorbing his story. "What exactly is your post? To be my babysitter?"

"No," he shot at her, sounding slightly insulted. "I was to watch the coast and make sure that if you came back, you could find your way to safety. Then I would bring you to the Watch."

"So, your job was to kidnap me?"

He cast a sideways glance. "If I was to kidnap you, you would certainly not be sitting comfortably at my table right now."

"Fair point."

"I told you, you will not be forced to do anything. The Watch isn't interested in unwilling participants to the cause."

"What am I supposed to do now?"

"Well, tomorrow we will meet with Shahad. He tells me he has a proposition for you. That is why he asked me to bring you tonight."

Pax gulped. "What kind of proposition?"

He shrugged. "I am not sure. But do not worry, he is a good man. With the Fellowship looking for you, I am sure he is concerned for your safety. After that, we will go to Zohn. He will teach you to control your gift, and you can travel home and never return, if that is your wish."

"But what if I want to come back?"

"Then you have the assurance of my protection and the protection of the Watch." He gazed at her intensely.

"Thank you." She grinned slightly, not sure how else to respond.

"We should rest." He rose from his chair and motioned her toward Dinah's cot. "You can sleep here for the night."

Pax removed her shoes as she settled on the cot. Ari moved to the bedding across from hers. He reached for a pail of water that was perched on a stool beside his bed, removed his tunic, and began to wash using a cloth. He paused and glanced over at her. "Would you like to wash?"

Pax looked away, not realizing she had been staring. "Oh, um. Yes. Thank you."

He hauled the bucket to her corner of the room, then moved back and turned toward the fire to give her privacy.

Pax quickly scrubbed at the grime that had caked itself to her legs.

Ari broke the silence, trying to ease the awkwardness between them as Pax continued to sponge herself clean. "What was your mother like?"

She sighed and thought for a moment. "Beautiful. Warm. She loved to sing, all the time. Honestly, I don't have many memories of her. I was so young when she—" she paused again, still unready to say the word out loud. "Left."

He nodded, stretching himself out on his cot, still facing the opposite direction. "My mother liked to sing too. When we were little, she would sit beside us every night, and run her hands through our hair, and sing a song about these black birds that were trapped in cages."

"That sounds like a sad lullaby."

"No, because it ended with their cages being opened, and

them soaring overhead above the waters and the trees and into the sky where they could not be caught again."

Pax dropped the cloth into the bucket. "How did it go?"

"Hmm?" He turned to her.

"The song. How did it go?"

"Well, I am not going to sing it, if that is what you want." She rolled her eyes. "Just tell me the words."

He thought for a moment. "It's been so long since I heard it. I'm not sure. Oh, the end was something like, 'And so the birds, they spread their wings, and their songs echoed through the trees, they sang—'"

"'One day, we'll all be free,'" Pax finished quietly. Her mouth dropped. She flashed back to the memory of her mother that had helped her get home, her arms engulfing her as she hummed the tune about the birds: *One day, we'll all be free. One day, we'll all be free.*

"Do you know it?"

She looked at him in disbelief. "My mom used to sing me that song."

"But that's impossible. That song is a Terrish lullaby mothers sing to their babies. She couldn't know it unless—"

Pax felt her heartbeat quicken. She didn't want to hope. She couldn't. "But she couldn't be . . . could she?"

Ari moved across the room and sat beside Pax on the pallet. "You said your mother disappeared? Just suddenly?"

She nodded. "Yes, I was young, so I don't remember her leaving. But my dad said she left a note . . ." she trailed off.

"What did the note say?"

She shrugged. "I never read it. I only know what my dad said. Something like she couldn't do this anymore, and to take care of me."

"She was saying goodbye."

"But if she was killed suddenly, she would not have planned to leave a note!" Pax rose from the cot and began to pace.

Ari stood. "Pax, it is still possible that she was killed when she arrived here."

"Yes, but she could have been leaving to come back here for some reason. And if she had a plan, then maybe she isn't dead. Maybe she's still here!" Against her better judgment, she felt hope swelling within her. She turned to find Ari looking at her with pity in his eyes. He was not convinced.

"Listen, Pax. You don't know the Fellowship. These people are ruthless. Even the most skilled Traveler could have still been captured."

She nodded. "I know. But what if she wasn't just a Traveler? What if she was one of you?"

He raised an eyebrow at her. "I'm not following."

"The lullaby. You said only Terrish people would know it."

"Yes, or maybe someone who had been around Terrish people."

"Right. But she would have had to spend a lot of time around Terrish people, and you said you had never seen a Traveler before me who wasn't inside the Fellowship, and those who were didn't come to the villages. So, is it more likely that she was an outsider who somehow could live among the Terrish people, or that she was one of you?"

"But our people cannot travel," he reasoned.

"Not unless you had Traveler's blood like Zohn."

He sat for a long time in silence, processing the possibility. Then he said, "Okay, so what is your plan?"

Pax blinked. "What do you mean?"

"I mean, are we going to find your mother?"

She paused. "I—I don't know. I mean, I don't know anything about this place, and what if we do all this work and put ourselves in danger only to find out she's—"

He put his hands on her shoulders. "If you are doing this, you have to know it is a possibility that she's dead. But if she is out there, and you didn't try to find her—"

"I would never be able to live with myself." She took a deep breath and looked up at Ari's intent gaze. "I have to do this."

He nodded. "I know."

She moved across the room and sat back on the pallet, simultaneously exhilarated and overwhelmed. "But I don't even know where to start, and I have to leave tomorrow or Ayana will freak out."

"Who?"

"Oh, my friend. Back home. She covered for me so I could come here."

"Well, I think we start by planning your next travel. I'll make some tea."

They sat up late into the night, mapping out a plan, fighting over the best course of action. It had become immediately apparent to Pax that Ari did not like following other people's orders. She would suggest a plan, and he would cast a sarcastic glance or snicker at her. So, out of spite, she would return his suggestions with equal amounts of disdain. It should have annoyed her, but something about the way he responded to her, even in disagreement, felt lighthearted. He didn't treat her like she was an idiot. Ari really just liked to spar. Despite the gravity of their mission, their back-and-forth banter felt like a welcome distraction.

The embers in the fireplace had died out when they finally reached an agreement. In less than a month, winter break was coming up and she would have time off from school. It would be a long time to wait, but she needed to make sure she would have enough time to execute the rest of their plan. She would tell her father she was staying with Ayana, and she was sure Ayana would cover for her again. Then, with Zohn's help, they would pour through the records and go from there. Pax sprawled out across the pallet, feeling the weight of almost two days without sleep spread across her exhausted body. She turned to Ari, who had propped himself up against the wall and was scrawling in a blank book with a bit of charcoal.

"Do you think I'm crazy?"

"Yes," he responded without looking up, though she could see a half smirk behind the pages in front of his face.

She rolled her eyes. "Seriously, do you think this plan will work?"

He sighed and looked at her. "I don't know. But if I had a chance to see my mother again, I would face down every guard in Terra to find her. You have been given a gift that many of us would kill for."

She stared up at the ceiling, thinking about what he said. She had spent so many years wishing she could see her mom again. Praying for an opportunity, a sign, anything that she was still alive. This was her chance. Even if it meant putting herself in danger, she owed it to herself to take a chance. She had felt like she was living a half life without her, like there was a whole part of herself that she didn't know. She felt like the goddess in the story Ari had told her, living without love and desperate to find it. This was her opportunity, and if it meant she had to cross the universe to find it again, she had to do it. She heard soft snoring coming from behind her, and turned to find Ari slumped over against the wall. She chuckled at the image of him passed out with his mouth open and reminded herself to make fun of him for it in the morning.

CHAPTER 12

"Do you know you talk in your sleep?" Ari teased as Pax stumbled groggily across the room and seated herself at the table the next morning.

Heat rose to Pax's cheeks. "Well, you snore," she shot back in a groggy voice.

He laughed. "Breakfast?" He held up a plate for her.

She rose and sat in the chair beside him and took a bite of bread. "So, what's the plan?"

He finished swallowing the chunk that was in his mouth. "Well, first we must dress. Then we will walk around the back to Shahad's home. It's not far from here. Then we—"

The front door swung open to reveal a haggard-looking Dinah carrying a bag on her back. She paused, eyeing Pax. "You are still here," she said with disdain. She closed the door behind her.

"Stop your whining, sister," Ari shot back. "We will be gone soon."

She dropped her bag to the floor and smacked Ari across the back of the head. Then she grabbed the rest of the bread on the table and devoured it. "And where exactly are you going?"

"To see Shahad."

She snorted. "Don't tell me he has recruited you for this ridiculous cause."

"I don't see what is ridiculous about trying to fight for a better world," Ari shot back.

"It's a death wish."

"I'd rather die standing up for our people than live like a coward," he said under his breath.

Dinah's eyes filled with rage. She slammed her fist on the table. "Do you forget how that turned out for our father? Our mother? Are you determined not to stop until they burn this village to the ground? You say I am a coward? I am the one who has kept you alive, kept you safe! And now you spit on all the sacrifices I have made?"

Pax shifted in her chair as they fired back at one another, wishing she could excuse herself. She felt like an extremely unwelcome intruder. But the pain in Dinah's voice was worse. This woman had seen so much loss, raised her brother, and woke up every morning knowing their family would never see justice. She was not a coward; her rage came from fear of losing the only family she had, perhaps her only reason to keep going. She wished Ari hadn't said that to her. She knew Dinah was no fan of her, but for some reason, Pax had so much respect for Ari's sister. Perhaps because she saw her mother in Dinah, or at least what she hoped her mother was like. She kept telling herself that her mother had left to protect her, to keep her safe from this place. She was suddenly angry at Ari for not realizing how lucky he was to have someone like Dinah. Before she could stop herself, she blurted out, "Stop it!"

The siblings looked at her in disbelief. She shifted under their gaze, now embarrassed for butting in. "I . . . I'm sorry. I just . . . can't you see how much she cares for you?" she said to Ari, gesturing toward Dinah. "I wish I had someone who—" Heat rose to her cheeks. "We should go."

"Yes," Dinah agreed. "You should. I worked all night. I need to rest."

Pax locked eyes with her for a moment. Dinah gave her a

brief nod. It would be a long road toward earning her respect, but Pax was determined. Dinah was only one of many people she was sure to encounter here who would not welcome her with open arms, and with good reason. They had all suffered too much. *Maybe there's something I can do to help.* Pax stiffened at the thought. She was already thinking about participating in the Watch's plan, before she even knew what it was. Defeat washed over her. She was so small and insignificant in the scheme of this entire world she knew nothing about. She had no power here, no influence, and just because she could travel, it didn't make her a superhero.

"Are you ready?" Ari's lips were set in a firm line.

Pax nodded, and they headed out the door. She followed him to the back of the cottage where he suddenly whirled around to face her.

"What was that about?"

"What do you mean?"

"Yelling at me in front of my sister. Placing your hand in my family matters."

"I know, I'm sorry. I just—"

"How dare you? You have no idea what it's like to—"

Pax gritted her teeth, her anger boiling over. "No, how dare *you* call her a coward! You have no idea. I know you lost your mom and dad, but you still have family who loves you and cares about you. Do you have any idea how precious that is?"

He appeared caught off guard and looked at the ground.

"You are taking that for granted. I wish I had a sister who cared enough about me to worry what I was doing, to yell at me for being stupid! I don't. I don't have a mother, and I have a father who—"

"Who what?"

She shook her head and pushed past him. "Nothing."

"Pax. Who what?" He chased after her and spun her around to face him.

She couldn't bring herself to look him in the eye. "My dad—he doesn't care about me. It's like . . . ever since my mom disappeared, he barely acknowledges that I exist. He walks around like he's this perfect father and all these people love and respect him, but if they really knew the truth . . ." She didn't know why she was sharing this with him. She had never openly admitted it to anyone. Even her best friends had to figure it out on their own. But saying it out loud was freeing. She looked at Ari and said, "It doesn't happen all the time, but sometimes if I make him mad, he . . . hurts me. That's why I'm saying you need to cut Dinah a break. I know what you're doing is really important, and you believe in it, but she loves you, and that is everything."

He stood quietly for several long moments, then stared at her fiercely. "You must not go back there."

"What? What are you—"

"To your father. You cannot go back."

She laughed at the foolishness of his suggestion. "Ari, I have to. That's my home. I can't just disappear. I have friends there, and I have to finish school."

"But you could be safe here."

"Could I? I mean, look at what we're doing. We're going to your friend's house where you're planning to overthrow your government. Am I any safer here?"

He sighed heavily and shook his head.

"Listen, I didn't actually mean to tell you that. I was just trying to get you to appreciate what you have. But I promise I'm fine. I know how to handle my dad, and I'm stronger than I look," she reassured.

He nodded. "It is your choice, of course. But you must know that if you ever need to leave—I mean, for good—you have a place to go."

"Thank you," she replied earnestly. Ari was frustrating, and argumentative, and half the time she couldn't tell if he even liked her, but the intensity with which he cared was something to be valued. He would never admit it, but he and his sister had that in common.

"Now, come. Shahad is expecting us." He motioned her forward.

Shahad sat across from Pax and Ari at a long table in the middle of his home. His cottage was larger than Ari's, with a couple of extra rooms built at the back to accommodate the swarms of children who were running around them. Pax smiled at the chaos as three little boys took turns chasing each other in a game of tag, or what they called "Capture the Tiger."

Shahad shouted at them over his broad shoulder. "Boys! Take this outside, please! *Vamineda! Vamineda!*" he instructed in Terrish. The boys squealed with laughter as they slammed the door behind him. Shahad let out a long sigh and turned to face them again. "My sincerest apologies. I could tell you it is not always like this, but that would be a lie." He chuckled.

"It's no problem at all. I wish I had a house full of siblings. It seems fun," Pax said.

"You are an only child, then?"

She nodded.

"And your mother has been gone since you were young, yes?"

Pax furrowed her brow at him.

"I told Shahad about you after your last visit," Ari admitted. "I'm sorry."

"Don't be offended with the boy," Shahad said. "He was trying to convince the Watch you were trustworthy. He put up quite the fight on your behalf, I must say." He let out a deep chuckle.

Pax looked over at Ari, who blushed and stared down at the table. "Then I guess I should thank him," she said. "And you too, from what I was told. He says you put him in charge of keeping watch for me on the shore?"

"Yes, but I have a feeling he would have done that anyway." The man cast a glance in Ari's direction.

Ari cleared his throat and quickly changed the subject. "So, we should really get started. Pax has to travel back home today."

"Of course," Shahad said.

Just then, a tall, statuesque girl approached the table carrying a tray with three steaming cups of tea that smelled spicy. The girl looked to be about Pax's age, but she was graceful and stunning.

"Thank you, my dear," Shahad said. "Pax, my daughter Taliah. Ari, I'm sure you remember each other."

The girl gave a brief nod at Pax before flashing Ari a wide smile. "I hope you are well, Arivhan," she said sweetly, batting her long eyelashes.

"I am, thank you," he responded politely and turned back to Shahad.

Pax couldn't help but feel pity for the girl when her face fell as she left. Ari was so one-track minded, he probably hadn't even realized the girl was flirting with him, and his matter-of-fact tone did absolutely nothing to encourage her intentions. Pax smirked. For all of his handsome features, Ari had none of the charm to accommodate them. He wasn't like Zeke, who was so attractive and charming that it was almost unfair. Ari was a bit prickly. But of course, that was its own kind of charm, she supposed. The kind that grew on you the more time you spent with him.

"So, Pax," Shahad started, pulling her out of her thoughts. "What has Ari told you of the Watch?"

"He said you're trying to overthrow the Fellowship," she said.

"Is that what he said?" Shahad raised an eyebrow. "Well, that is a very strong way to put it. Makes us sound like savages."

Ari averted Shahad's gaze. "I didn't exactly say it like that. I was trying to give her the idea without telling her everything. I thought you would explain it better."

"I should say so." He chuckled at Ari's discomfort. "Pax, Arivhan is one of our more zealous members, as I am sure you have already learned. The heart of what he says is true, but we are hoping to do it with a bit more finesse. 'Overthrow' makes it sound like we are planning to storm the streets and put their heads on spears."

"So, what exactly are you trying to do?" she asked.

"You have not seen much of it yet, but the Fellowship is a well-organized system on the inside. You have only been around people in the village, so you have only heard about the evils within the system. And do not mistake me, they are wicked. But public opinion of the Fellowship within Travelers' circles is extremely high. If we stormed the city walls screaming 'Revolution!' the citizens would turn on us immediately. That is, in essence, what the first Watch did over a decade ago, and it ended in mass bloodshed for our people. This time we will be smarter."

"But I don't understand," Pax said. "How can the Travelers not see how awful they are?"

"It is simple. The Fellowship controls the stories Travelers hear about us. They grow up hearing a very different version of our history. They are taught that their founder came in offering medicine and civility to our people, and that we turned on them because we were killers. They are told that our culture is violent, that we sacrifice our children to our goddess, and that the Fellowship, in all of their goodness, keep trying to civilize us—to save us from ourselves, but they can't. So, they keep us separate."

Pax pursed her lips. "They teach them to be afraid of you so they will never want to meet you or hear your side."

"Yes. They learn nothing of the ways that the Fellowship enslaved us, starved us, and slaughtered our children. They believe we are the villain, and the Fellowship is the only defense between us and them."

"So, what is your plan?"

He smiled. "We plan to infiltrate from within."

"How will you do that?"

"We've already started. Many of the half-blood members of our villages have moved within the capitol's walls. They take jobs as orators, teachers, record keepers—slowly changing the public opinion by correcting the history."

"That's smart," Pax said, impressed. "But what about the rest of you? There were dozens of villagers at the meeting that night."

"We recruit. We plan. We train. Make no mistake, just because I say we won't be storming the walls of the city doesn't mean we aren't preparing for a fight. We are under no pretense that the Fellowship will go quietly just because we succeeded in swaying the public to our cause. They are tyrants, and tyrants never meet peaceful ends."

Pax shivered. "So, where do I come into this equation?"

He laughed. "I like you. You cut right to the heart of the matter. The members of the Watch working within the capitol have been doing marvelous work, but if we are going to succeed, we need someone who can gain full access into their world. Someone who looks like the Fellowship, who talks like them, someone who could use the privilege of their gift to potentially wield influence."

"A Traveler," Pax muttered, anxiety creeping up her throat. She knew where this was headed, and she wasn't sure she was ready for what they were asking of her. She looked at Ari for reassurance only to find him staring at her with an expectant gaze.

Shahad placed a large hand on her arm. "Listen to me, Pax. I know what we are asking of you is a huge burden to bear. That is why I want you to know that you are not obligated to say yes. You can walk away today and never return. And even if you do not wish to be a part of this, you will still be under our protection. I swear it to you. But we have been working to unravel the Fellowship for almost a decade now on our own. We have figured and refigured all the possible plans and solutions, but we realized we cannot do it alone. We need to have allies at every level who are willing to be a part of our cause." He paused for a moment, then looked deeply into her eyes. "We are not asking for you to be our hero, Pax. Just a helper. We will do the rest."

She sat back in her chair, contemplating his proposal. She tried to swallow the lump in her throat, but she was too overwhelmed by the thought of being a part of this. "I—I don't know. I came back here because I wanted to find out about myself. And now I want to find my mom. I don't know if she's here, but she might be, and that's what I came to do. But now you want me to . . . start a revolution with you?"

"I know it might be more than you can think about right now," he assured. "You do not have to give me an answer today. But I will make you a deal. If you help us with this, we will help you find your mother. I believe Ari will commit to helping you either way," he said.

Ari was already nodding at Pax with determination. "You have my word."

"The Watch is a very large network. If they know you are one of them, you will have their trust, and you will get a lot further in your search much faster. We can put you in front of the right people, give you all the resources you need."

Pax breathed a heavy sigh and clasped her hands tightly in front of her, unable to meet Shahad or Ari's gaze.

"Say nothing now, Pax. When you return—if you return—you can give me an answer then. I know it is a lot to think about. You probably need time.

"Yes," she said quietly, finally meeting his eyes. "Thank you for understanding."

"We should go soon," Ari said. "It is broaching on mid-morning. Zohn will be expecting us."

"Of course." Shahad stood and placed a hand on Pax's shoulder. "Thank you for listening, Pax. Safe travels," he said with sincerity.

She mustered a smile. "Thank you."

As she followed Ari out the door, Shahad called, "Oh, and Pax. I know it would be tempting to tell yourself you do not have the courage to do this. But, my young friend, that is a lie."

She met his eyes and gave him a genuine smile. "I'll see you again soon." And they left his home.

As they made their way toward the Mother's Temple in silence, Ari kept eyeing her curiously. After some time, he said, "What are you thinking?"

"I'm not sure. It's a lot to take in."

"Of course." He nodded. "He was telling the truth, you know."

Pax looked over at him. "About what?"

"You are not a coward."

She scoffed. "How could he possibly know that? How could you?"

"Shahad has a way of reading people. But the fact that you are still here says all I need to know. You could have chosen not to come back."

"Well, I don't exactly have control over whether or not I come back."

He shook his head. "But when you show up, you don't just exist. You fight, you search for truth. You don't know how rare it is to find people who are willing to ask hard questions and want real answers. That means something, and I'm not just saying that because I want you to join us."

His expression told her he meant what he said, but she wasn't convinced. He only knew the person she was here, in Terra. He didn't really know who she was. Pax was not a fighter. There was none of the fierceness in her that she saw in people like Dinah, and Ari, and even Ayana. She had spent her life hiding, depending on the strength of people like Zeke just to get by. She felt like a fraud here. She was less afraid of what could happen if she joined the Watch than she was of what would happen when they realized she was not the person they thought she was.

The streets were mostly empty and quiet. "Where is everyone?" she asked.

"This is our holy day. Most people spend the mornings inside resting, preparing for the evening feast."

"Feast?"

"Later tonight, many will gather in each other's homes and share a meal, tell stories, play music. It's a time to connect with each other and give thanks."

"That sounds nice."

"Well, you are welcome to stay if you'd like. Dinah and I are visiting a friend tonight. We like to celebrate the holy day a little differently." There was mischief in his eyes.

"And how is that?"

"We go to my friend Kitara's home to gamble and drink spiced wine."

"That does sound fun, but you know I have to go back."

"I understand. You are a *prudena*." He snickered.

She eyed him. "A what?"

"It means you are straight-spined. You do not like fun."

She huffed. "That's not it. I like to have fun, okay? I go to parties all the time back home," she lied. "As a matter of fact, I was at a party the last time I traveled here."

"As you say," he teased.

She rolled her eyes as they approached the temple.

He turned to her. "Are you ready?"

She swallowed hard. "I think so."

Then he opened the door and led her back down the tunnel to the underground rooms.

When they entered Zohn's quarters, he was seated at his desk with a single spectacle over his eye reading a leather-bound book. As they approached, he lifted his head and offered them a welcoming smile. "Pax! Good morning to you!"

Pax returned his smile, genuinely. She was relieved to see him again after the events of the morning. It was nice to be around someone like Zohn. He was warm and honest, and Pax enjoyed his company. "Good morning."

He made his way around the desk until he stood in

front of her. He patted her hand. "How are you this morning, child? Better?" he asked in genuine concern.

She nodded. "Yes. Actually, I think we should talk."

"Oh?" His pale blue eye peeked curiously over his spectacle.

"Yes." Pax seated herself beside Ari at Zohn's table. "See, I think . . ." she paused, worried that Zohn might think she was crazy. But then she remembered he was also a Traveler, and not only that, but a little old man who lived underground. At the very least, her theories might entertain him. "I think my mom might still be alive."

"Is that so?" he said. "Tell me."

Pax explained the circumstances around her mother's departure, the letter, the lullaby, and her theories. The old man listened intently, his eye fixed on her as he thoughtfully scratched the stubble on his chin. When she finished her tale, he appeared deep in thought.

"What is your mother's name?" he asked after some time.

"Leanah. Leanah Graves."

The lines in his forehead crinkled. "That's not a name I remember. But of course, I have recorded the names of thousands of people in my lifetime." He chuckled. "You have come to the right place, nonetheless. I will search the records. Perhaps by the next time we see each other, I will have some good news."

Pax smiled at the thought. "Thank you so much."

"Of course. Now, speaking of you getting home, we should get started."

She sat up straighter in her chair, excited. "Right."

"Are you leaving right now?" Ari asked.

"Well, not right this moment," Zohn answered for her, slightly amused. "It will take her some time to practice, of course."

"Right." He sat back, looking embarrassed.

"I was doing some reading this morning," Zohn said. "It's been quite some time since I've traveled, believe it or not, so I needed to refresh my memory. But this book is for you." He grabbed the small leather-bound book from his desk and handed it to her.

"What is it?"

"I had to do quite a bit of digging through my collection, but I finally found it tucked away in one of my book chests."

"You mean you have more books somewhere down here?" she asked, amazed.

"Of course. You didn't think the entire history of Terra could fit on these shelves, did you?"

She shrugged. "I guess not."

"But this is not a history book. This is actually a textbook of sorts."

Pax took it and flipped through the pages, relieved to find that it was in English.

"I commandeered this copy from a classroom inside the capitol. I thought it might be of use someday. Turns out I was right. See, at around the age of twelve, young children with the gift are taught how to use it, and this is their guide." He patted the cover.

"Well, that will be useful."

He laughed. "I'd imagine so. But, of course, you will not have time to read all of it today. So, I will guide you through the basics. Now tell me about your experience with traveling so far. How have you been able to do it successfully in the past?"

"At first I could only do it in my sleep."

"Hm . . ."

"Is that not normal?"

"Well, I wouldn't say it's not normal, but it is a bit unusual for someone to travel without any intention whatsoever. We assumed most outsiders with the gift arrived through some form of meditative state. Now, many of us—in fact, I'd say most people—can project their consciousness in their sleep to other realms. That's what dreams are, but for you to fully travel—you must have an extraordinary gift." He looked at her intently.

She shifted under his gaze. "I don't know. I mean, I can't control it at all. It's been terrifying not knowing if I'll wake up here or there."

"I should think so," he said. "Is this your only experience with traveling?"

"No. Well, I mean yes, at first. But I did some research on my own, and then the last time I was here, I figured out some kind of way to . . . I don't know, use my memories to travel."

"Fascinating. And how did that work?"

She explained how she was able to allow the memory of her mom singing to guide her home.

"And is that what you did to come back here?"

"Sort of. Only I thought about . . . Terra. I mean, my memories of Terra. You know. People, places . . ." she trailed off. She didn't know how to say she had been thinking about Ari without it sounding weird, but she hoped Zohn wouldn't press for more information.

"I see. Well, what's interesting is that you just stumbled upon the foundations of traveling without any training."

"I did?"

"You did. Fortunately, I don't think it will be difficult at all for you to grasp the fundamentals. Now, why don't you make your way to the bed over there." He gestured to the little cot in the corner of the room.

Pax obeyed. "Do I need to lie down?"

"If that is what feels comfortable," he said. "The goal is that you remain in a position that you feel relaxed in so you will not be distracted by your body. Your mind needs to be able to gain full control."

"Okay." She settled into a seated position with her legs crossed in front of her, allowing her hands to rest in her lap.

"Now, I will guide you into a sort of meditative state," he said softly. "You will not be traveling just yet. It is just to get you familiar with what your body feels when it is beginning to shift."

"Is this something like the Gateway Experience?" she asked, remembering the article Ayana had given when she first experimented with traveling. The atmosphere now felt very similar.

"The what?" Zohn said.

"Oh. It's this program that's supposed to help your mind travel, I guess."

"Ah," he replied. "You will find that there are many pathways to achieve the sort of mental clarity one must have in order to travel in your world. Prayer, meditation, and even certain medicines have been used to assist people with projecting their consciousness. But none of these things will ever result in traveling without the gift. That being said, if you do have the gift, any of these methods could work. It's just a matter of finding what works for you."

"Oh . . . cool."

He chuckled. "Now close your eyes. Allow your body to relax into the floor. Feel it settle beneath you. Once you feel at ease, I want you to think of a memory that brings you comfort. Preferably, something from your world."

Pax closed her eyes and immediately summoned the same memory of her mother she used the first time she'd traveled. The soft hum of the lullaby filled her mind, but her heart could not relax. She wondered if her mother would be able to find her, *if* she was still alive. She shook her head, trying to focus.

"What are you thinking about, child?" Zohn asked.

"I was thinking about my mom."

"I think you should find a different memory. Your whole body is tense. Your body cannot follow a mind that is not in control."

"Okay." She sighed and shifted in her seat.

It took a moment, but she decided to focus on her friends. Not Zeke. That would surely cause her more anxiety. She summoned a memory of Ayana from Christmas break two years ago. Ayana and her mom had invited her over, which had become their tradition. They were sitting around the tree, wearing matching silk pajama sets that Ayana begged Sima to get for the three of them. Sima excitedly ran over to the tree to retrieve two small boxes wrapped in ornate silver paper with gold ribbons and trim. Pax and Ayana excitedly unwrapped the boxes to find matching necklaces of delicate gold bars with their names engraved. Pax remembered feeling so overwhelmed and loved. They had continued with their Christmas revelry, smiling and laughing, because to them, giving her a gift wasn't a burden or an obligation because she was going to be there. They probably didn't even have to think twice about it. It was at that moment when Pax realized they considered her family.

She smiled, remembering the warmth of that day. Her skin began to tingle. She pressed into the emotion of the memory, and the familiar sense of weightlessness rushed over her. She heard Zohn say something to her, but he sounded far away, as if he was at the end of a tunnel. Suddenly, there was a loud crash and her body smacked back down to the floor. Despite the soft blankets beneath her, her head had made hard contact with the ground. "Ow," she murmured, rubbing the back of her skull.

Zohn's face came into focus. "Are you all right, my dear?"

"Yeah. Just had a hard fall, I guess. What happened?"

He laughed. "Well, your body began to dissipate right in front of us. Scared your friend out of his skin. I had to slam those books to the ground to disrupt your travel before you were gone for good."

"Oh." She looked over at Ari, whose mouth was gaping open. "I'm sorry."

"Don't be sorry. You simply proved to me what I had already suspected. You are a very powerful Traveler."

Pax's face heated at the compliment. "So . . . . I guess I'm ready?"

"I should say so." Zohn chuckled.

She sighed and stood, approaching Ari. "Thank you for everything," she said. And she meant it. She would never have found out about her mom, or much less still be alive, if it weren't for him.

He smiled. "I will start searching the coast for you in four weeks' time. And if you don't come back . . . goodbye," he said gruffly.

She looked into his eyes. "I will come back. I promise." She turned to Zohn, remembering an important question. "Zohn, how do I stop myself from traveling in my sleep?"

"Well, I can't be certain since I have not met anyone who could travel unconsciously. But I imagine it should happen less often now that you are learning to control your travels. It's a bit like working a certain muscle. The more you do it, the more control you have over it. But now that you know what traveling feels like, if you start to feel your consciousness reaching that direction, focus yourself into your physical body and will yourself to wake up. Then reset your intentions. That might also take some practice, though. If you wake to find yourself where you do not wish to be, then try to travel back. Does that make sense?"

"Yes, I think so."

"Well, then. I think it's time for you to be on your way." He smiled warmly. "I don't think you really need me here to guide you, so Ari and I will make our way out, but it has been a pleasure."

"Thank you for all your help."

"Of course. Oh, and don't forget your book."

She quickly retrieved it from the table and watched Zohn and Ari leave.

Ari paused and turned back. "The Mother be with you, Pax."

She tilted her head, trying to read the expression in his eyes. Was it sadness? "Thank you. I'll see you soon," she promised.

He gave her a tight half smile, which told her he was not convinced, and he turned and followed Zohn out of the room.

She sighed, clutching the book in her hands. She looked around. There were no windows because it was several feet underground, but she figured it must be getting close to noon. She didn't have much time to waste before Ayana would start to worry. It was only then that it dawned on her: it might not be noon at all when she arrived back. She kicked herself for not thinking of it before. Time had always differed between the two worlds. Anxiety threatened to take over. She wasn't sure what she would be coming back to since she'd ended up traveling a bit unexpectedly. Had Ayana already started panicking? Did she call the cops again and send out a search party? Pax prayed that would not be the case as she settled herself back on the ground. She summoned the memory of them at Christmas, pressing into the way her skin began to prickle. This time, she could feel her insides vibrating, as if they were getting ready to break apart. She smiled, recognizing how much easier it was this time. She sighed as the weightlessness overcame her and she remembered what Ari had said about her looking like water becoming vapor. That was exactly what it felt like, that she had simply willed herself to evaporate. The warm glow of Zohn's room seemed farther and farther away until suddenly she was shrouded in darkness. She felt lighter and lighter as she drifted through the dark void until it felt as if she was nothing at all.

CHAPTER 14

A shrill voice pierced through the silence. Pax winced. Her anxiety spiked at the thought of what might be waiting for her when she opened her eyes. She could make out two voices: Ayana's and a deeper, huskier one. Both seemed upset. She sighed and opened her eyes. Ayana and Zeke were standing just a few feet in front of her, but the yelling had stopped. Pax sat up from the couch, on which she had been lounging on Friday night.

"What's going on, guys?" she asked.

But there was no answer. They just stared at her as if they had seen a ghost. *Oh, right,* Pax thought. They had just watched her appear out of thin air. They were in shock.

"Oh my God," Ayana muttered. Then a smile slowly spread across her face, and she bounded across the room. "Oh my God! Oh my God! Oh my God!" She practically slammed Pax back into the couch and wrapped her arms around her. "You actually friggin' did it!"

Pax laughed. "I did."

Ayana straightened up. "At first, I was like, maybe she's outside somewhere, and then when I couldn't find you, I was like . . . well, maybe she did it. Then you didn't come back, and I was like, well, I hope she did it. I wasn't sure, but I didn't want to call the cops just in case you had done it, so I decided to wait, and I'm so glad that I did because, oh my God! You did it!" She panted, out of breath from the nearly inarticulate rambling.

"Well, thank you for not calling the cops." Pax laughed.

Then she realized Zeke was still standing across the room, his face pale, eyes rounded in shock. "Zeke, what are you doing here?"

"I—I came to talk to you," he started, sounding dazed. "I borrowed Abby's car because I had this whole thing I was gonna—well, anyway, I got here and you weren't here, and Ayana said you were traveling. Then you know I freaked out because that's not real and you were missing, so I was like, 'We have to call the cops!' Then Ayana was like, "No, you can't!' And then we were yelling and then . . . there you were. You were not here, and then it was like . . . poof." He waved his hands, still in shock.

"Well, I'm glad you're back," Ayana said. "But I think you guys have some things to discuss here, so I'm just gonna go outside."

"Thanks," Pax said. Once Ayana left, she stared at Zeke from across the room in silence. He was still looking at her as if she . . . well, as if she had appeared out of nowhere. She was unsure where to begin. "Do you want to sit?" she offered, motioning to the seat next to her.

He crossed the room and sat down.

"So . . ." she started.

"So, you can actually—"

"Yep. I can travel through space with my mind," she finished.

He exhaled and leaned back on the couch. "You know how insane that sounds, right?"

"I mean, yeah, but you also just watched me do it, so . . ."

"I don't know what I saw," he said.

"You seriously still don't believe me?"

"I didn't say that. It's just . . . it's a lot to process."

"I know. I'm sorry. Take all the time you need."

He rubbed his hands down his jeans and sank into the couch. They sat in silence for so long Pax was contemplating if she should get up and leave. Then he finally sat up. "Do you want a drink or something?"

She nodded. "I'd love one."

He made his way to the fridge, scanning the contents until he had located two soda cans in the back. He popped the top and took a long swig. She smirked at him. Zeke always hounded her and Ayana about drinking too many sodas. He said it was like putting liquid garbage into your body.

"Slow down there, buddy. You know that stuff is poison, right?" Pax teased.

He was unamused by her joke. "Give me a break, okay? I just found out that everything I know about the world is a lie."

She rolled her eyes. "That's a little dramatic. Besides, you're not the one who is disappearing into thin air. Way to make it about yourself, though."

"You're right. I'm sorry," he said, and then made his way over and offered the other soda to Pax in a gesture of friendship. "I've been a jerk."

Pax took a sip. "That's an understatement."

He walked over and grabbed the sides of her face with his hands until their eyes locked. Pax's breath quickened. Then he said, "I have been a gigantic, smelly asshole."

"Gross!" she shouted, pushing him away.

"Uh, excuse me? I'm in the middle of an apology," he retorted with false offense.

She pursed her lips in amusement. "Right, my apologies. Proceed."

"Where was I? Oh, right." He cleared his throat, and then at the top of his lungs, yelled, "I am an asshole!"

He continued screaming self-deprecating insults into the air, and against her will, Pax bubbled over with laughter, and soon they were both bent over in hysterics.

When they had finally caught their breath, his eyes met hers. "I am so sorry for not believing you. And for breaking your trust. And for like, all around being a terrible friend, and making this whole thing about me."

As usual, Zeke's sincerity had won her over.

Suddenly, Ayana peeked her head through the door. "So, uh, I hate to interrupt whatever's going on in here, but we should probably get going. We're running a bit behind schedule, considering it's about half-past three and you were supposed to be back at noon. I've got a paper I've been putting off all weekend, and if I don't get started soon, I'll probably give up and just take the F."

"It's 3:30?" Pax said. She thought when she returned it would surely be almost nighttime because that was how it usually worked when she traveled. The more she learned about traveling, the more questions she had.

"Yeah, so . . . can we go?" Ayana prompted again.

"Right." Zeke straightened himself and grabbed the keys to his mom's Civic, and the three made their way out the front door.

"I already packed all the stuff you brought," Ayana said, handing her the small black bag.

"Thanks," Pax answered, grabbing it.

"Do you want to ride back with me?" asked Zeke, who was buckling himself into the driver's seat.

"Yeah, that sounds good," Pax replied.

Ayana smiled. "Well, drive safe. And remember, hooking up in the back seat can get you arrested for public indecency!" she called over her shoulder.

"Shut up!" Pax said, praying Zeke hadn't heard that as she made her way to the passenger side. As she slung her bag into the back seat, Zeke turned the key in the ignition, and set off toward home.

As they made their way down the road, Zeke grilled her with questions. "So, where exactly do you go when you . . ."

"Travel?"

"Is that what you call it?"

"Well, I mean, that's what everyone calls it in Terra. That's the place where I go."

"Huh. So, what's it like?"

Pax thought for a moment and smiled. "It's beautiful and terrifying. There are these rust-colored sand beaches, and the sea is almost green. And the village is full of people who just exist together like a big family. They have parties together every week. But it's also been torn apart by their government. It's full of people like me—people who can travel—but all they want is power. They stole Terra from the natives, and now they kill them and imprison them so they can keep control of it."

"That sounds dangerous," Zeke said. "So, what do you do when you go? I mean, when did you even start?"

"I guess I've been seeing Terra in my dreams for years. But the first time I actually traveled with my body, I think it was the day you found me on the floor at my house."

"The day you told me about the guy," he remembered. "I'm sorry I didn't believe you then."

She shrugged it off. "Why would you? I mean, I don't even think I believed myself until I saw Ari again."

"That's his name? The guy who grabbed you?"

"Yeah."

"You mean you've been hanging out with some guy who physically assaulted you?"

"Okay, he didn't physically assault me. He's not like that," Pax reassured. "He was just scared. He was trying to keep me from getting killed."

"What do you mean 'getting killed'?"

Pax froze. She hadn't meant to tell him that part. Zeke seemed interested to hear about her traveling, but he was still Zeke. He'd freak out if he learned that she'd been in danger. "Yeah, so there are these people who run Terra called the Fellowship, and they don't want other Travelers to come there."

"Why?"

"Because they think new people could be a threat, I guess." She tried to sound nonchalant. "Anyway, Ari kept me safe and helped me find people who could teach me to control my gift, so it's fine."

He sighed. "Yeah, I guess it's good you went then, so now you know how to keep yourself from just randomly showing up there ever again."

She shifted uncomfortably in her seat.

"You aren't planning on going back to that place, right?"

She paused for several moments, not sure she was ready to delve into the whole story with Zeke when they had just gotten on speaking terms again.

"Pax, are you serious? You're going back? What, do you want to die?" His voice grew more panicked.

"No, that's not it, it's just . . . it's complicated, okay?"

"What, is it because of this Ari guy or something?"

"What? No. Ari has nothing to do with it. It's just—"

"Well, then what could possibly be so important that you are willing to risk your life for it?"

She felt herself growing frustrated with him, but then she remembered Dinah. She remembered her shouting almost the same thing to Ari. She could still see the fear and panic in her eyes. Her voice softened. "Look, can we just not do this right now? I'm not going anywhere right now, and I'm so sick of fighting. Can you pause on being Big Brother Zeke for a little while and just be my friend?"

"I'm not your brother," he said so low she almost didn't hear him. She looked over to see his eyes boring into the road with an expression that inexplicably made her chest tighten. She looked away and turned the radio up so loud that no further conversation could be had. She was kicking herself for starting yet another fight with him when they had just made up. Frustration emanated from him as his hands clutched tightly on the steering wheel. She kept her eyes straight ahead until they pulled into Zeke's driveway.

Zeke opened his mouth as if he wanted to say something, then quickly closed it again. Then he turned to her and simply said, "I, uh, guess I'll see you at school tomorrow?"

"Definitely. Bye," she said, waving awkwardly before she made her way back to her house.

Her father wasn't home yet. That was one less thing she would have to deal with right now. She entered her home and immediately stripped out of the dress she had been wearing for almost three days. She wrinkled her nose, disgusted by her current state, and was immediately thankful to be somewhere with running water again. She practically sprinted to the bath, ran the water, and sank down into the tub, allowing her muscles to relax. Then she remembered the book she had stuffed down in the pockets that were sewn into Dinah's dress. She dried her hand on the fabric she had discarded at the foot of the tub and fished around in it until she retrieved the small leather-bound book.

She ran her fingers across the etching on the cover that read, *The Traveler's Guidebook*, in a delicate gold script. She opened the book and flipped through the pages. The first chapter was the story Zohn had told her about the history of Travelers, only it was much more embellished, touting the brilliance of John Dickinson and how he was "chosen by God." She scoffed and flipped further into the pages, skimming through basic instructions for traveling, Traveler's safety, and other logistic pieces. Then she stopped at a subheading in the chapter on "Advanced Traveling Techniques": *Choosing Your Coordinates.* She eyed the section with fascination. It read:

> "Once you have mastered the basics of traveling to and from Terra, the well-practiced Travelers may begin to broach upon the very complex art of selecting specific locations within Earth or Terra. If you have previously traveled, you may have found that you begin your travels at the same point each time, and then return to the location where you left. This is because these places have high concentrations of energy. Your travels, as well as the travels of others, create portals which then serve as launching points. As discussed in chapter 3, traveling functions through preestablished points in the universe. To our knowledge, this evidence holds true. However, when you have traveled between two points multiple times, and your mind has mastered the energetic path-way between each location, you may begin to adjust the launch point and return point within each world.
>
> "This is done much the same way as basic traveling. However, when you begin the visualization process at the start of your travel, you must choose the exact location you wish to go. It must be an access point you are very familiar with or you will end up in the standard access point. You must concentrate your energy on the location, focus on the sensory details: what it smells like, the sounds, the colors. At first, your body might

resist the shift, but practiced Travelers will be able to press past
the resistance. Then once you feel the energetic pull toward
your access point, fixate your mental energy upon a single
point in that location. Coordinates work best, but a specific
location in a room, such as a chair or bed, have been known to
work as well."

Pax sat back in the tub, contemplating what she had just
read. She thought about how convenient it would be if she
could simply bypass the wall altogether on her next trip. It
would certainly be nice not to begin every visit to Terra with
a near-death experience. She decided she would practice this
technique for the next few weeks without actually traveling.
Simply letting herself meditate on a set location—Ari's house,
she decided—until she felt the energy shift. She'd set her alarm
at fifteen-minute intervals, so even if she did travel, she would
be brought back quickly. She smiled, feeling confident in her
plan, wishing for the next few weeks to pass quickly. She made
a mental note to talk to Ayana about covering for her during
winter break.

Pax was interrupted from her thoughts by the sound of her
stomach growling. She hadn't eaten anything since early that
morning. Hurrying her way out of the tub so she could find
something to eat, she dressed in a pair of comfy joggers and an
oversized vintage tee that had a little frog in a cowboy hat that
read, "Howdy Y'all!" It was stupid, but the shirt always made
her laugh. Soon after, she made her way to the kitchen. She
eyeballed the window, noting that her father was still not home.
She checked the clock: 6:00 p.m. Surely, he was off the plane by
now. She shrugged. Maybe he'd had some kind of delay, which
was just fine with her. The less time she had to see him, the
less she had to stress about why they still hadn't talked about

her disappearance from the party last week. Was he playing mind games with her? Was this a sick form of punishment he had cooked up? She made herself a sandwich, grabbed a bag of chips, and devoured the whole thing while standing over the kitchen sink.

As Pax stared out the window, she saw Abby leaving for her evening shift. She thought about her tense conversation with Zeke and was filled with a heavy remorse. Fighting with him over the last few weeks had been miserable. And just when things started to get okay again, she messed it all up. She shook the feeling away. She had a ton of work to do before school in the morning. Her travel to Terra had taken up the entire weekend.

She made her way to her bedroom and pulled out her books, working through math and biology homework for a couple of hours, but she couldn't stay focused. Her eyes kept drifting over to Zeke's bedroom window, adjacent to hers. She stifled the urge to walk over there and work it all out for as long as she could, but when she finished her homework and just sat in her quiet room staring at his house, she resigned against her better judgment. She slipped on a pair of old sneakers and headed out the door.

Pax hesitated as she approached Zeke's house. She was so sick of all the crap between them that she just wanted to settle it now. It was possible that she might not come back from her next trip to Terra, and that was only a month away. She couldn't stand the thought of leaving with bad blood between her and her closest friend. She knocked tentatively. When there was no answer, she knocked again with more force. On the third knock, the door swung open. Zeke answered in his PJs, his wet hair brushed back on his head, indicating he had freshly showered. He looked surprised.

"Oh! Um, hey," he greeted her.

"Hey," she started, unsure of what to do next. She made a mental note to start actually preparing for this kind of conversation from here on out.

"Do you want to come in?" he offered, stepping out of the doorway.

"Sure." She walked into the dimly lit living room. "Where's Maria?"

"She's staying at a friend's house tonight."

"Oh . . . cool."

Zeke sighed. "Did you need something?"

"I—" Her voice caught in her throat. "I just want to talk to you about earlier today. I was acting weird and cut you off, and I'm sorry for that. But I wouldn't be going back if I didn't have a good reason. I am not the kind of person who just makes stupid, impulsive decisions for no reason, Zeke. You know that."

"I know," he said.

"Okay, so here's the truth. I think my mom is still alive, and she's hiding in Terra for some reason."

He blinked. "What?"

She exhaled a long breath. "Yeah."

He found a seat on the couch, then motioned for her to sit next to him. "Explain."

She sat down, took a deep breath, then started from the beginning. She relayed everything Zohn had told her, how she thought her mother had died on Terra's shore, then the realization about the lullaby her mom would sing. She talked for what felt like hours, and Zeke remained stoic but fixated on her story.

When she finished, she said, "I know it's crazy, but it can't be any crazier than discovering I can travel through space. And if that's possible, why can't this be?"

He sighed and took her hands. "Look, Pax, nobody knows more than me how hard it is to lose a parent, and how much time you can spend imagining ways to get them back. But even if she was a Traveler like you, it sounds like there's a high chance that she might've been killed. I know that's hard to hear."

She pushed his hands away. "Weren't you even listening? I know what the odds are. I know this might be insane, but if there is even a sliver of a chance she's there and I didn't find her, I'd never be able to live with myself." Her voice wavered, filled with emotion.

"I hear you. I do. But Pax, this place is dangerous. If they are against people like you, there is a higher chance you'll die before you even get a chance to look for your mom. Is that what you want?" His voice was filled with panic.

"Come on, of course I don't want to die. But I need to find her. Surely you of all people can understand that."

"You know what? I do. I actually get it more than you could even imagine. I spent years looking for my mom while we were in foster care. I thought if I could just find her, we could all be a family again. And you know what? I found her."

Pax raised her brows. She had never heard this story. "What?"

"Yeah. The year before Abby took us in, I found her in a park, sitting on a bench with a needle sticking out of her arm." He rubbed his hands over his face. "She was so high she didn't even know who I was."

"Oh my God," Pax whispered. She grabbed his hand. "Zeke, I'm so sorry. I had no idea."

"Don't," he said. "I'm not telling you so you can feel sorry for me. I'm trying to keep you from making the same mistake I did. I know it can be really tempting to believe that everything would be fixed if you just had your mom. But you don't even know her. Parents can be just as screwed up as the rest of us. Maybe she left because she was saving you from herself."

She patted his hand. "I am so sorry about what happened to your mom. Really, I am. But I can't explain it—it's like everything in me is telling me that I have to do this."

"No."

"What?"

"You heard me. I'm not going to let you go and get yourself killed."

Pax stood and crossed the room. "Um, last I checked, you aren't my dad. Why do you treat me like this?"

"What do you mean? I'm trying to look out for you. This is what we do, Pax. We look out for each other."

"But it's more than that. You treat me like I'm some kind of child. Like I'm so fragile, I'll fall apart any second if you aren't there to hold me together. Like I'm your charity project."

He laughed humorlessly. "Is that what you think? That I look out for you because I feel sorry for you or something?"

"Yes," she said.

He gritted his teeth and crossed the room to meet her, then leaned in until he was only inches from her. "I do not think you are a charity case," he said in a low voice.

"You don't?"

He shook his head, his breath shuddering. "And I don't think I'm your dad or your brother."

Pax swallowed hard and looked into his eyes that were now smoldering green pools. "Then what do you think?" She wanted to sound strong, but her heart was sputtering so fast that it came out no louder than a whisper.

He looked at her for several long, unbearable moments, his breathing becoming shallow where Pax's had stopped altogether. Then, without warning, his hand wrapped behind the base of her neck and his thumb grazed her cheek, and with urgency he pulled her face closer until they were breathing the same breath. He looked in her eyes, waiting for a sign from her. Pax stiffened, then nodded without thinking, giving him the permission he needed to close the gap between them. Then, in a single second, Zeke's lips were glued to hers.

It had happened so quickly. Her best friend in the world was kissing her with the passion that could only come from years of longing. She didn't want to like it. She hadn't had time to process whether she was ready for things to change between them.

No. She wasn't ready for this. But before she could even think about pulling away, her body betrayed her. Her breath let out in a wild gasp, and suddenly her lips were moving against his too as her hands twisted into his damp hair. He smiled against her mouth, feeling the satisfaction of her returned affection, as he wrapped his other arm around her back and pulled her closer.

Pax's heartbeat pounded in her ears with a desire she had never experienced before. She had been kissed before, sure. In the eighth grade, she briefly dated a boy named Charlie from her art class. He liked emo rock and was always chewing green-apple-flavored gum. Kissing Charlie felt like something she had to do because they were supposed to like each other. She'd kissed boys a handful of times at parties, but it always felt strange, unfamiliar. This was entirely different. It was soft and warm and perfect. She could kiss Zeke for a hundred years and never have enough of the way it felt. There was so much history between them, Pax always thought it might be weird if they kissed, like kissing a brother. But it took her by surprise how right it was between them. The heat climbed up her body as he gently pushed her against the wall, and his warm hand found the bare skin of her hip bone beneath her shirt. She pressed herself closer to him, but he pulled away and rested his head against hers, panting as he tried to catch his breath.

He stroked her cheek and looked into her eyes with their foreheads pressed together. "I think you are the bravest person I've ever met," he said. "I think you're beautiful, and so funny, and smart. Way smarter than me." He laughed. "You are my best friend, and I would do anything for you because there is no one else who makes me feel so . . . at home. I spent years feeling lost and alone, but then I met you. Being in the system for so long, I learned that when you find a place that feels like home, you try to hold on to it. You are home to me, and that's the reason I do all of this because I want to be home for you too. That's what I think."

A smile broke across her face. "Some speech, Hernandez," she teased.

He smirked, then kissed the tip of her nose. "Yeah, it was all right." They laughed in unison, then quieted. He kissed her forehead and brought her eyes to meet his again. "Please, please don't go back."

Her heart tightened as she remembered what they had been fighting about in the first place. She sighed. "Zeke . . ."

"Please," he whispered. "Stay here with me. We can be together. We can look out for each other. We could be so happy."

Tears welled up in her eyes because she knew it was true. They had been friends for so long. Zeke knew her better than anyone. She could walk away from all of this right now and actually start living her life. She could graduate and go to college, and they could be together and leave her dad and his mom and all of the darkness in their pasts behind. Then the tears spilled over. As beautiful as that picture was, she had to do this. And she knew it was going to break his heart. She wanted more than anything to wrap her arms around his neck and kiss him one more time, but that wouldn't be fair.

She untangled herself from his grasp, took his hands in hers, and squeezed them. Then in a broken whisper, she said, "I'm so sorry." She saw his heart shatter behind his eyes just before she turned and sprinted out the front door.

Once outside, she stopped and finally let the sobs that had been building in her chest escape her. She hated herself for what she was doing to Zeke, but she couldn't shake the feeling that she had to go back, even against her better judgment, even if she would be happier not knowing. She just knew she had to find her mom. The next few weeks were going to be even more painful. Seeing Zeke in the halls, having to avoid the sad, painful expression in his eyes, would be torture. She sobbed as she made her way across the damp lawn back to her house. Her father's car was in the driveway, but she didn't care. She just wanted to curl up in bed and sleep for the next three weeks. She already decided she was going to wait until her father left and then fake a sick call to the school in the morning by the time she walked through the door.

Before she could even finish the thought, she saw her father seated at the kitchen table, waiting for her. Her chest clenched.

"Sit," he instructed calmly as he gestured toward the chair across from him.

Pax shuffled forward slowly and lowered herself to the seat. "How was Chicago?" she asked. She tried to keep her tone even and casual, but her voice quivered.

"It was fine," he responded as he took a sip of his whiskey, neat.

Pax shifted uncomfortably in her seat. She was so nervous she could only manage a nod. Why wasn't he saying anything?

They sat for several unbearable moments until her father

finally cleared his throat. "I have something for you," he announced. He reached into the bag that was positioned against his chair and retrieved a stack of papers that he placed on the table in front of her. In a loopy script on the top of the page, it read: *"Whispering Pines: A home for troubled teens."*

"What is this?" she asked.

"I've been looking for a solution to your . . . issue. After I learned about your disappearance from that party, I talked to some experts and had them assess your records. We all think a little bit of distance and the chance to learn some new coping skills in a supportive environment would be really good for you," he answered, as if it had been rehearsed.

"What?" she nearly shrieked.

"Paxton." Her father adjusted his tie uncomfortably. "You and I both know you need help. Help that I can't give you."

Her breathing quickened. "You mean you *won't* give me."

"Excuse me?" His voice turned harsh.

Pax wanted to shrink back from the challenge in his voice, but she was emboldened by her anger. "Let's stop pretending you care about me for five seconds and acknowledge what this is really about."

He chuckled humorlessly. "And what is that?"

"I am an inconvenience to you. I always have been. My *episodes*, my art—I embarrass you. You see me as a threat to your career, and now that you're up for your position on the school board, you want me out of the way because you are a selfish—"

Suddenly, she was violently interrupted by the sound of glass shattering against the wall just inches from her head. Pax jumped. Her father's hand that had been holding the whiskey glass was now empty and clenched into a fist.

His chest was heaving. "That's enough. It's already been

arranged. You are going to this facility. Tomorrow. Go pack."
He slicked his hair back with his hand, then headed to his room.

Tears pricked her eyes as anger welled within her chest.
"No," she responded.

He turned on his heels. "It wasn't a question. You *are* going."

"No, I'm not. If you want me to go, you are going to have
to drag me out!" she shouted. She didn't know what had come
over her. Maybe she was just sick of her dad treating her like
something he could throw away. But when she met his eyes,
she knew she had messed up.

There was a fire in his eyes she had never seen before. Before
she could move, he had advanced upon her and grabbed her
by her wrists. "You want me to drag you there? Fine." He slung
her against the wall.

She groaned as she tumbled to the ground with a thud.
She winced at the throbbing in her head where her skull had
slammed into the floor. Usually when he used force with her, it
was to shut her up. But this time, it only fueled her own anger.
"I hate you."

He towered over her, meeting her gaze with cold indifference.
"You know, when I was your age, your grandmother used to tell
me that if I hated her, it meant she was doing something right.
She said, 'The rod of discipline was a blessing to a rebellious
heart.' It is clear I haven't been firm enough with you because
look what you have become."

She gasped. "What I've become? That's rich coming from
you. You're a monster." She smiled spitefully. "And I can't wait
to tell everyone in Golden Valley exactly what kind of man you
really are."

She watched as any semblance of civility left his eyes. He
slammed the heel of his dress shoe down into her rib cage. She
groaned, then gasped for air, trying to find her breath again.

"I hate that you make me do this," he said as he grabbed her by the arm and wrenched her upward until they were face-to-face. "You know I only want what's best for you."

Anger coursed through Pax's veins, fueling her to taunt him further. "You mean what's best for *you*," she spat at him.

The fire in his eyes burned stronger. "You're just like your mother. So goddamn difficult." He threw her across the hallway and into her room. She landed with a loud thud, her skull crashing against the wall as her body slumped forward. Through the ringing in her ears, she heard her father mutter "shit" and shuffle toward her.

"Pax. Pax!" he shouted as he shook her roughly.

She groaned in response and looked up at him. For the first time in her life, her father looked afraid. His perfectly crafted persona had finally cracked. Though her body was radiating in pain, part of her felt a sense of satisfaction in knowing that her father's reputation could be ruined.

He straightened his back and cleared his throat as he backed out of the room. "We'll talk about this more in the morning. But make no mistake, you are going to that facility." He closed the door behind him, leaving her lying on the floor.

Pax fought for breath. Her chest heaved as she felt herself slipping from consciousness. She reached up and grabbed the Traveler's textbook from her dresser and stuffed it into the waistband of her jeans. She closed her eyes. Her father might come for her in the morning, but she would not be here when he did.

She slowed her breathing and fought against the fog that was taking over her brain. She remembered the instructions from the manual about how to set travel points, and she evoked the memory of Terra. The warmth of Ari's home, the smell of freshly baked bread, the glow from the hearth. She forced

herself to keep breathing in and out evenly, struggling to keep
the image in her mind. Her head grew heavier and her body
screamed in pain. But she pushed, imagining herself lying on
the soft pallet on the floor, the colorful tapestries surrounding
her. Tingles crawled down her spine, and she suddenly felt as if
she were being ripped in half. In all the times she had traveled,
it had never felt like this. It was like every molecule in her body
was exploding and her skin burned as the darkness swallowed
her whole. She wondered if she could die in transition between
two worlds. But soon she felt herself come back into her body.
A soft surface formed beneath her, and a warm glow filled the
room.

"Pax?" a familiar voice called from across the room.

All she could do was groan as she looked toward the voice.
Soon she was face-to-face with Ari. His eyes were wide with
concern. She opened her mouth to speak, fighting against the
exhaustion that was sweeping over her.

"Pax," he called again, but this time it sounded like his voice
was coming from inside a tunnel. She strained to open her eyes.

"You will be all right, Pax," Ari whispered in reassurance. It
was the last thing Pax remembered before her body gave out.

CHAPTER 15

One day, two days, three days. Pax didn't know how long it had been. All she knew was darkness. From time to time, she saw flickers of light and warmth, heard soft murmurs of voices around her, and felt the cool touch of hands on her forehead and the warmth of rich broth sliding down her throat. She didn't know where she was, and the only sign that she was still alive was the pain radiating through her. Her limbs were heavy like lead, and her head felt as if it were filled with water. In her fleeting moments of consciousness, she tried to open her eyes or her mouth to speak, but her efforts only made her more exhausted, and before she knew it, she was enveloped in sleep again.

It went on this way for what felt like years, in and out of consciousness. Until she heard a gentle voice singing above her.

One day, we'll all be free.

Her eyes fluttered open to see a woman with black hair standing over her, stroking Pax's hair. Pax sighed, knowing her body must have finally given out. This must be the afterlife. "Mom?"

The woman smiled softly. "No, child. I'm not your mother."

Pax's brow furrowed, and she tried to sit up but winced as a sharp pain hit her side. She groaned.

"Shh," the woman coaxed her back down. "Don't get up. You have two broken ribs."

Pax's eyes widened. She pulled down the warm woolen

blanket that had been laid on her. Large strips of bandages covered her entire torso. "Where am I?"

"You are in the temple shelter. My name is Felyine. I am Shahad's wife. I'm a healer, and I have been looking after you. You're safe," she said gently.

Pax was confused until she recalled the underground shelter. She was in a dimly lit room with a small hearth, a trunk, and a table. She was lying on a small cot on the left side of the room. She breathed a sigh of relief, realizing she had made it to Terra. "How long have I been here?"

The woman turned from the table where she had just finished pouring water into a clay cup. "I believe you were with Dinah and Ari six days ago." She sat down beside her, gently lifted Pax upward, and poured the water into her mouth.

Pax accepted the water gratefully. She was parched. Once she'd had her fill, she sat backward and looked at the ceiling, finally processing what she'd been told. A week. She remembered her father had beaten her severely; it was a wonder she was still alive. She thanked the gods that she had managed to travel through that.

"Where is Ari?" she asked.

"It is well past midday now, so he is probably just leaving the docks. But he usually comes at night to look after you."

"He does?"

She nodded, taking a small cloth and dabbing at Pax's head. "Yes. It's a wonder he hasn't dropped from exhaustion yet. He sits by your side every night."

A pang of guilt hit Pax. She hated the idea that he had inconvenienced himself to look after her.

"Oh, thank the Mother you're awake!" a gravelly voice called from the doorway.

Pax smiled. "Zohn." She tried to sit up again but winced, remembering her injuries.

He approached her. "Easy, child. Don't hurt yourself on my account." He stooped down and clasped her hand. "How are you?"

"I've been better."

He chuckled and shook his head.

"How did I get here?"

"Ari realized your injuries were out of his depth," he said. "So he called for Shahad and brought you here in the dead of night. Nearly scared me into an early grave. He did the right thing, though. Traveling with injuries as you did could have put you in far more serious condition, you know."

She shook her head. "I didn't know."

"Oh yes. It is very ill advised to travel if you have been injured. It's a bit like voluntarily tearing yourself to shreds, then letting gravity glue you back together."

"Yep. That sounds exactly like how it felt."

He nodded. "You've been well cared for," he added. "There are Watch members who have been caring for you day and night. I'm sure they will be pleased to know you've awakened. The result of your travel had you near death, but it would seem you are recovering well."

Pax mulled over his words. Watch members. People who didn't know her or probably didn't even trust her had dedicated their time to helping her live. She was overwhelmed. "Thank you. I . . . don't know what to say." She craned her neck to look over at Felyine, who was preparing new bandages. "Thank you, Felyine."

Felyine smiled. "Of course. You are a friend of the Watch."

"I am?"

She chuckled with amusement. "You clearly have the trust of Ari and Zohn, which means a great deal. A man who has survived as much suffering as Zohn does not give trust lightly."

Pax looked over at Zohn, who had a twinkle in his eye.

"And after speaking with Shahad," Felyine continued, "I could tell you had completely won him over. So, I have made sure that the rest of the Watch knows you are our ally."

"But I haven't given Shahad my decision—"

"Decision or not, you will be under the care and protection of the Watch, as promised," she assured. "Now, I will be going. But when you are feeling up to it, we will speak again." She made her way toward the door, then turned to Pax once more. "I'm relieved that you are okay," she added with sincerity.

Pax smiled and watched Felyine leave. Then she turned to Zohn and lowered her voice. "Have you heard anything about my mother?"

He pursed his lips and shook his head. "No. I'm sorry. There is no record of her here."

She sighed and dropped her head back against the pillow.

"But that doesn't mean she is not here," Zohn continued. "It just means she is probably not from Rehama. There are citizen records in the west, too, and the capitol."

"Oh." She thought for a moment. "So, I just have to find a way to get to those records."

Zohn nodded. "Yes, but that is not an easy feat. Many of the village records from Nomadesales were confiscated in raids. The only thing that remains are current citizen birth logs, and most likely financial records. And if all the records are in the capitol, you will risk your life to see them."

Pax tossed up her arms in exasperation. "Well, there has to be a way."

He looked at her dubiously. "Perhaps there is, but your body is not ready to go hunting in enemy territory, child. You must give yourself time to heal—"

"She lives."

Zohn and Pax looked up to see Ari leaning casually against the doorway with a smirk curling the left side of his lip.

"For now, I guess," Pax joked, meeting his eyes.

Zohn motioned for Ari to grab his arm to help him up. "I must be going now. But do not worry, my friend. You and I will have plenty of time down here together." He chuckled. "I don't think I have ever had a neighbor down here, unless you count the occasional carousers who drink too much during our gatherings. It will be nice to have some company."

Pax smiled after him. "Well, then I'll see you tomorrow, neighbor."

Ari took Zohn's place beside her as the old man disappeared down the hall. "It's good to see you with your eyes open," he joked.

She smirked. "Thanks, I guess?"

"So, what happened? The last time I heard from you, we had agreed that I'd see you in three weeks. The next thing I know, you appear unconscious on my bed as I am dressing for work."

She attempted to sit up a little, feeling silly trying to hold a conversation with him while she was lying flat on her back. Ari helped her. Then he grabbed another pillow and wedged it between her and the wall.

"Thank you," Pax responded through the discomfort of being tended to this way. When Ari had settled back down on the ground beside her, she began to explain. "Well, it was my dad. He was threatening to send me away. I pushed him too far. I barely had enough time to grab my book before I . . ." she trailed off suddenly, remembering. *The book.*

The Last Traveler

"It's on the table over there," Ari gestured, reading her mind. "You had it in the waistband of your trousers when we went to bandage you. I thought you would want it when you woke."

Pax's cheeks reddened, suddenly realizing that Ari had most likely seen her naked.

"Dinah," he said quickly. "She bandaged you. I just helped. I didn't . . ."

"Thank you both for what you did. I don't know if I'd be alive if it hadn't been for you."

Ari shook his head. "It's disgusting . . . what he did to you. You know, if he were here, the village counsel would exile him. In the old days, they'd cut his hand off. I wish—"

"Ari!" Pax scolded.

"Do you not think he would deserve it?" he said, gesturing.

"I mean, I'd be okay with exile so I'd never have to see him again, but cutting his hand off? That feels a little extreme."

"That's why the punishment is not used anymore. But hurting a woman is a serious offense to our people. Women are sacred. They make life, like the Great Mother. If you do wrong against a woman, you do wrong against God. It's blasphemous." His words burned softly.

She thought about her last exchange with her father. She was proud of herself for the way she had stood up to him. Then she remembered the anger in his eyes as he crushed her ribcage. Even if she told someone who could help he might find a way to turn it around on her. It was her word against his. He was a respected member of their community. The principal of the year. And she was on her way to a girls' home. But then she realized that was what her dad wanted her to think. He manipulated everyone around them into believing Pax was the problem because he wanted her to be too afraid to speak.

Her silence was his shield. The thought made her enraged and devastated all at once. It was too much.

"Pax? What is wrong?" Ari's question pulled her from her thoughts.

Her jaw clenched and her eyes brimmed with tears. "I don't know if I want to go back. At least not now."

Ari scooted closer and gently squeezed her shoulder. "I am so sorry. But I told you last time, you have a place here if you need it. You can stay in the shelter with Zohn as long as you need, and eventually the Fellowship will forget about you, and you can come out of hiding. You can live here with us forever."

Pax exhaled heavily. *Forever*. She was so grateful for what Ari was offering her, but he didn't realize what it meant. She might not have had a great life in Ohio, but it had still been home to her for sixteen years. Now she was faced with the possibility of leaving it all behind. Her school, her friends. Ayana. Zeke. Her breath caught. *Zeke*. She recalled their last talk. The things he'd said to her, the way he'd kissed her, and how she'd rejected him. Her heart filled with longing and regret.

"I can see you need some time," Ari said, pulling her away from her thoughts. "Someone will be coming to bring you dinner soon."

"I'm not hungry," she responded weakly.

"Well, I will have them leave it for you. I've been staying in here while you slept, but I can move to the room across the hallway if you'd like," he said.

She nodded, unable to respond.

"If you need me, just call."

When he was no longer in sight, Pax managed to slide back down in the bed. She stared at the dark ceiling as she came to terms with the truth that was upon her. The life that she knew was probably over. She was no longer Paxton Graves, high school junior from Ohio. She was no longer Ayana's best friend. And she would never get to be Zeke's girlfriend. She was Pax, a Traveler, and that was it. That was all she knew about herself now. She was starting over. New home, new friends, new life. She was so overwhelmed she didn't know if she could ever accept it. But she would have to. Because if she traveled back, she could be sent away to live out her life in a care facility, far from her friends and any semblance of a real life. Of course, if the Fellowship found her, she wouldn't have any life at all.

"Damned if I do, damned if I don't." She laughed under her breath. She was suddenly overcome with exhaustion from the past couple of hours. The deep aches and throbs ebbed and flowed through her body until she was taken into a fitful sleep.

Pax's heart stopped as she awakened to her father looming over her. She was in her own bed at home.

Her father's eyes were as enraged as the last time she saw him.

Pax desperately tried to sit up, flinging her arms and legs to fight him off as his large hand clamped over her mouth and nose, restraining her to the bed. She let out a muffled scream against his hand to no avail. Her heart slowed and her chest burned as her lungs desperately fought for air. Tears streamed down her cheeks, and she tried to scream again. Her body was shaking, and her father was saying something she couldn't quite make out. She forced her body forward, pain ripping through her torso.

Her eyes flung open, and she gasped for air. She was back in the passage, and Ari was kneeling beside her.

"Pax!" he called.

Still hyperventilating, she said, "He was there, he was in my room, and he . . . he—"

"Shh." He gently eased her back down on the pillow. Her ribs ached in protest. "It was a dream, Pax. You were dreaming."

She worked to steady her breathing. "I'm sorry. I just never know if it's real."

"Are you all right?"

She nodded. "I think so." She wrapped her hands around her middle, the pain of her sudden movement radiating through her.

Ari stood and crossed the room to the table. "Here, I'll do your bindings again. It will help with the pain."

He returned to her side with a long strip of fabric and a glass bottle. She watched as he set them on the ground next to her bed and knelt beside her.

"I'll have to sit you up for this, but I've never done it while you're awake, so it might hurt," he said. From the bottle, he poured something into the clay cup beside her bed, then brought it to her mouth. "Drink this. It's a tonic Felyine mixed up for you. It's made from the Testalos flower. It should help."

Pax lifted her head and took a slow sip from the cup. She nearly choked when it splashed onto her tongue. The flavor was strong and pungent, like alcohol and dirt and herbs. She wrinkled her nose as she finished what was in her cup, shivering as it burned down her throat. Then she met his gaze.

He seemed unsure of how to proceed. "I . . . um. I'll have to lift your tunic to get to the bandages."

Heat rose to her cheeks. "Oh."

"I'm sorry," he said, seeming uncomfortable. "It's just,

Felyine says we have to keep your ribs tightly bound so they will heal properly."

Pax sighed. "It's okay. I'll just hold it up to keep things . . . covered."

He nodded, his eyes on the floor. "I'll need to help you up first." He gently slid his hands underneath the upper part of her back and neck, slowly scooting her upward.

She shifted beneath him, frustrated. "I'm not a baby. You don't need to support my neck."

"Sorry," he said, moving his hand to support her left side instead. "The last few times I did this, you were not conscious, so holding the neck was necessary."

"Oh . . . right." She felt guilty for the way she had snapped at him. She wasn't used to being tended to in this way. Her father wasn't exactly warm and fuzzy. When she was sick, she mostly stayed quarantined in her room and cared for herself. Having a boy like Ari care for her felt foreign and strange. To be honest, if he wasn't here binding her wounds, she wouldn't be convinced that he was capable of such gentleness. He was usually teasing her and making jokes at her expense. But now, he looked at her with so much concern in his eyes, it was bizarre. She grimaced as he slowly wrenched her body upward, inch by inch, until she was in a seated position. She tried to support herself but found it difficult to straighten her back.

Ari quickly recognized that she was struggling and shifted her back until she was supported by the wall behind her. "Is this all right?"

"Yeah."

"I need you to . . ." He gestured toward her shirt.

"Oh." She lifted the thin fabric of her tunic until it was resting just below her chest. Ari knelt down again and quickly unwrapped the binding. When the old fabric was discarded on the floor, Pax gasped. Her entire torso was a giant purple bruise tinged with yellow around the edges. She shivered, remembering the impact of her father's boot against her stomach.

"It looked worse when we first found you," Ari said.

Pax scoffed. "I can't imagine it looking worse than this."

"You're lucky you didn't see yourself. You looked . . . unrecognizable, at first," he said with concern in his voice.

"Really?"

He nodded as he wrapped the new bandage snugly around her. Pax winced each time he lifted her back from the wall. "Zohn said it was because of the travel. The first few days, I did not know if you would make it. Your whole body was swollen. Your arms, your stomach, your face . . ." His fingers rose to brush the skin of her cheekbone, causing Pax to flinch involuntarily, then he quickly pulled back and finished tying the bandage.

"Ugh. I bet I look amazing right now," she said, trying to change the subject. She rested her head against the wall.

"You look . . ." Ari's voice trailed off as he searched for the words. "Strong," he finished. "Like a fighter."

She smirked. "Thanks."

"Finished."

Pax realized she was still sitting against the wall with her shirt pulled up. She quickly rearranged herself until she was covered again. Her head spun, and she slumped back against the wall. "What was in that stuff?"

He smirked. "Something strong, made from the Testalos flowers outside. Felyine usually gives it to people with bullet wounds."

"You have guns here?" Pax asked, her words slurring slightly.

"We don't. The Fellowship does. It's their weapon of choice during the raids."

"Oh," she replied, unsure of what else to say.

"Are you hungry?" he asked, deciding to drop the subject.

As soon as he said it, her stomach rumbled as if it had just registered that she hadn't eaten today. "Yes."

He turned to pick up a tray from the table and brought it to her. "I thought you would want real food, so they brought some things. But start slow. You've only had broth for about a week now."

She eagerly reached for the dried fruit and chewed. She hadn't realized just how ravenous she was until the first slice hit her tongue. Soon she was shoveling chunks of food into her mouth as if she had lost control of everything except her insatiable hunger. She noticed Ari smirking at her, and quickly covered her mouth with her hand in embarrassment.

"Can I ask you something?" Ari said.

She nodded as she swallowed a mouthful of food.

"What does 'ho-die yole' mean?" His mouth stumbled over the unfamiliar phrase.

"What?" She stared at him in confusion.

He crossed to the corner of the room and returned with a pile of fabric in his hand. He unfolded it to reveal the T-shirt she had been wearing when she traveled from home. A little frog in the cowboy hat cheerfully waved at her with the phrase "Howdy, y'all!" written in a speech bubble. It seemed so absurd in this context that she burst into laughter, which caused her to wince in pain.

Ari rushed to her side. "Are you all right? What is so funny?"

She slowly breathed in and out, trying to contain her giggles. "It's just—that shirt is just a stupid joke."

"A joke for who?"

"For me."

He smirked. "You are a strange girl."

"Yeah, I get that a lot," she said with a smile. She didn't know why, but when Ari said it, being a "strange girl" didn't sound all that bad.

They sat in companionable silence as she finished the remains of her meal. Once she swallowed the last bite, she asked, "So, what now?"

"What do you mean?"

"Well, our plan to meet up in three weeks got sidetracked, so . . ."

"I suppose that's up to you."

She sighed. "Right."

"Have you decided anything?"

"I think the decision has been made for me, don't you?" she asked wryly.

"Why is that?"

She swallowed down a cube of meat. "I can't exactly go back now, so what other choice do I have?"

Ari's brow furrowed. "You still do not understand, do you? We are not going to make you join us. They have forced us all of our lives to do things we don't believe in, to fight battles that are not ours. If you are going to help the Watch, it has to be because you believe in it."

"What happens if I don't want to join the Watch?"

"You can still live here as a part of our village."

"But what about the guards? And the Fellowship?"

"You will always be at risk. Just like us."

"So, it's not really a choice, is it?"

He shrugged. "It is not a choice for anyone in Terra. The choice to be safe, to actually decide if or how we will live, is taken from us at birth. Every person you have met here has had to make the same decision you are facing right now: to sit back and take it, or to fight. Only, we don't have the luxury of escaping if it gets difficult."

Pax's chest tightened. "I'm sorry. I didn't mean to be a jerk about it. I hadn't thought of it like that."

His tone softened. "I know you have not had an easy life. But you must realize that if you stay here, you will not be pitied for it. The nature of your gift gives you choices the rest of us will never have until the Fellowship is taken down."

Ari's words did not offend her. She had spent her entire life wishing people would stop looking at her like the girl whose mom left. She had been pitied for it for as long as she could remember: by classmates, teachers, even her best friends. For the first time, she was surrounded by people who saw her and expected something more from her. It was terrifying but also strangely empowering. "I still need time to think," she whispered.

"I know. I'm sure nothing will be asked of you until you have recovered. But think seriously about your decision. I don't know what the Watch has planned, but I know it will be dangerous, and I cannot promise that—"

"I know," she interrupted before he could finish the thought.

He stood to take her empty tray. "You should try to sleep."

Her eyelids were drooping from all the food and whatever was in the concoction she had just taken. She carefully slid down onto the cot. When she winced, Ari jumped to grab her hand, helping her the rest of the way down. He didn't seem the slightest bit uncomfortable with the gesture now, but he had been lifting her up and down, changing her dressing, and feeding her broth for over a week, so decorum was probably out the window at this point.

He rose to his feet and looked down at her. "Goodnight, Pax," he said.

"Goodnight," she responded in a small voice, feeling foolish for the way her heartbeat quickened. The way he said her name spread warmth all the way down to her toes.

CHAPTER 16

"Good morning," Dinah offered in a neutral tone.

Pax was awakened by footsteps scurrying about, and when she'd opened her eyes and saw Dinah, she inwardly groaned. "Morning," she muttered. She couldn't tell from Dinah's expression whether this would be a pleasant interaction.

"I heard you had awakened yesterday. You gave everyone a scare, you know," Dinah said firmly. "But it is good you are up."

"Um, thank you."

Dinah shook her head. "Well, we couldn't let you die, could we?"

Pax didn't know what to make of that.

"Well, since you are awake, it will make these morning duties easier." Dinah approached her.

"Morning duties?"

Dinah looked at her for a moment, expectantly. "Do you need to relieve yourself?" she asked impatiently.

"Oh." Of course that was what she meant. It hadn't occurred to Pax that someone had needed to help her do that. "Um, yes." She blushed deeply. Of all the people to be here while she peed, Pax thought Dinah might be the worst.

"Felyine says if you feel strong enough, you can move about the room so we don't have to use the waste pan."

"The what?"

Dinah pointed to a shallow, slightly dipped basin that was resting against the wall on the other end of the room.

Pax's embarrassment grew. "Dinah, I am so sorry you had to do this."

To her surprise, Dinah laughed. "You are not the first person I have cared for, believe it or not."

Pax relaxed a little. "Well, thank you anyway. I'm sure you have better ways to spend your time."

"Shh, none of that," she scolded softly. "Now, come. I'll help you up."

Getting out of the bed was excruciating at first. Her ribs ached, her legs wobbled beneath her like jelly, but she was relieved to be on her feet. Dinah guided her down the corridor to a room that appeared to be a communal washing area. There were two large steel tubs and then three toilet setups similar to the one at Ari's house separated by partitions. "So, you do have inside bathrooms here," Pax muttered, mostly to herself.

Dinah chuckled. "Only in the shelter. We couldn't have people walking out to relieve themselves if they were supposed to be in hiding. Of course, I hear it is more common in Travelers' homes." She wrinkled her nose in disgust. "I will leave you here. I've been boiling some water because I thought you might like a bath. Felyine thinks it will help loosen your muscles as well."

Pax's eyes lit up. "Yes, thank you," she responded.

Dinah made quick work of filling the tub and helping Pax undress. Pax groaned as Dinah lifted her into the tub, but as she sank into the water, she felt her muscles immediately relax under the warmth. Pax was so relaxed she had forgotten to be self-conscious about Dinah's presence in the room until she was beside her again, holding a cloth and soap.

"Oh, you don't have to do that. I can—"

"Hush, now," Dinah said firmly. "You can barely lift your arms. It will go much quicker if I do it."

Pax sighed and tried to relax again as Dinah slowly leaned her forward and worked a lather into her hair.

"I hear you will be staying here," Dinah said.

Pax nodded. "Yes, I think so. But I promise once I'm better I'll find a place to live, and I'll work. I won't bother you at all."

Dinah looked at her for a moment. "Do you think I am so cruel that I would turn you out on the street?"

"*No*," she responded. "It's just . . . I know that my being here hasn't exactly been easy for you."

Dinah sighed. "Yes. I will admit that your presence was a shock at first. It was frightening to me, you being a Traveler, and suddenly in our lives."

Pax furrowed her brow. She had a hard time imagining anyone being frightening to Dinah, least of all herself. The woman was made of granite. Her piercing glare and gritty demeanor could make grown men quake.

"I've never met a Traveler before, and I thought if you had the chance, you would betray us," Dinah continued. "Ari is all I have. He is stubborn and stupid, but he is the reason I breathe." Tears filled her eyes. "I could not bear to lose him."

"Dinah, I would never betray you or Ari. I owe him—and you—my life. If you hadn't taken me in and brought me here, I wouldn't be alive right now."

She nodded. "I know this, and I feel shameful for how I acted toward you. When you appeared in our home barely breathing, and when I learned it was your own blood who did this to you—" She gritted her teeth and shook her head in disgust. "I know we are not your family, and you are a stranger in this world, but you deserve to have a home. And if you want it, you can have one here with us." Her eyes were sincere.

Pax's chest heaved, her heart swelling with emotions. She was overwhelmed by what Dinah had said. A home. Pax had lived for sixteen years feeling like an afterthought and an outcast in her own house, and it wasn't until this moment that she realized she had deeply longed for a home, a place where she was truly wanted. She experienced flickers of it with her friends, but even the places where she felt loved and wanted couldn't be her home.

"Shhh," Dinah said softly, placing a hand in her hair. "You'll hurt yourself."

Pax hadn't realized she had been crying until a sharp pain stabbed her abdomen. She looked up at Dinah. "Thank you so much." It was not nearly enough to express her overwhelming gratitude, but it was the only thing she could muster.

Dinah smiled and stood. "Enough of this now. I'll have to call Felyine in to reset your ribs if you keep at it."

Pax smiled and wiped her eyes. "Okay."

"Now, you must be hungry. Let's get you dressed." Dinah offered her hands. By the time Dinah had dried, re-bandaged, and dressed her, Pax was starving. Her stomach rumbled as they made their way back down the corridor. When they returned to her room, Zohn was seated at the table sipping a steaming cup of tea. He smiled when he saw them.

"Happy morning to you!" he offered cheerfully.

A wide smile spread across Pax's face at the sight of the old man. "Good morning."

"I was hoping you'd be up for company today. I thought we might break our fast together." He waved a hand at the tray in front of him, which held an array of cheese, fruit, and some kind of pastry that smelled like heaven.

"That would be great."

Dinah helped Pax into the chair opposite to Zohn.

"Dinah, my dear, won't you join us?" Zohn asked.

"And be seen with the likes of you? I have my reputation to protect, and you are nothing but trouble," she teased.

He laughed. "You are right about that much. Thankfully, my young friend is stuck with me. She will keep me company, even if it is against her will."

Pax laughed. "As long as you keep bringing food, I'm happy to be here."

Zohn laughed loudly. "Oh good, you're funny! That will make your time here much more bearable."

"Well, I must go now. I have to sew at least fifty more dresses before the festival." Dinah rolled her eyes.

"The Mother forbid that the capitol women go to the celebration looking anything less than an over-frosted birthday cake," Zohn teased.

"Well, you know how they love their frosting," Dinah snorted as she headed toward the door. "Don't keep her up too long. She is still in need of rest."

"Of course."

As Dinah exited the room, Pax immediately reached for the pastry. In between bites, she asked, "What is the festival?"

"It's the celebration of the Travelers' establishment in Terra. Three whole days of celebration of their own grand accomplishments," he grumbled as he poured tea into Pax's cup.

"So, Dinah has to make the dresses?"

"Yes, along with many others here in the village. It is one of the main trades here. Much of the labor we do here is on the capitol's behalf. The capitol is celebrated for their fashion and opulence, though none of it is from their own work."

"That doesn't seem right."

"Yes, well, it is the way things are. They give themselves

credit for building a world their own hands have barely touched."

She shook her head. "How were you ever part of that world?"

He sighed. "Well, when you're in that world, it is your reality. Travelers are only taught of their own sovereignty and excellence, and they never so much as see people from the village outside of serving roles. They believe their willingness to provide work for the villagers is generous, only further establishing their ideals."

"So, you used to be the record keeper for them?"

"Yes, for over twenty years."

"What was that like?"

"At first it was wonderful work. I felt like I was doing something important, you know. I was in charge of what stories were told and how we told them. I had my hand in history books, current events—everything. And I'll say it was far easier to do the work there, with all the resources that were available."

"So, how did you—"

"Come to be in Rehama? Well, I slowly realized the stories we were telling were not the whole truth. The Fellowship had a heavy hand in my work. They wanted to be sure that what was presented to the public was always in line with their narrative."

"And what was that?"

"That the Travelers were the good guys. That they had established a utopian society through their own excellence."

"But they're not."

"How can you be sure?"

Pax furrowed her brow. "Well, all these horrible things they've done. The people they've killed. They stole this place."

"Yes, but had you come here and encountered a Traveler first, I'd imagine you might not believe that. On an individual level, many Travelers are good people. They are kind, they believe in peace and harmony among their citizens, and they make a pretty good show of maintaining that."

"So, what are you saying?"

"I'm saying that on an individual level, the Travelers may be as good as you and me, but the system in which they live, and the way it is maintained, is monstrous. But the average citizen will never see that because the story they are told consistently from birth is that they are exceptional and we are the monsters, and they are so far removed from the rest of us that they could not possibly comprehend it."

"But you did."

"You forget, I am not a full-blooded Traveler. My mother was my anchor to this world. I grew up hearing stories of this village and the people here. It was a part of my identity, but as I grew older, I learned to hide those parts of myself. The way my peers looked at me, I was a stranger to them, a threat. They assumed I was dangerous. They would run from me. My teachers treated me like I could not learn simply because of who my mother was. I had to fight to get half of the opportunities my peers did, and I had to learn to assimilate to survive. And when I worked my way up to this respectable position, I was determined to prove to the Travelers that I was one of them, and to prove to people like me that they could do it too. Then, of course, I learned that the reason the odds were stacked against me was because of my position."

"What do you mean?"

"About ten years ago, I was tasked with documenting the uprising in the villages. I observed the raids firsthand. I saw the horrors committed against the villagers at the hands of the guards. Senseless brutality." His face tightened as he continued. "I realized quickly that the goal was not to subdue the unrest, but to destroy the threat. They burned down homes and wiped out entire generations of families. Families of people who looked like my mother. People like me. I documented the stories exactly as I saw them, but my superiors told me that I must have been mistaken. They said the villagers had grown violent and attacked the guards, that they threatened to commit a Traveler genocide and take over so the guards had to use force to stop it. But I was there. I saw it with my own eyes. I had planned to tell the whole truth to the public, but before the story could be released, the commander visited me. He told me that if I released my lies and propaganda to the public, there would be repercussions."

Pax's eyes widened. "What did you do?"

"I did it anyway. I released the story early, and without approval, because I knew it had to be told. Then, of course, I was imprisoned. The Fellowship was convinced that I was some sort of spy for the Watch and demanded to know who I worked for. I was tortured for three days. That was when this happened." He gestured toward his missing eye.

"How did you get out?"

"Danathu, Ari and Dinah's father, broke me out and brought me here. He was the leader of the Watch during the uprising. He offered me safety, and I offered my services to the Watch."

"Ari's father was the leader of the Watch?"

"Yes. He was a good one too, and his mother, Imani, was the leader of Rehama. They led the rebellion over a decade ago. The Fellowship would never admit this, but they were terrified of how much power Danathu and Imani held in Rehama."

"It's just . . . Ari never told me."

"Well, my dear, he didn't know until recently. When it was apparent that the Fellowship was hunting down and killing the leaders of the uprising, Danathu took great care to ensure his children would not be implicated for their own survival. The remaining members were given strict orders never to tell Ari or Dinah about it. But then Ari went poking about on his own. He is certainly his father's son."

"Wow." Pax imagined how proud it must have made Ari to learn that about his father. She made a mental note to ask him about it later. "So, what happened to your story?"

"It was destroyed. The Fellowship told people I was a traitor to the capitol, and that I had been working against them to plan the uprising."

"Oh my gosh. I'm so sorry."

"Don't be. I'm not. I wanted to be part of something significant, and now I am."

"Do you ever think about what would have happened if you had stayed?"

"Of course. I could have stayed there, kept working for the capitol, lived out my life peacefully. But that would make me part of the problem."

"What do you mean?"

"There was a time when I didn't know any better. I was ignorant back then. But if I had learned the truth and still chose my comfort over the lives of other people, that would have made me complicit. I can live uncomfortably. I can live with the risk, but I couldn't live with my people's blood on my hands."

"But aren't you scared they'll find you and kill you?"

"Every day. But important work is always dangerous." He winked at her. "And speaking of which, I must get back to it." He forced himself up. "They've got me working on something for the festival that is sure to be a shock," he said deviously.

"The Watch is planning something for the festival?"

"Oh yes." He chuckled. "I'm sure Ari will tell you all about it when you are well enough. But for now, focus on your rest. Do you need help getting back to bed?"

Pax almost laughed at the thought of frail old Zohn trying to help her to bed on his unsteady legs. It would likely end with them both on the floor. "No, I'm all right. I think I want to sit up for a while."

"Very well. I'll see you." He slowly inched his way out.

Pax exhaled heavily, slumping back in her chair now that she was finally alone. She had been holding herself upright so Zohn wouldn't see how tired she was. She wanted to hear his story, but the effort she had exerted just to stay in her seat was catching up with her. There was a short distance from her chair to the pallet on the floor. To her tired body, it seemed miles away. She slowly shifted herself forward, but even the smallest movement was like thousands of pinpricks in her ribcage. She sat back and breathed, then spotted the glass bottle of medicine Ari had given her last night. She carefully extended her arm and reached the tip of the bottle, inching it closer with her fingertip, but then knocked it over.

She scrambled for the bottle. Thankfully, it was tightly corked, so nothing had spilled. She removed the cork with her teeth and spat it out onto the table. Unsure how much she was supposed to take, she poured a few drops into her cold cup of tea. She brought the cup to her lips and grimaced. The smell was pungent. She quickly tipped the cup upward and shot-gunned the entire concoction at once, which caused her stomach to twist and gurgle as liquid burned down her throat.

She looked over at the pallet again. It was likely she wouldn't be able to get into bed until the concoction had worked its magic. So, she settled back into her chair and grabbed her Traveler's manual from the table. She opened it to a heading called "Timing Your Travels." It seemed like it might be useful, but instead she found it extremely dull. Her eyes scanned the first page over and over again, but she couldn't seem to retain any of it. Soon, her eyelids grew heavy, and before she knew it, the tincture had done its work.

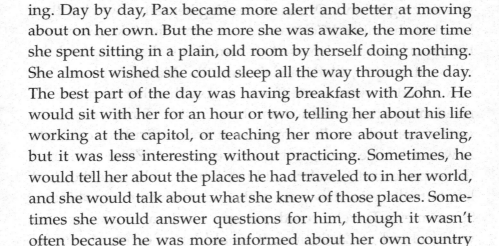

The week passed by at a snail's pace, torturously long and boring. Day by day, Pax became more alert and better at moving about on her own. But the more she was awake, the more time she spent sitting in a plain, old room by herself doing nothing. She almost wished she could sleep all the way through the day. The best part of the day was having breakfast with Zohn. He would sit with her for an hour or two, telling her about his life working at the capitol, or teaching her more about traveling, but it was less interesting without practicing. Sometimes, he would tell her about the places he had traveled to in her world, and she would talk about what she knew of those places. Sometimes she would answer questions for him, though it wasn't often because he was more informed about her own country than she was, much to her embarrassment. When she told him this, he laughed and explained that it was his job to know. One branch of record keeping was responsible for destroying the evidence of Travelers from Earth's records. They were a bit like the CIA for Terra, protecting classified information and going on missions into unknown territory.

Pax and Zohn had grown into comfortable companionship together. But then, inevitably, he would have to go back to doing his secret work for the Watch, which she still knew nothing about. And she would be left on her own until Ari arrived in the evening.

Zohn had dropped off books for her, records of old village

legends and histories. He said it would be good for her to know more about this place if she was going to stay. She spent a lot of time reading.

She learned that Rehama was one of the oldest nations in Terra and handled most of the clothing and produce that went to and from the capitol. It was fascinating to learn about Terra and its history, but she would feel pangs of sadness from time to time when she thought about the home and the people she was leaving behind. Of course, leaving her father was hardly a loss, but she missed Zeke and Ayana. She didn't know exactly how much time had passed. It turned out that Terra and the planet it was on, Madara Gaia—or "the Mother's planet," as they called it—was in a different galaxy than her own, and its rotational pattern was longer than Earth's. Terra's days and weeks were physically longer, so it was difficult to calculate how much time was passing between them. Zohn explained that experienced Travelers could shift back to the time they had left, but otherwise they were at the mercy of their own abilities. Sometimes a Traveler could end up a few hours, days, or even weeks ahead of Earth time. It would be an extremely useful skill to practice, Pax thought, until a wave of sadness hit her as she remembered she might not be going back for a while..

She didn't know what her friends knew or didn't know at this point. She hoped they would assume she had traveled and they weren't worried, but there was no way to be certain. How could she get the message to them? Perhaps when she was well enough, she could travel and leave a letter on Zeke's door, but she couldn't risk seeing her father again. Not until she decided what to do. Sometimes she wondered how freaked out he must have been when he came to her room the next morning and saw she had disappeared. It brought her a strange sense of satisfaction to imagine him standing in her bedroom doorway, staring at her empty bed, trying to wrap his brain around how she could have possibly vanished into the air. He probably thought she had escaped from the window and ran away. In a way, she had, but thankfully it was to a place he would never find her. Even though the days here were long, and her recovery had been painfully slow, it still felt more like home to her than anywhere else. People who barely knew her looked after her day and night, some of whom she had actually never met before she was injured, and yet they treated her with kindness and respect. Like she was a part of their community, and she supposed she was.

At the week's end, Pax sat at her table staring blankly at the book in front of her, restless and desperately bored, when Ari suddenly appeared with a mischievous smile. "I have a surprise for you if you're up for it."

Pax's eyes lit up. "Yes. Please. Anything."

"I thought you might say that." He laughed and ran over to help her to her feet. Now that she had regained her strength, she no longer needed to lean all of her weight on him, so she simply took his arm to keep her steady. He walked her down the long corridor toward the main room.

It wasn't pitch-black at the end of the hall like it usually was. The lamps must have been lit.

"What are we doing?" she asked.

"You will see." He urged her forward.

The sound of voices and music grew as they moved toward the brightly lit room. When they finally approached the entrance, Ari let go of her arm and flung the large wooden door open.

"Surprise!" he yelled.

Faces, some familiar and some not, were seated at tables or standing against the walls, laughing and drinking.

"You could not come to the gambling and debauchery, so we brought it to you," he said excitedly as he guided her into the room.

Pax laughed. "Gambling and debauchery? How did you know it was just what I wanted?" she said sarcastically.

Several people smiled and greeted her. She waved at a few people whom she'd recognized had brought her food or changed her dressing throughout the week.

"I just know these things." He shrugged. "Now, let's see if we can loosen up that spine, hm?"

She rolled her eyes, remembering his insult. *Straight-spined.*

"Do not listen to him, Pax." Dinah came up beside her, offered her a drink, then slung an arm over Pax's shoulders. "Ari thinks anyone who isn't willing to jump naked off the village wall is boring. He's a fool," she teased.

"And Dinah thinks anyone who doesn't spend all of their time worrying about whether the sun will rise tomorrow is a fool," he retorted back.

Dinah glared at him and brought her cup to her lips, draining the entire contents of the glass in a single gulp. Cheers rose around her as she slammed the cup down on the table in front of her and smirked at him. Ari raised his hands in a temporary draw. Then she stalked off to the corner of the room to greet a tall, attractive man who was beaming at her. He draped himself around her and whispered something in her ear that made her laugh. Pax had never seen Dinah so relaxed. It was almost off-putting.

"Who's that?" she asked, gesturing toward the man as she took a hesitant sip of the drink. Her eyes widened in pleasant surprise. It was sweet and warm, and tasted like berries, spices, and honey.

Ari snorted. "That is Tahim. He is Dinah's lover."

"I didn't know she was in a relationship."

"I do not think they would call it that. Tahim would have probably married her years ago, but Dinah keeps refusing him."

"Why?"

He shrugged. "She says she is not ready, but I think it's because of me."

"You?"

"Yes. She thinks she needs to keep looking after me. I have tried to tell her otherwise, but she just rolls her eyes and says I'm not ready to be on my own."

"Do you think maybe she's the one not ready to be on her own?" Pax said.

He paused. "I guess I had not thought of that."

"And who is this goddess who graces our sacred tradition on the holiest of days?" a voice called from the far corner.

Pax and Ari turned, and Ari smiled. "Kitara!" he shouted, crossing the room.

Pax followed behind. Kitara was a boy about Ari's age but a few inches shorter. His sapphire eyes lined with charcoal glimmered brightly. His tunic was made of shimmering gold and tied with a colorful sash that secured a long train to the back of his pants that billowed down past his feet. He looked stunning. Regal, even. Ari grabbed the beautiful boy's face with both hands, then kissed him on his forehead.

Kitara laughed jovially and gathered him into a hug, slapping Ari on his back. "Hello, my friend. Now step aside. I must meet this divine creature I have heard so much about." He glided past Ari until he was directly in front of Pax. "You must be the famous Pax. I am Kitara." He grabbed the train of his sash and bowed in front of her.

Pax stood dumbfounded for a moment. "Nice to meet you." she offered quietly. "I'm sorry, I just . . . you are so beautiful," she blurted. She blushed and stammered. "I—I mean . . ."

He laughed musically. "No, no, please do not take it back. I live on the praise of beautiful women."

She smiled, allowing Kitara's infectious charisma to put her back at ease. "I just didn't know people dressed like this here."

"Yes, well, not all of us prefer to dress like dirty little dock boys all the time." He cast a disapproving glance toward Ari, who huffed.

"This is my best tunic," Ari said.

"How sad for you," Kitara teased. "Now, if you'll excuse me, there is someone over there who is in desperate need of my attention." He pushed past them, then made his way across the room and enveloped a tall, lanky boy in a passionate embrace.

"Oh, is that his boyfriend?" Pax asked.

"One of many," Ari shook his head as he came to stand beside Pax again. "So, what do you think?"

"He's not at all what I was expecting."

"Yes, Kitara is definitely unexpected. We have been friends since we were boys."

"I don't know why, but I just kind of assumed that the Fellowship wouldn't let people like Kitara . . ."

"Exist?" he offered. "Well, they don't. If you saw Kitara out by the docks where we work, you wouldn't recognize him. But it's safe in the village. Many of us here are what our people call *totamira*. It means 'all-loving,' or that we do not have a preference for lovers. Love has always been celebrated in our village, in all forms. It wasn't even considered strange until the Travelers came."

"So, you are also *totamira*, then?" she asked curiously.

"That's why I joined the Watch."

"For people like you and Kitara?"

"And for you, and everyone the Fellowship wants to hide away and punish just for existing."

Pax felt the warmth in her toes again. "You're a really good friend."

He looked down shyly and lifted his mouth into a half smile. "Well, enough of this heavy talk. We are here for debauchery. Are you ready to lose some money?" he joked.

She snorted. "Sure. I mean, I don't actually have any money, so that's fine by me."

"Well, you can offer other things: jewelry, information— some people here would even accept a kiss as payment. You could offer that to Kitara since you think he is so beautiful." He nudged her.

Pax blushed. "I don't think he would want to kiss me."

Ari laughed. "Believe me, Kitara wants to kiss everyone."

"He speaks the truth!" Kitara shouted from the table they were approaching.

Ari helped Pax into her seat, then settled beside her as the cards were being dealt. He leaned over and told her the game was called Tatan and explained the rules. Pax tried to follow, but she was completely lost by the end of his explanation. It appeared to be similar to poker, only way more confusing.

"I know it sounds difficult, but you will catch on, I promise," he reassured.

He was wrong. Pax was constantly laying down the wrong cards, calling bets at the wrong time, and desperately trying to keep up. Of course, the drinks that kept mysteriously appearing in her hand were not helping. By the end of the game, her head was spinning, and she owed money to almost everyone. Out of kindness, most of them agreed to cancel her debts, but Kitara and Ari were not as easily swayed.

"You know, a kiss is always an option!" Kitara offered. "I've been told I'm a marvelous kisser, am I not Ari?"

Ari groaned. "We shared one kiss, *one* time as repayment, and he has never let it go."

"I will never give up on our love, my friend!" Kitara teased. "Unless, of course, the lovely Pax is willing to consider my offer?"

She rolled her eyes. "Pass."

He put his hands over his heart as if he had been shot in the chest. "I am hurt!" Then he flipped his hand as if to wave the insult away. "It is no matter to me. I have other options." He raised his eyebrows and turned his head toward the boy from earlier who had been eyeing him from across the room all night.

Ari shook his head. "We will end it here, and you can pay us back later."

"No! I demand payment!" Kitara hit his fist on the table in false rage. "What about a little exchange of information then?"

Pax looked at him questioningly. "What do you mean?"

"You are a Traveler from another world, yes? Tell us something we don't know!"

She sat back and thought for a moment. "Hmm . . . well, back home we have these pocket-sized devices where we can talk to anyone from anywhere around the world, and we can get any information we want at the press of a button."

Kitara looked unimpressed. "No. That is not interesting. Try again."

"Well, why don't you ask me something and I'll tell you?" she offered.

He smiled deviously from behind his glass and took a large swig. "Excellent. So, tell us, Pax. Do you have a lover back home?"

She wrinkled her nose at the word *lover*. "I am from a different planet, and that is what you want to know?"

He thought about it for a moment, then nodded. "Yes, that is my question. I believe we would *all* be interested to know," he said mischievously. Ari's eyes were firmly fixed on the table, feigning disinterest.

"Well . . ." she started. "I wouldn't say I had a 'lover.' But there was someone."

Kitara clapped his hands. "Tell us about him. Or . . . her?"

"His name is Zeke and . . . well, it's nothing now because I'll never see him again." Her voice wavered and the table went silent. Pax felt her discomfort growing at the show of vulnerability, and all she wanted to do was get out. She stood too quickly, and a stabbing pain shot through her ribs. She doubled over and gripped the table for support.

Suddenly, Ari was by her side. "Are you all right?"

She gritted her teeth. "Yes, I'm just . . . getting tired."

"Of course. Let me grab my things." He gestured for someone to help before he moved across the room.

Kitara rose from his chair and offered a hand to her, helping her back up. "I am sincerely sorry, Pax. I did not know of your life back home. I should not pry."

"No, no. It's all right. It's just still hard to talk about."

He nodded. "Well, you are lovely, and I am so glad you are here. If for nothing else than to keep my friend company. He's very fond of you."

Pax shifted uncomfortably on her feet. "Yes, he's been a very good friend to me."

Kitara smirked slightly. "Yes, he is nothing if not a good friend."

Ari slipped beside her, gently grabbing hold of her forearm. "Are you ready?"

Kitara gripped his friend's shoulder good-naturedly. "Good night to you both. Let's do this again!" Then he made his way toward the refreshment table and the boy who had anxiously been waiting for him.

"You don't have to go just because I'm tired. Why don't you stay with your friends?" Pax assured him.

Ari shook his head. "Everyone is getting ready to leave now. We all must prepare for the week ahead. Besides, tomorrow is a big day."

She looked at him. "It is?"

"There's a Watch meeting here tomorrow night to discuss the festival. Surely, Zohn must have mentioned it?"

She shook her head. "He must have forgotten."

"He is getting old, I suppose." He laughed.

"Hey, he's got a lot to remember, what with accounting for the entire history of everyone and everything in the village," she chided.

"You are right. I'm sorry. So, I take it you and Zohn are getting along well down here?" he asked, guiding her toward the door. Several people stopped them to drunkenly bid them goodnight, offering sloppy cheek kisses or wobbly bows as they went.

"Yes, he's really good company," she said as they finally made it to the door.

"I believe you. He seems like he has many good stories."

"So many. He's done everything. He's kind of my hero." She laughed.

Ari chuckled as he led her into her room. "And what of you?"

"What do you mean?"

"Do you have any good stories?" he asked, helping her settle onto her cot.

She laughed. "None."

"That can't be true," he persisted as he seated himself on the ground beside her bed.

She collapsed backward, then slowly rolled to her side and groaned. "Seriously, aside from being abandoned by my mom, my life has been exceptionally uninteresting until very recently. Why the sudden interest in my life?"

"Well, I realized I don't know much about who you were before you came here. I mean, I did not know that you were with someone."

"I'm not," she corrected. "Zeke was just . . ." She paused, remembering the kiss they'd shared and the look on his face when she had walked away. Her heart felt heavy. She couldn't lie and say that he was just a friend. "He was my best friend."

"Oh?" Ari perked up in interest.

"Yes. He was good and kind, and he made me feel safe." She laughed humorlessly. "Listen to me, I'm talking about him as if he's dead. For all I know, he probably thinks I'm dead."

"So, no one knows you traveled here?"

"I don't know, exactly. I made a pretty quick escape."

Ari stretched out on the floor, laying his hands beside his head. "So, this Zeke. He was your Kitara?"

She laughed. "Not exactly. My other best friend, Ayana, is my Kitara. Life of the party, center of attention, impeccably dressed." She smiled, thinking about her friend.

"You loved him, though?"

"Of course." She glanced over to see his mouth set in a line. "But not like that. At least, I don't know. Not yet. I think maybe I could have, though. He wanted that."

"But you did not?"

"It's not that I didn't. It's just . . . he wanted me to stay. He thought it was too dangerous to come back here, but I had to. And he didn't understand."

Ari contemplated quietly. "I am sorry you had to leave them."

She shook her head. "It's been hard, but I'm glad I came. I can't explain why, but I feel like I'm supposed to be here. Having met all of you and being a part of this world, I can't imagine not being here. I just wish I had the chance to say goodbye."

"Do you think you will ever try to go back?"

She thought for a moment. "I don't know. Probably, but not until I'm old enough to be on my own. That way, my father can't send me away and I won't have to live with him."

He nodded. "Yes, you should never have to go back to him."

"So, the meeting tomorrow . . . will I have to make a decision by then?"

"I think they will probably expect that, yes."

She sighed heavily. Suddenly, the warmth of Ari's hand was enveloping hers. She turned to face him and found his golden eyes gazing into hers.

"It does not matter what you choose. You will still belong here."

She squeezed his hand briefly, returning the gesture before releasing his grasp. Then she turned her gaze toward the ceiling, allowing the ease of Ari's presence to comfort her until they both fell asleep.

CHAPTER 17

When Pax woke in the morning, Ari had donned a fresh tunic and was pulling his hair back from his face, readying himself for work.

"Good morning," she said as she sat up from her cot.

He turned to her and smiled. "How do you feel?"

"Fine. No pain today."

He smirked. "I was actually talking about your head. You had a fair amount of the wine last night."

She grinned sheepishly. "Yeah, my head's okay too."

"Good." He chuckled. "I must head to the docks, but I will see you later tonight. I'll come to fetch you before the meeting starts."

Her chest tightened at the thought of the meeting, but she quietly replied, "Okay."

He knelt beside the bed and put a hand on her shoulder. "Try not to worry about it, all right?" he offered, as if reading her mind.

She nodded.

"Oh, and you might want to wash before then. You smell of stale drink," he teased, shoving her slightly before he rose and headed toward the door.

Her cheeks flushed with embarrassment, and she picked up the book beside her bed and hurled it toward him.

He dodged it quickly as he sprinted out the door, laughing maliciously. "See you!"

"Bye," she called after him in annoyance, then buried her face in her hands.

She lifted the collar of her shirt and sniffed, then wrinkled her nose. He was right. She sighed and lifted herself from her cot, then set to work heating water for her bath.

Thankfully, when her injuries began to improve earlier in the week, Dinah had shown her how to care for herself so she would need less assistance. She sat in the bath until the water grew tepid and her skin began to prune. She made quick work of wrapping her bindings, and then put on one of the fresh dresses Dinah had brought for her. When she made her way back to her room, she was surprised to find it empty. Usually by mid-morning, Zohn had already prepared breakfast and tea for them and would be sitting at the table greeting her with a smile. Perhaps he had gotten caught up in his work, she thought. She decided to prepare breakfast for them.

She went to the shelf positioned on the opposite end of her small room and surveyed the food. There was some fruit, a bit of bread and preserves, and a meager stash of loose tea leaves in a jar. Her supplies were dwindling. Likely, someone would come tonight to restock for her, but until then, this would have to do. She prepared the food, assembled two servings onto the wooden serving tray that sat on the table, and walked it a few doors down to Zohn's room. She stood at the door, unsure for a moment. It was slightly cracked, but she felt weird about barging in, as she had never come to his room unannounced before. She knocked quietly to announce herself, then opened the door tentatively. She paused when she saw him hurriedly shuffling papers and books around his table, as if he were trying to hide something.

"Oh, um, I can go if you're busy. I just thought I would bring you some food," she explained nervously, hoping she hadn't offended him.

"No, no! I was just . . . finishing something," he replied. "Please, sit." He gestured toward the empty chair across from him.

Pax walked hesitantly toward him, noting the dark circles around his eyes. It looked like he hadn't slept in days. "Long night?" she asked as she placed the tray between them.

He nodded as he reached for a slice of toast. "Indeed, but breakfast is a welcome distraction." He smiled.

"I don't suppose you'll tell me what you've been working on?"

Zohn chuckled. "Unfortunately, I have been sworn to secrecy. However, should you decide to attend the meeting tonight, you will find out."

She looked down at her plate and chewed in quiet contemplation.

"I do have something to show you, though," he said, bringing Pax out of her daze. He pulled a folded paper from his desk. "I reached out to a friend who still works in records at the capitol. I received word from her yesterday about your mother."

Her heart squeezed in anticipation, and she leaned across the table. "And?"

"There is no one named Leanah Graves in the capitol."

Her face fell. She had been so distracted by everything else, she had almost given up on the search for her mom. She wasn't willing to admit to herself how hopeful she had been that Zohn had found something, only for him to tell her he hadn't. Truthfully, she was crushed.

"But," Zohn started, "she sent me a list of all the people

with the name Leanah who live in the capitol and surrounding villages. There are two, and one of them never married or had a record of bearing children, so we suspect this other one might be a good place to start." He tapped his frail fingertip against the second name on the list.

Her head jerked upward and her eyes widened. "Of course!" she said, almost too loudly. "She wouldn't go by Leanah Graves here. She and my dad aren't married, and I guess technically, in this world, he doesn't exist." Her heart sputtered, daring to hope again.

"Pax," Zohn started hesitantly. "I hope you know I will do everything I can to help you find your mother, but please keep that hope at arm's length, dear. We still don't know if your mother is even—"

"Alive? Yeah, I know." She nodded. "Even if I never find her, or I find out the worst is true, I feel closer to her just by being here. Being part of her world feels like I'm finding myself. Does that sound stupid?"

"Not at all." Zohn smiled.

"So, when can we go try to find her?" She eyed the names on the list. It looked as if someone who was desperately trying not to get caught had hurriedly scrawled them in ink. The final number in what appeared to be the address of the second woman was blotted out.

"Well . . . I'm not sure. Since we will be in town for the festival, we could start then. But the Watch already has something planned, and to be honest, we are still not sure if the Guadaros are looking for you. It might be best to keep you out of sight for a while."

She sighed and cast her eyes down at the floor.

"Oh dear, I hope I didn't disappoint you too much. I want to help you, truly, but above all else, we must keep you safe."

Pax looked up at him and nodded, trying to mask her sadness behind a tight smile. "Yes, I understand."

He sighed and reclined back into his chair as he finished the last sip of his tea. "So, are you excited for the meeting tonight?"

She bit her lip. "I don't know."

"Then I don't suppose you have made a decision since we last spoke?"

She shook her head. "Every time I think I'm leaning in a certain direction, I think about how big the choice feels and what it will mean. It's like . . . I don't know. Either way, I'm leaving someone behind. Either way, I'm disappointing someone."

Zohn brought his clasped hands to his lips and nodded, contemplating. "And have you yet thought about what you want?"

She was confused. "I've been contemplating this for weeks now. What do you mean?"

"What I mean is, take away all the people you fear you will be disappointing. Your friends back home, your mother, the Watch . . . remove all of those other factors and think about you, Pax. What is it that you want? Which path makes you feel alive? Not necessarily happy, because if there is one thing I have learned, it is that happiness is fleeting, but it can be found anywhere you are. But what is the direction that makes you feel hopeful? When you think of each path, what is the one that is urging you forward to the person you want to be? Whichever one that is, that is the path to take."

She sighed into her tepid cup of tea.

"Oh, and if the reason you are saying no to a certain choice is because you don't think you are strong enough, that is not a reason." He smiled.

She returned his smile with a timid one of her own. She wished she could feel as confident in her decision-making as

Zohn seemed to be. Anxiety bubbled up in her stomach as she felt the sudden weight and urgency of her need to decide, hovering over her like a thick, dark cloud. Pax stood and quietly collected the remains of their breakfast and placed them back on the tray. "I should really let you get back to work."

Suddenly, Zohn's cool hand rested over her own. She met his earnest gaze. "I know there are voices in your head telling you that a bad decision will be the end of the world. But for what it is worth, I have made a million bad decisions in my life and still somehow found myself in the place I felt I belonged. And the people who cared for me the most didn't care even an inch about what choices I made, or didn't make, in the end."

Tears stung her eyes. "Thank you. I should go."

"Will you be all right?"

She nodded. "Yeah, I just think I need to take some time to be alone and think."

"Of course. Good luck to you, dear. I will see you tonight," he said.

"I'll see you," she muttered before making her way back to her room.

The hours blurred together as Pax paced back and forth across the room, debating her decision. She tried to distract herself with books but found her mind drifting to the meeting tonight. She contemplated what Zohn had told her and remembered the reassurances from Ari. She knew in her heart what she wanted to do, but she couldn't get away from the feeling that making this decision meant saying goodbye to people who cared for her deeply. The sense that she was betraying them gnawed away at her insides. She sighed as she sifted through the stack of books and papers she had been studying for the past few days until she found a pen and a piece of paper. She knew her friends would never understand why she did what she did, but she needed to reconcile these feelings, somehow. She positioned the pen over the paper and started, "Dear Zeke . . ."

After finishing her letters, Pax felt more resolved in her decision. Even though she didn't know if they would ever be read, she found the closure she had needed to explain her decision, even if it was only for her. It was tempting for Pax to believe she was leaving her old life behind for good, but even as she thought it, she knew it wasn't true. Not only because she loved her friends, but because she wouldn't allow herself to run from her father forever. It scared the hell out of her, but she knew that one day she would face him again, and when she did, she would tell everyone the truth. Even if no one else believed her, she would do it for herself. But that was a fight for another day. Today, she was choosing something bigger than herself. She wiped her face and readied herself for what was to come.

A while later, Ari knocked at her door and entered, carrying sacks of pantry items and two plates of hot food. "How was your day?"

"All right," she replied, placing the items on her shelf.

When the food was unloaded, they settled at the table and picked at the food Dinah had sent for them in silence. After some time, Ari asked the question that had been lingering between them. "So, have you decided?"

She saw the hopefulness behind his intent gaze, and she nodded. "Yes, I think so."

He looked at her expectantly. "So?"

She smiled. "You can wait."

He scoffed. "So dramatic."

"That's for telling me I stink earlier," she retorted.

He rolled his eyes and popped his last bite of chicken into his mouth.

Suddenly, there was a knock at the door. Their heads turned toward the sound, and Pax called, "Come in!"

Her heart stuttered as Shahad's large frame filled the doorway. "Good evening to you, Pax," he called.

"Hi," she replied quietly.

Shahad entered the room, closely followed by Felyine, Zohn, and another man she had never met.

Felyine stepped forward from the group. "Sorry to intrude, but we'd hoped to have a moment with you before tonight."

Pax stood to meet them. "No, that's all right." She bowed her head toward each of them as they entered.

"How are you faring with your injuries?" Felyine asked, stepping forward to gently examine her abdomen through her dress.

"Better, thank you. Your tonic was really helpful."

"I am pleased to hear it. I wish I had more time to visit you, but Dinah has assured me that you were improving well. She insisted on taking charge of your care, you know."

"I'm really grateful to her, and all of you," Pax said. "I don't know what I would have done without your help."

Felyine nodded pleasantly as she seated herself at the table. "Please sit." She gestured in invitation. Pax quickly obeyed. "I had not wanted to bother you with this while you were still healing, but I trust you remember Shahad's invitation for you to join the Watch?"

"Yes, I've been thinking about it a lot."

"Good. Well, as I am sure you know, tonight is a very important meeting for the Watch. But it is important that we only have those present who are committed to the cause. It is a matter of trust and safety. We would not want to endanger anyone with information that could implicate them if they were questioned."

Pax nodded gravely. "That makes sense."

"So, you understand then, that we must know your decision now."

"Yes, I understand." She glanced toward Shahad, confused why he was standing in the background. She thought he would be the one to whom she revealed her decision. Maybe they thought Felyine would be more reassuring.

"What have you decided?" Felyine asked intently.

Pax looked around the room, meeting the eyes of Zohn and then Ari. They looked at her with reassurance and expectancy. Her heart sputtered wildly and her mouth went dry. "I have seriously considered it, and I've decided that—" She took a deep breath, feeling the weight of her next words as she spoke them. "I would like to join the Watch."

Felyine's tight expression relaxed into a smile. "Wonderful! We are so honored that you will join us."

Ari was grinning from ear to ear.

"Thank you for having me. I hope I can make you all proud," Pax said.

Felyine shook her hand. "I want to assure you, as leader of the Watch, I will do everything in my power to keep you protected, as we do with all of our members."

Pax's brows furrowed for a moment. "Oh. I'm sorry, I hadn't realized you were—"

"In charge?" Felyine chuckled.

"Yes, well, it's just that when I spoke to Shahad, I thought he might've been." She felt slightly embarrassed at her admission.

"That's all right. Shahad is one of the elders of the Watch, and he is a wonderful recruiter, which is why you see him doing a lot of the talking."

Shahad spoke up from the corner of the room. "It is my good looks and charm that hooks them in." He winked.

Felyine shook her head. "Anyhow, we are so pleased that you will be joining us. We will hold a small initiation ceremony at the start of our meeting to honor your decision."

Pax shifted on her feet. "If I had known, I might have put on a different dress or something," she muttered awkwardly.

Felyine smiled warmly. "You look lovely. We have much else to discuss, so it will be short. Are you familiar with a Mother-bond?"

She shook her head.

"I'm sorry, I'd hoped Ari would have filled you in on how this all worked." She shot him a disciplinary look.

He held up his hands defensively. "I didn't even know if she wanted to join until five minutes ago."

She tutted. "Well, you will have to explain now, as we are getting ready to start. Ready, Pax?"

She took a deep breath. "I think so."

Felyine and the other members of the Watch started toward the door. "It will be fine," Felyine reassured. "Oh, and Ari, you will be leading Pax's initiation."

His mouth dropped. "What? I've never done that."

She shrugged. "Well, the way I see it, you and Pax will both be doing something unfamiliar, as you have given her so little time to prepare. It's only fair."

Pax snickered from behind him, and Felyine winked at her as they exited the room. Zohn gave her hand a gentle squeeze as he passed by. Pax felt so strange. She knew she had just made a life-changing decision, but she felt exactly the same. Only more nervous, and even more out of the loop than usual. She took a deep breath, then turned at the touch of Ari's hand on her shoulder.

"Welcome to the Watch." He smiled.

She smiled back. "Thanks. I can't wait to hear all the nice

things you're going to have to say about me during my initiation," she teased as they followed behind the leaders, heading toward the meeting room.

He snorted. "Oh, you will hear it, but you won't understand any of it since I'll be speaking in Terrish."

She scoffed. "How can that be fair? It's *my* ceremony."

"No. It is the Watch's ceremony, and speaking in Terrish is a rule." He shrugged.

She pretended to pout at him as they found their way into the meeting room where they had gathered the night before. Most of the members had already filed in and were finding seats. She scanned the room, trying to find somewhere to sit when her eyes landed on an empty space on the third row next to a boy dressed in a plain beige tunic, his shoulder-length hair pulled back into a neat braid. It wasn't until her gaze landed on the pair of mischievous, smiling blue eyes that she recognized him. "Kitara?" Ari had been right. Kitara was nearly unrecognizable outside of his festive attire.

Kitara wrapped an arm around her as she sat. "Hello, my dear. So, I take it this means you have decided to join our little club?" He raised an eyebrow.

"I guess so!"

He smiled in return. "Wonderful."

"Well, it would be. But apparently, I won't even know what's happening during my initiation. Ari is refusing to do it in English."

Ari sighed as he sat beside them. "I'm not refusing, I can't. It's the rules."

Kitara smacked his friend playfully. "But how will she know about all the lovely things you think about her?"

"That's what I said!" she laughed.

"Do not worry, my love, I will translate for you."

"Thank you. See? At least someone around here knows how to be a gentleman," she teased.

Ari shook his head. "Be serious for a moment because I have to tell you about the Mother-bond before we start."

"Oh, right. What exactly is that? Some kind of blood oath?"

"Well, sort of."

"What?"

"Relax. There is no blood. And really, you already know it."

"I do?"

"Yes. Do you remember a while back when Dinah had you swear to the Mother? And you did the ritual with your hand to her heart?"

She thought back. "Yeah, I think so."

"That was a Mother-bond."

"Oh . . . I hadn't known it was that serious."

"Well, like most oaths, it is as serious as the oath-maker takes it. Our people take them very seriously. We call it a Mother-bond because we believe those who take the oath are bound in spirit by the Great Mother until the oath is fulfilled."

"What happens if it isn't?"

"Exile," he responded gravely.

"Oh," she sighed, widening her eyes.

"Do not worry. There has not been an exile in years. The Watch protects its members and this village from threats. Being a part of it is an honor, and most people don't have a problem keeping the oath because the Fellowship has nothing we want."

She released the tension in her shoulders. He was right. She was honored to have been chosen as a member of the Watch, and the Fellowship definitely had nothing to offer her.

Shahad offered greetings to everyone. Kitara leaned forward and whispered translations in her ear. It was mostly logistic things until she heard Shahad say her name. She stiffened at the sound as he motioned for her and Ari to stand. She did so shakily as they made their way to the front. Kitara followed a few paces behind so he could translate for her. She watched as Ari nervously shifted his way toward the front of the room and cleared his throat. He paused for a moment, looking over the crowd, then began.

Ari started: "If there is anything I can say about Pax, it is that for more than one reason, she was . . . unexpected. I had never expected to find a girl lying face down on the shore of the Outerlands. I did not expect to ever meet, never mind speak, to a Traveler." The crowd laughed as Ari shifted his gaze toward her. He swallowed hard before he continued. "I did not expect to find and join this wonderful family because of her. And it was most unexpected that she became one of my dearest friends."

Pax's breath caught as Kitara translated the last part. Tears pricked at her eyes.

"I want to thank you all for letting her in, and giving her a chance, and making her one of us." Ari stepped toward her and said in English, "And, Pax, thank you for giving us a chance too. We are honored to have you."

Lost for words, she swallowed the lump in her throat and nodded. Tears trickled down her cheeks as she scanned the crowd, meeting the accepting gaze of Zohn, Shahad, and Felyine, and finally Dinah, whom she hadn't expected to be there. Dinah smiled at her, and Pax noted that she, too, was holding back tears.

"Now let's get to the important part," Ari prompted, shifting back to Terrish. The crowd stood, causing Pax to step a few paces backward. In surprise, she felt herself step directly into Kitara's body. "Sorry," she muttered. He chuckled and placed his hands on her shoulders, guiding her forward until she was face-to-face with Ari. He smiled at her and asked, "Are you ready?" under his breath.

"Yeah." She nodded, wiping the tears from her face.

Ari's expression shifted to a grave one, noting the gravity of the moment. He placed his hand on the center of her chest, then gently guided her hand onto his chest with his other hand. She felt the warmth of his skin and the gentle thud of his rapid heartbeat thrumming against her fingertips. Ari said as Kitara translated, "Pax, do you swear by the Great Mother to uphold the values of the Watch? To place the safety and protection of its members above all else? To uphold its commitment to uproot injustice and defend the defenseless among us to the best of your abilities?"

As Kitara finished translating, she looked to Ari, who was waiting expectantly. She remembered what was next, and she took a deep breath before boldly declaring, "I swear it by the Mother."

Ari nodded. Then Kitara whispered, "Beautiful. Now you will make the oath to Felyine."

She turned to Felyine, who was standing behind her with her hand extended. Pax took it and allowed Felyine to guide her hand to her chest, then Felyine placed her hand over Pax's heart in return. Felyine waited for a moment, then prompted her with a nod. Pax said, "I swear by the Mother."

Felyine nodded and smiled. Then, in English, said, "And the Watch swears by the Mother that you have our protection and our allegiance as long as you should live."

Then voices all around her opened and echoed in unison, "On the Mother, we swear," as they lifted their hands toward her.

"Pax, welcome to the Watch," Felyine announced, and a chorus of applause erupted around them.

Pax was overcome by the welcome and brushed away tears again as she made her way back to her seat amid pats on the back and offers of congratulations. Ari and Kitara came and sat on either side of her.

"So, was this what you expected?" Ari whispered as Shahad opened the meeting again.

She shook her head. "I hadn't expected to feel so much like I . . . belonged."

Kitara leaned over and whispered, "And I hadn't expected to hear such beautiful words come from this boy's mouth! We have been friends for nearly seventeen years, and he has *never* said anything to me like what he said tonight."

Ari shifted uncomfortably. "Yes, well, I've never been forced to talk about our friendship in front of a crowd of people."

Kitara rolled his eyes. "Yes, I'm sure that is it."

They all turned their attention to the front of the room, where Felyine cleared her throat. She spoke to the crowd in Terrish, and this time Ari translated for her. Felyine spoke about the Watch's plan for the festival, which was set to begin in four days. The Watch had planned a protest that would take place during the largest celebration in the center of the capitol. The day before the celebration, the commander of the Fellowship would make a big speech and host a presentation celebrating the history of their arrival in Terra. The festival was always heavily guarded, so the Watch decided to hold the protest the following day during the performance at the city square. People would be drinking and celebrating, and the guards would be much less vigilant. It would be bold and incredibly dangerous.

As Felyine assigned different jobs to certain people and groups in the room, Pax wondered what she would be doing during this time. Would she be in the crowd? Would they want her out of the way? After all, she was a new member. What could she really do aside from, maybe, hold a sign? Some people were put in charge of ensuring that all the necessary supplies were packed, some would secure transportation, and others would make costumes and clothing to ensure the Watch blended into the crowd. Dinah, who had apparently decided to join the Watch after all, had been assigned to that group. She watched one by one as each person in the room was given a job, but her name was never called. She sighed heavily as Felyine called the meeting to a close. She supposed they might want her to stay back as she continued to recover. She was mostly fine aside from a few aches, but maybe they were trying to be cautious. Maybe they didn't want to throw her in with the sharks right away, or maybe they just didn't trust her yet.

She rose from her seat. She was pulled from her thoughts by a tug on her arm. Ari had been trying to talk to her, but she hadn't noticed. "Are you all right?" he asked.

"Yeah, I'm just . . . processing everything," she lied.

"Well, Felyine mentioned she wanted to meet with you in Zohn's room."

Pax asked, "Do you know why?"

He shook his head. "She just said to tell you. I'll be joining you."

She felt her heart stutter, wondering why Felyine would want to meet with her in private. "Well, should we head that way?"

He smirked. "Nervous?"

"A bit," she admitted.

They wove their way around the crowd and made their way back down the long corridor to Zohn's room. Felyine, Shahad, Zohn, and, surprisingly, Dinah, were waiting for them.

Felyine smiled. "Come in."

Ari and Pax made their way to the two empty chairs, shifting under the weight of everyone's eyes.

"Did you enjoy the ceremony?" Felyine asked politely.

Pax smiled. "I did. It was . . . really nice," she said, wishing they could skip the pleasantries and get to what they were doing here.

Felyine nodded. "Yes, your friend certainly had some lovely things to say about you."

Her cheeks warmed. "Yes." She cast a glance toward Ari, who was shifting awkwardly at the remark. At least she wasn't the only one.

"Well, I'm sorry to call you in here so mysteriously, but there is something I wanted to discuss with you about the festival. I have a job for you."

"Oh? What's that?" She perked up in her seat.

"Do you remember when Shahad told you we needed someone whom we could send to the places Terrans aren't allowed?"

She nodded, remembering the conversation explicitly.

"What's interesting about the festival is that citizens of every territory are required to attend, but there are certain . . . boundaries. Any non-Travelers are required to stand at the outer sections of the city. It is roped off and heavily guarded to ensure this boundary. Only Travelers and those in their employ are allowed in the city center. They insist it is for safety purposes," she explained, clearly insulted by the rule.

Pax furrowed her brow. "So, how exactly are we going to do the protest?"

She smiled. "Leave that part to me. We've got that under control. The only missing piece is how to deliver an important package to our person on the inside."

"I'm assuming that's where I come in?"

"Exactly. We need someone who can sneak into the city center without being stopped by the guards."

"But aren't I still on their radar?"

"From what we have gathered, we think you have been moved to a low priority. There is far less patrol around the village, and they stopped making the announcement with your description about a week ago. We think they assume you have not returned. Nonetheless, you will not be easily identified." She straightened. "Dinah has prepared something for you."

Dinah leaned forward. "The women in the Traveler cities like to wear decorative pieces during the festival week. It helps them stand out in the crowds. I made one for you, and we will do your hair differently and paint your face. By the time I am done with your styling, you will look exactly like one of them."

"You want me to blend in by standing out?" Pax asked.

They all chuckled. "Something like that," Felyine replied. "I cannot lie and say it will not be dangerous, but Ari will be there as your guard. He will pose as your manservant. Many women in the city have one in their employ. Should anything happen, his job is to get you out of there as quickly as possible. I can give you more details when the time comes, but I just need to know if you will do it?"

Pax met Felyine's expectant gaze and breathed deeply. She remembered a conversation she had with Zohn from what seemed like ages ago. When she'd asked him if he was afraid, his response echoed as if it had been etched into her core.

I can live uncomfortably. I can live with the risk, but I couldn't live with my people's blood on my hands.

Even though the Terrans might not be her blood, they were her people now. In truth, she had already made this decision as soon as she said yes to the Watch. She would not live with the regret of choosing her own safety over their liberation.

"I'm in," she said.

"Excellent. We can give you more details in the coming days, but you have had a very eventful evening, dear." She gently squeezed Pax's hand.

Pax warmed and returned the gesture, accepting the offer of familial compassion from her leader.

"I think you should get some rest. We all should," Felyine said.

They exited Zohn's room one by one, bidding each other goodbye. Soon it was just Ari and Pax. They bid Zohn goodnight and walked back to her room. They readied for bed in silence. She thought about telling him he could go home tonight if he wanted to, but for some reason, she couldn't bring herself to say it. She lay on her bed, and he made up another pallet on the floor for himself beside it. They stared at the ceiling. They hadn't said a word to one another since they left the ceremony. Her heart was jumbled but strangely full as she tried to sort through the events of the evening. Then she turned to face him, and he shifted himself until he met her gaze.

"Thank you for all of those things you said tonight," she said.

He pierced her with a look that she couldn't decipher and replied, "I meant it."

She suddenly felt the urge to be close to him, and before she knew it, she had shifted to the far side of the bed, casting her eyes over, extending a silent invitation. Ari paused for a moment, contemplating the offer. Pax's breath stopped, immediately self-conscious. But before it could melt to regret, Ari shifted himself over until they were lying side by side on their backs, arms touching. He turned his left palm upward, and Pax moved her right hand until it was securely clasped in his.

CHAPTER 18

I n the days that followed, the shelter was constantly bustling with people shuffling in and out, making plans, packing bags, and sewing clothing. It was busier than Pax had ever seen it. She tried to help as much as she could, but more often than not, she just felt like she was in the way. Zohn had been locked away in his room, trying to complete whatever project he was working on for the festival. Once it was complete, he'd told her, he would deliver it to her to keep safe until the day of the protest. Until then, she had to busy herself any way she could.

She tried her hand at sewing costumes with Dinah but was graciously dismissed after pulling a loose thread on a dress and accidentally unraveling a seam. She was all right at baking but couldn't keep up with the men and women scurrying about the kitchen, throwing together dozens of breads and cakes at a time. Eventually, she found herself with Ari, Kitara, and a group of others who were packing items into boxes and doing inventory. She hadn't realized what a massive operation this was until she was counting around fifty dozen oatcakes that would be making the trip over with them. Ari told her it was mandatory for all able-bodied citizens within two-days' distance of the capitol to celebrate the Founder's Festival. They were given the week off to prepare, travel, and attend the festivities.

"What is the point of forcing people to go to a festival?" she asked as she hefted another box of supplies onto a nearby cart.

"For appearances," Ari replied. "Everything the Fellowship

does is to keep up the image of a peaceful realm where everyone lives in harmony and worships them. We all must play our part."

"But not this time," she replied.

He laughed. "No, not this time."

The two days passed by more quickly than Pax thought they would, as everyone prepared for the trip ahead. She was doing her part as best she could. In the evenings, they all had dinner together in the meeting room. She met more members of the Watch, like Sheera and Bahan, who were not much older than her but had just gotten married and were expecting their first child. They would be traveling in the same caravan as them, and she liked them a lot. They were calm and pleasant people, which provided a much-needed balance to the rest of the group. She met Dinah's boyfriend, or whatever he was to her. She was still baffled by Dinah's quick transformation from the tough, no-nonsense caretaker to the lighthearted and easygoing girlfriend. She laughed around him a lot, and it was easy to see why. He was charming and playful, and he put everyone at ease.

At night, she and Ari had fallen into an unspoken habit of sharing her room. He would lay beside her bed on the floor and ask questions about her life back home, and Pax found it easy to let him into her world. She talked about her friends, school, her art. Ari was fascinated by her penchant for building things out of trash. Actually, he was just fascinated—and slightly horrified—that there was enough trash just lying around that she could use to build things. Pax laughed at that. She even opened up about the more difficult things in her life, like how it felt to lose her mom, and how terrified and isolated she felt when she first started experiencing her dreams about Terra, before she learned she was a Traveler.

She asked him about his father and how he had been the

leader of the Watch. To her surprise, Ari opened up to her. He was proud to be Danathu's son, and he wanted to honor his legacy well. They would talk until they fell asleep, sometimes hand in hand. She remembered the first time they met when Ari had told her that hands were for family and lovers. She wondered which one she was to him. But she didn't dare bring it up with him because she took too much comfort in feeling him by her side at night, and she didn't want to mess it up. She just wished she knew what it meant to him . . . or to her. She decided to push those questions to the back of her mind until after the festival. She had much bigger questions plaguing her thoughts at night anyway.

The little slip of paper that Zohn had given to her the morning before her initiation was burning a hole in her pocket. Zohn had said the woman who might be her mother lived close to the city square. The thought of being there in just a few days filled her with longing. Would she recognize her mother if she ran into her on the street? Would her mother know who she was? What would she say? She imagined slipping away to find her while they were in the city square, but the thought was ridiculous. She didn't know the first thing about navigating the capitol, or if her mom even looked the way she remembered her. She probably didn't; it had been ten years. Besides, Pax had a role to play and had made a commitment to the Watch, and she intended to keep it.

The next morning, she shoveled down the food someone had brought by from the kitchen.

Ari smirked as she shoved a large chunk of cheese into her mouth. "Do you have somewhere to be?" he teased.

She shot him a dark look. "You would be anxious, too, if you hadn't seen the sunlight in almost three weeks. I've been dying down here. Besides, I'm excited to actually see more of Terra."

He snickered. "Well, don't get too excited. The city is a heap of trash compared to the village. There's no ocean, or animals, or trees, or anything. It is just a wasteland."

"Yeah?"

"You'll find out soon enough. But for now, we must go. The caravan will be loading soon."

They made their way down the corridor and through the meeting room, and for the first time in what seemed like ages, climbed up the steps until they reached the temple door. Pax shielded her eyes from the shock of bright rays of sun assailing her pupils. After weeks of only dimly lit rooms, seeing the sun again felt like being reborn. She inhaled sharply, letting the crisp, fresh air fill her lungs. She followed Ari out the front but quickly skittered to a halt and stared in shock.

Ari paused and turned to face her, noting the look of confusion in her eyes. "Are you all right?"

"Um . . ." She looked up and down at the monstrous tube-shaped vehicle. She hadn't known there were any kind of motorized vehicles in Terra. There was a fleet of what she could only describe as school buses rounded on both ends. Though they were a bit rusty, she could tell they had once been all shiny white. Whatever they were, they looked comically out of place amid the rest of the village.

"Have you never seen a transport before?" he asked, pulling her out of her trance.

She laughed. "Of course I have. I just didn't expect to see this here."

"Well, these are sent from the capitol, but we have smaller ones in the village."

"You do?"

He furrowed his brow at her. "Of course. There are not many, because most of us prefer to walk since the village is so small, but there are some. Shahad uses a smaller transport to go to villages and recruit."

"No kidding," she replied in amusement.

"We're not animals, you know."

"No, no, of course. I'm just realizing how much I still need to learn about this place."

"Well," he said as he grabbed her bag and guided her toward the bus. "Consider this trip a part of your education."

She seated herself beside Ari, still dazed from the bizarre juxtaposition of seeing a big white bus in the middle of a village in which she hadn't seen so much as an electric stove since she'd been here. The driver of the bus, an older Terran man, introduced himself as Tyvek and gave a few instructions about safety and rest stops they'd be making on their almost nineteen-hour trip. Before she knew it, they were barreling down the dusty road, headed for the city.

The trip was painstakingly long. Pax remembered when she used to ride the bus to elementary school. She had always brought a book with her to pass the time. She regretted not thinking to bring one with her now. She and Ari made conversation, and many in their caravan sang songs and played card games, but now they were nearly ten full hours in and everyone was getting restless. They'd just had dinner and still had hours to go. Young children were fussing as they squirmed in their mothers' laps. Some couples were bickering in their seats, and others had given up hours ago and resigned to sleep for the rest of the trip.

The first half of the trip was filled with the gorgeous terrain of Rehama. Miles of dunes sprinkled with patches of lush greenery stretched into the distance to meet a large body of water. But when they came to the border, the land grew dry, flat, and barren. They came upon a massive encampment surrounded by fencing next to a large stone building. Miles behind the building, on the other side of the fence, were lines of smaller stone buildings that appeared to be lodging. Swarms of men in black uniforms walked about behind the fence. Some stood on the outside of it, holding guns and watching the buses pass.

"The Guadaros' encampment," Ari informed her.

"They live here?"

"Some of them do. But they are everywhere. The capitol, Rehama, Nomadesales, even the Madares Isles."

"I don't know why, but I assumed they traveled to and from all this land."

"Oh, Guadaros are not Travelers. They do not have the gift."

"Really? None of them?"

He chuckled with good nature at her ignorance. "No. No Traveler would want to do a job so beneath them. Those born with the traveling gift are given jobs with much more power."

"Well, it seems to me like those guards have plenty of power." She gestured toward one of the men who held a large gun.

He shook his head. "Guards answer to the Fellowship. They do not make rules or decisions; they only enforce them. Of course, they take every liberty in exercising what little power they have over the rest of us."

"So, how exactly does all of this work? You say Travelers are given powerful jobs, but the guards are not Travelers . . . but they are from the capitol? I thought there were just Terrans and Travelers."

"Not exactly," Ari said. "There are many different levels of power here. The Fellowship is at the very top. Then below that are other Travelers in the capitol. Then there are those who were born in the capitol but do not have the traveling gift. Those are people like the guards, the merchants. Then at the bottom is us."

"So, everyone who is not a Traveler or born from a Traveler is just . . . nothing?"

He nodded. "Of course, if you are a Terran who closely serves those in the capitol, or provides them with highly valued services, you are allowed more freedom, but you are still at the bottom."

"And everyone in the capitol, even the non-Travelers, are okay with that?"

"Why would they not be? As long as they are not at the bottom."

"Being forced into a certain life just because you were born without the right gift or the right parents just seems wrong."

"It is wrong. But even the things that we've known since birth are wrong can seem right if enough people believe it."

Pax sighed at the profound sadness in that revelation and settled back into her seat. The encampment was miles behind them now, but the land remained utterly bare and uninteresting. Staring out the window felt like a chore. Her mind drifted to her mother and the slip of paper she had hurriedly stuffed into the pocket of her tunic before they left the shelter this morning. She fingered the soft edges of the paper now, which had grown worn from her grasping it between her hands and rubbing the page between her fingertips. It comforted her just knowing it was there. It was like having a little piece of her mom with her. Like the old sweatshirt she'd left behind at home. She pulled the paper out of her pocket and glanced over at Ari, who was leaning his head against the window and staring blankly out at the setting sun. Then she carefully unfolded the paper and stared at the names and addresses that were scrawled on it.

"What is that?" Ari asked, causing Pax to nearly jump out of her own skin.

"Oh, um . . ." She debated making something up, but then decided she didn't see the point. "It's the names of two women. Zohn got them from one of his friends who still works for the Fellowship. He thinks this one might be my mom." She pointed to one of the names of the list.

"Do you mind?" he asked, gesturing toward the paper. She hesitated for a moment, then handed it to him. He squinted at it, trying to make out the words on the page against the light that was growing dimmer in the setting sun. "Hmm . . . Did you know this place is only a few blocks from the square?"

"What?"

"Yes, this is workers' housing just outside of the village square. Many people who serve Travelers live there. You know, close enough to get to work, but not so close that the Travelers feel uncomfortable." He rolled his eyes.

"Oh." Her heartbeat picked up. It had been one thing to know that her mother might be somewhere close by. But the thought of her being this close was almost unbearable.

"When are we going?" Ari asked quietly.

"What do you mean?"

"You want to find her, yes?"

"Of course I do. But what about the Watch and the demonstration?"

"Your role is to deliver something before it starts. My role is to keep you safe. If we hurry, we might have just enough time to make it to this place and back to the meeting point outside the square."

"You say it like it's easy. What would I do when I got there? She probably wouldn't even be there."

"Probably not, but you could leave a note. Tell her who you are and that you have been looking for her, then leave a meeting point in the village."

"But what if it's not her?"

"Then I guess the woman wouldn't come, yes?"

"But what if she reports it to the guards?"

Ari pondered a moment. "You would have to make it like a secret message. Something that only your mother would know."

She sat for a moment, stumped. She hadn't seen her mother since she was six. They didn't have any secrets together. All she had was her mother's old sweatshirt. Then it dawned on her. She pulled a bit of charcoal from her bag, ripped a strip of paper from her Traveler's guide, and scrawled: "I have your Ohio State sweatshirt. Meet me in the West Village temple one week from today. –PG"

She lifted the strip of paper and read it over. Ari skimmed the page over her shoulder. "Do you think it will work?" Pax said.

"I have no idea what it means, but I think so."

"You really think we can pull it off in time?"

"It is your mother, Pax. We have to try."

She leaned her head against his shoulder. "Thank you."

CHAPTER 19

"Pax. *Pax*." Ari nudged her gently.

She popped her head up, shoving a mess of black hair from her eyes. "Huh?"

"We're here."

Blinking, Pax opened her eyes. Once they adjusted to the light, her mouth dropped. She swung her head from left to right, taking in the sight before her. She wasn't sure what she had been expecting to see when she reached the capitol, but it certainly wasn't this. She leaned over Ari to drink in the endless lines of pristine white buildings, hundreds of stories high. Just outside their transport, the busy city streets were bustling with thousands of people. Sleek cars and buses lined every corner, and a high-speed railway train zoomed past just over their heads. Its track seemed to stretch the length of the entire city. This didn't look anything like the Terra she thought she knew.

"What on earth?" she gasped in shock.

"Disgusting, isn't it?" Ari said.

"Are you kidding? Everything is so shiny and so . . . nice."

"Yes, they do like their things to be shiny, I suppose."

Soon, Tyvek instructed everyone to exit the bus. Pax and Ari filed out, following the crowd into the street. As they moved farther into the city square, there were large screens mounted on the sides of the buildings surrounding the square. Drones mounted with cameras whizzed over the crowd, filming their arrival and broadcasting it to a stream connected to one of the screens. Pax wished she could explore the square more, but they were moving away from the square and the shiny buildings toward an area that had been sectioned off. A line of people miles long ahead of her shuffled toward a grassy meadow lined with long tent-like structures. Hulking guards clad in black holding large guns aggressively shouted at them, urging them forward. The guards were fully intent on keeping them as far away from their shiny white city as possible. The Terrans might be here, but they would not be seen by those inside the city square.

The guards ushered them through the line at a snail's pace toward a check-in area blocked off by heavily guarded partitions. When they reached the front of the line, Shahad tossed a large stack of papers toward the man on the other side of the check-in table. The two moderators held small transparent devices that projected a list onto the screens. One moderator peered over his spectacles and scrunched his nose down at the paper.

"You are from *Rehama*, then?" he sneered, saying the name as if it were some kind of disease.

Shahad nodded. "Sector C."

"Right . . ." The moderator glanced over the list, counting and checking off names.

Pax shifted on her feet, restless from standing for so long. Suddenly, there was a gentle whirring just above her head. She looked up and flinched to find a silver disk-shaped drone hovering beside her. It looked like a metal frisbee with a short antenna at the top, and it emitted a soft blue light as it whirred about.

"Can I help you find your way, General?" prompted the disk in a robotic voice.

All eyes turned to her in suspicion. She looked at Ari for assurance. He simply shrugged, at a loss.

The moderator holding the list turned his eyes to her. "Are

you lost, miss?" His voice had completely changed when he addressed her.

"Um, no, I'm from Rehama."

"Strange. Our helping drone seems to believe you are someone else." He eyed her. "It has recognition technology to identify Traveler citizens." His tone turned accusatory. Pax stood in silence, unsure of what to say. Then the man waved a hand, motioning to a guard. The guard advanced upon her swiftly, seized her by the arm, and gruffly tugged.

"No!" Pax protested. Barely two minutes in the city and she was already being arrested. Her heartbeat climbed up her throat as she scrambled to find a way out of this mess.

"Get back!" the guard shouted as he attempted to pull her away. Thankfully, all the commotion had caught the attention of the crowd, causing bystanders to swarm the area. This bought Shahad enough time to push in and grab her other arm. "She is half-bred! She is half-bred!" he shouted over the buzzing of the crowd, just loud enough to catch the guard's attention. The guard stopped and turned toward Shahad, who was boring him down with a look so intimidating it caused the guard to stop in his tracks. The noise died down.

"She was abandoned by a Traveler parent and sent to our village," Shahad lied coolly. "I have known her since her infancy. This happens to her every year, but I can assure you she is legitimate."

The man leaned in toward Pax and lowered his tone. "Miss, are you with these people against your will?"

Ari chuckled and the man shot a glare at him.

"No," she spoke up before the man could respond to Ari's slight. "I am as he says. I am half-bred." She rolled her r's and elongated her vowels, attempting to emulate a convincing Rehaman accent.

He eyed her up and down, then looked back at the snooty man at the registration table for further instructions.

The little man moved out from behind the table and advanced upon her until his face was only inches from hers. He squinted at her from behind his spectacles, sizing her up.

"Hmm. I suppose these things can happen with half-breeds. The drones have been known to glitch from time to time. Helper, dismissed." He waved the drone away, and it whirred off back into the city square. "Sector C is clear!" he called.

The guard released his grip on Pax and waved them into the clearing.

Pax sighed in relief, then made eye contact with Ari, who stifled a laugh. "What?"

"Your accent is terrible," he whispered.

She rolled her eyes. "I'll work on that."

The hoard moved forward until a guard stopped Shahad. "Hold out your left hand," he said.

Shahad obeyed, and the guard pressed a long silver tube, like a ballpoint pen, into his skin and pressed a button at the top. There was a soft beep as something injected into his palm. Shahad set his teeth into a grimace.

Pax's eyes widened. "What are they doing?" she whispered to Ari.

"Putting trackers in. It is how they ensure we don't go to places that are off-limits. There are scanners all over the capitol. If you step out of place, they will know."

"Does it hurt?"

"Yes," he answered quietly as they approached the guard.

Pax met the guard's intimidating gaze, and a shiver crawled down her spine. He smirked at her reaction.

"Your hand," the guard demanded.

She lifted a shaking hand and bit down hard on her lip as

the cold tube pressed into her palm. She yelped at the sharp stab that pierced into the muscle. The guard chuckled with satisfaction and motioned for her to move along. She glared at him, wishing she could kick him, or do anything to wipe that stupid grin off his face.

As they approached the rows of makeshift lodging, Pax rubbed the swollen skin on her hand where the tracker had been injected. "So, they'll just track me forever now?" she asked no one in particular.

"Not forever," Shahad said over his shoulder. "The tracker is designed to dissolve over time. At least, that is what Zohn told me."

The sound of his name reminded her she hadn't seen Zohn since they had departed Rehama.

"Where is Zohn?" She scanned the crowd to see if she could spot his hunched figure.

"He is not with us. He is technically still a fugitive, so he can never return to the capitol . . . with their knowledge," Shahad added with a mischievous grin. "Go find a spot inside before all the cots fill up. I will see you both at the opening ceremonies tonight."

Pax and Ari nodded and approached the tent marked "Sector C-1." Inside was a long line of nearly hundreds of cots separated by curtains for privacy. Food was being served at the front of the tent, and people sat eating at long tables just outside the entrance. Small portable toilet rooms and curtained showers lined the back of the tent.

Pax and Ari moved through the crowd, searching for empty cots. Though it was far from luxury housing, with nearly a third of their village sharing a living space, it was well organized and efficiently made. This was just how things were done here, Pax realized. She remembered what Zohn had said about how the city people only saw the peaceful and beautiful parts of Terra. She could understand how a person who grew up in a place like this might never stop to wonder if things were not as they seemed. She wondered what her mother thought about this city.

"What are you thinking about?" Ari asked, seating himself on the cot beside hers.

She looked at him. "I was just wondering, if this is what the capitol looks like, with all of these nice things . . ." She paused, realizing her question might be offensive.

"How do the rest of us live with so little?" he finished for her.

She nodded.

"Well, it is not only that we are forced to live with less. We believe we live life to our fullest when we are not surrounded by useless luxury. I'm sure you know the capitol likes to keep Terran people separate. When they pushed us out of the city, they pushed us out of everything. Land, opportunities, and access to any luxury you see within the walls of the city. In the village, we made everything you see with our own hands, with our own materials. Of course, when we want something, we can find our own way to get it," he said mischievously.

"What do you mean?"

He laughed. "I'll show you." He nodded toward the tent exit, and she followed him out.

She stayed close to Ari as they came into the field bustling with thousands of people. Children chased each other around, and men and women hauled their bags, searching for their shelter. The commotion was overwhelming.

Ari led her through the field until they came to a strip of merchant tents selling all types of different goods. Colorful, glittering tapestries woven by hand, leather shoes and sandals advertising discounted prices. The tables of goods were endless, but they didn't stop at any of them. Instead, Ari led her around the corner to a little tent tucked behind the others and guided her inside.

"Hello, my young friends!" a man with a deep voice greeted them from behind his merchant table. "Looking for anything specific today?"

"No," Ari replied. "Just looking."

The man laughed in a way that unsettled Pax. "Ah yes, many are curious about my treasures. Is this your first time?"

Ari shook his head. "No, we have been before."

"Well, call me if you find something you like." The man drifted to a chair in the corner of the tent to give them space and opened a book, though he kept his eyes on them.

The merchant table was stocked with an amalgamation of unexpected items: digital cameras, blenders, vacuums, televisions, even MacBooks with Wi-Fi adapters.

"How did he get this stuff?" she whispered.

Ari leaned in. "He's a Traveler."

"He just goes and steals it and brings it back here to sell?"

"I suppose. I mean, it's not an honest living, but it is a living."

"Does the Guadaros know?"

He nodded. "There are dozens like him in the city. Half-cast Travelers who aren't welcome by their own people, who can't find a job, and are desperate to make some money. They get arrested all the time."

"So, this is how non-Travelers get their technology. Have you ever bought anything?"

He chuckled. "When I was a boy, Dinah bought me a snack from one of these tents. It was like tiny bits of bread, only they were very crunchy and tasted like cheese."

Pax smiled as he struggled to describe what must have been a bag of chips. "And did you like it?"

"I talked about them for weeks after."

She laughed. "Remind me next time I travel home, and I'll bring you a whole box of tiny, crunchy cheese breads." She was hit with another pang of sadness, as she remembered it might be a long time before she traveled back.

Ari quickly changed the subject. "I do not have much use for these items, but I know Zohn and some of the other senior members of the Watch have employed the services of a Traveler like that man to gather a few items for our display."

Pax suddenly remembered the morning she went to have breakfast with Zohn and he had covered something on his desk. She could have sworn it was a laptop, but at the time it didn't seem possible. It was beginning to make sense. Now she wondered what he was working on.

"Thank you!" Ari called as they made their way out of the tent. The man waved from his chair, following them with his eyes as they left.

"I mean, if you think about it, it is kind of the perfect crime," Pax said.

"What do you mean?"

"Well, where I'm from, we have guards and cameras looking for people who steal things, and most of them get caught. But if you're a Traveler, you just—poof—disappear. And you're from a different galaxy, so they don't have your name or any way to trace you. It's actually kind of brilliant." She laughed.

Ari laughed at her. "So, are you telling me you have found your new path?"

She pushed him lightly. "Of course not! I'm just saying."

"You would certainly make better money than I do at the

docks. Perhaps we could be partners. You get the items and I sell them out of my house. We will split the profits."

"Perfect. When do we start?" she teased.

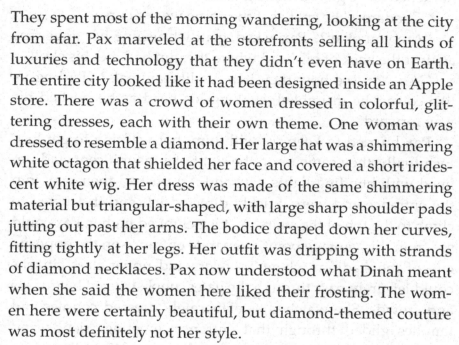

They spent most of the morning wandering, looking at the city from afar. Pax marveled at the storefronts selling all kinds of luxuries and technology that they didn't even have on Earth. The entire city looked like it had been designed inside an Apple store. There was a crowd of women dressed in colorful, glittering dresses, each with their own theme. One woman was dressed to resemble a diamond. Her large hat was a shimmering white octagon that shielded her face and covered a short iridescent white wig. Her dress was made of the same shimmering material but triangular-shaped, with large sharp shoulder pads jutting out past her arms. The bodice draped down her curves, fitting tightly at her legs. Her outfit was dripping with strands of diamond necklaces. Pax now understood what Dinah meant when she said the women here liked their frosting. The women here were certainly beautiful, but diamond-themed couture was most definitely not her style.

After an early evening meal back at their tent, an announcement sounded from the speakers mounted on the city buildings. A nasally male voice called out, instructing everyone to assemble at the stadium for the opening ceremony. Everyone rose to their feet and followed the throng of people toward the inner city, past flashing lights and screens of colorful advertisements. The air grew thinner as the heat from the crowd gathered around her. The overwhelming stench of sweat-drenched bodies bumping and jostling every which way, the endless cacophony of shouting rising to a roar, and above it, the tireless string of obscenities and demands from the guards who urged them all forward. The crowd pushed Ari too close to one of the guards, who shoved him forward with the butt of his gun. Ari stumbled and gritted his teeth. His eyes darkened as he glared at the guard.

"Guadaros," he spat as if the name were a curse.

"Are you okay?" Pax asked, gently brushing her fingertips against the back of his head where the gun had met his skull.

"Yes. You see how they treat us like animals? Herding us like cows," he grumbled, shaking his head as he pushed his way forward.

Pax hurried to keep up with him, not wanting to get lost. Eventually, they came upon the sight of a magnificent stadium lined with blinding lights. Pax and Ari pushed their way into the entrance and were quickly directed left and instructed to climb to the top of the stairs. As they climbed higher, Pax could see from this vantage point a separate entrance on the opposite end of the stadium where Travelers and upper-class citizens could leisurely pass through the gates, unobstructed by guards and crowds. She watched as elaborately dressed couples and families glided through that entrance, greeting friends and finding seating close to the center of the arena. When they were nearing their designated spot in the highest section of the arena, Pax was already so exhausted from the trek that she could have collapsed into a heap on the floor and cried. The Travelers went to such lengths to ensure the Terrans remained out of sight. It was disheartening and dehumanizing to watch the Terrans—her friends—be treated as they were. Her aching legs climbed step after step until they reached a section nearly at the top row. Despite her exhaustion, she smiled when she spotted Kitara along with other members of the Watch.

"Pax!" Kitara called, gesturing toward her. "In a sea of thousands, we found each other. It is fate!"

She chuckled. "How are you?"

"Dirty and tired and sweaty. And yet, you are as stunning as ever."

Pax rolled her eyes. "Please."

"And how is your little servant boy?" He leaned forward to Ari. "I heard about your very special job tomorrow, my friend," he teased.

Ari shot him a look. "You are jealous. I know you would kill to be inside the city."

"You know me too well. I would commit murder to be your manservant. I hear they get to dress to match their ladies. The things I would do for a gorgeous sparkling suit."

"What?" Ari said in a mix of shock and disgust.

Kitara snickered. "I just wanted to see the look on your face."

Ari glared at him, but whatever comeback he'd mustered was quickly drowned out by the squeal of a microphone overhead. The crowd flinched as a little man with fiery red hair and clad in a fitted gray suit nervously chuckled into the mic.

"Sorry, folks! Thank you all for your patience, and for those of you who come from afar, welcome to New America!" He proudly lifted his hands over his head with a flourish. The crowd below them—the Travelers—roared in excitement.

New America. The more Pax thought about the name the more unsettling she found it. But it made sense. The Travelers who settled here did so with the intention of making a better America somewhere else. She wasn't sure they had succeeded so much as made the same America on a different planet. It was history repeating itself across time and space.

She scanned the crowd of villagers. Some children in the

crowd of Rehamans cheered and whistled, happy to be part of the commotion. The older Rehamans who knew better sat in silent protest, and most offered only a halfhearted applause, exhausted from the years of taking part in this charade.

The little man continued in a tone so forcefully overexcited that his nasally voice cracked. "We are so humbled by how many have made the long, long journey for our little celebration."

"As if we had a choice," Ari muttered under his breath.

"But I know that none of you are here to see me." The crowd cheered in protest and the man laughed heartily and raised his hands in false humility. "Oh, please! You flatter me! Now let me call up to the stage the man of the hour, our fearless leader, Commander Dickinson!"

The crowd reached a fever pitch as a tall, subdued man slowly approached the microphone. Camera lights flickered throughout the crowd across the stadium in blinding flashes that made Pax squint.

"Good evening, citizens and guests alike." The man's voice emulated warmth but sounded slightly strangled. The massive screens zoomed in on the man's face. He was in his sixties, but something about his face and his cold, dark eyes made him seem much older. His smile was wide and seemed so tight that if you touched it, his cheek might crack. His silver hair was slicked back and perfectly coiffed, and his black tux was tailored and sophisticated. He evidently made a great effort to appear trustworthy. But behind his pristine facade was a flicker of something sinister. Pax gasped. Commander Dickinson reminded her of her father.

"We are honored to have you all here for our Bicentennial Founder's Festival celebration," he continued. "When my great-grandfather, John Dickinson, founded this land nearly one hundred years ago through his tireless work and innovation, he did so with a vision: to create a better world. I stand before you today so humbled by the knowledge that we are living out his legacy in New America!"

He spread his arms wide to receive the raucous cheer that the crowd brought forth.

"The land we came from was rife with poverty, inequality, and conflict, and though we honor our ancestry, we have fought tirelessly to establish a society founded in peace and prosperity for all people. Today, you and I are reaping the fruits of that fight! In our hundred-year history, we have never experienced war."

The crowd below screamed with outstretched hands.

"Not a single citizen of New America has ever gone hungry or homeless, and most of all, we have lived in harmony with the good people of Native Terra, to whom we owe a tremendous debt of gratitude for doing their part to make this nation great! Let's give them a round of applause!"

The quiet, seething rage of hundreds of Terrans grew so tangible it made Pax's skin heat and prickle. Ari's fists were clenched so tightly his knuckles were white. Kitara's eyes were fixed on a crack in the cement floor. A middle-aged man a few rows down rose to his feet to leave the stadium but was promptly met at the head of the aisle by a guard who towered over him, glowering through his helmet.

"Back to your seat, sweat neck," the guard spat through gritted teeth.

The man's eyes blazed and he stood frozen, his chest heaving up and down as rage coursed through him. Then he turned on his heel and slumped back into his seat, looking tired and defeated. The guard's face spread into a wide grin as he stepped back to his post.

"What did he call him?" Pax whispered to Ari.

"Sweat neck," he grumbled. "It is what they call us because we work outside. Doing their labor for them," he seethed.

Pax took in the scene before them. Hundreds of levels below, the crowd was electric. Wild with excitement and joyous in celebration. But in the rafters, it was almost quiet. The faces in the crowd ranged from anger to despair, but many seemed beyond that level of emotion. They had heard this song and dance every year for the past hundred years. They had run out of rage; they had cried all of their tears. They were just tired. They were in the same stadium, but it might as well have been a different universe. The Travelers of New America were blind and deaf, and she saw now more than ever why the Watch needed to wake them up.

The tension of the moment slowly faded into boredom as the ceremony dragged on. The commander recognized the achievements of notable citizens this year, and there had been quite a few. The excitement of the lower tier never wavered as they roared with applause for various inventors, doctors, and leaders. The crowd swelled with praise for the inventor of the new facial recognition software, and the doctor who was working on gene therapy to remove wrinkles and sunspots. Pax had to admit the achievements were impressive, but had they even considered expanding their newfound accomplishments to those outside of their borders? How much good were they actually doing if their wealth and prosperity came at the expense of everyone around them? The faces below were bright with joy and pride for their city, and she wondered if they even knew their success was coming at such a tremendous cost.

The ceremony ended with a star-studded performance of New America's most talented celebrities. Dancers, singers, musicians, and actors all came together for a big unity concert à la "We Are the World."

The crowd cheered at the egregious display of good-willed patriotism. Ari made fun of the performers, putting his finger to his ear and contorting his face as he sang into a fake microphone. Kitara gushed over the costumes. Pax, however, was so physically and emotionally spent that all she could do was stare blankly at the over-the-top display. It was late into the night when the crowd was finally permitted to leave.

The walk back to their tent felt longer and even more grueling than the one to the stadium. Everyone dragged their feet despite the shouts from the guards lining the walkway. By the end, she and Kitara were practically holding each other up.

His head lolled backward dramatically. "Let me sleep in the street! I don't care anymore!" he shouted.

Pax laughed humorlessly. "I might join you."

Ari shuffled beside them, hands in his pockets. His hair had come loose from its tie, and wild chestnut locks were stringing down his face, sticking to his cheeks and neck where sweat had collected from the heat of hundreds of bodies for the past several hours. Pax nudged him. "You okay?"

His eyes met hers briefly, and he gave her a short nod. "I hope this is worth it," he mumbled.

Kitara gripped his friend's shoulder reassuringly. "It will be," he said with conviction.

When they reached their tent and walked through the crowd of people readying themselves for bed, Kitara pulled Ari and Pax into a warm, sweaty embrace and bid them both goodnight. Pax collapsed onto her cot, allowing her body to sink into the firm, itchy cushion as much as it could. Out of the corner of her eye, she saw Ari strip off his dirty tunic and flop onto his bed, too exhausted to change into fresh clothes.

She sneaked a long sideways glance to study his bare chest as he mindlessly sat up to refashion his dirty tresses into a loose bun atop his head. The skin on his chest was the same warm golden-brown as his arms.

He must not wear a tunic out at the docks often, she thought.

Her mind drifted to an image from what felt like another lifetime ago: Zeke, in his room, changing into his athletic wear for soccer. The cut of Ari's body was not like Zeke's. He certainly had the same muscles, but they weren't the long, lean bands carved from hours of gym time and training. Instead, they were stacked thickly upon his arms, shoulders, and chest showing years of physical labor. Level-headed and humble as he was, Zeke always took pride in his body. He'd never say it out loud, but Pax could always tell by the way he carried himself. Though Ari was just as strong, there was no vanity or pride regarding his body. It was simply the way it was. He was strong because he worked, and that's all there was to it. Of course, not everything was so cut and dry with him. That was another way he differed from Zeke.

Zeke was factual, disciplined, everything was black and white and made sense. His mind was always clear, he always had the answers, and he was always two steps ahead. That was part of what had always made her feel so safe with him. There were no questions, only answers. And in her life, which was always so unpredictable, she'd needed that.

Ari, on the other hand, was all passion and emotion—act first, plan later. She chuckled at the memory of their first encounters, and how terrified she'd been trying to keep up with him, making things up as they went. But somewhere along the way, they'd fallen into step together, and instead of feeling like she was always two steps behind, she was running in stride with him. It didn't feel like Ari had any more of a plan than she did, and it was strangely empowering. Perhaps because for the first time, Pax felt like she was actually calling the shots in her own life. And instead of questioning or doubting her, he just trusted her.

Ari turned to her and quirked an eyebrow. "Everything all right?"

She flushed, realizing she had been staring at him. She felt an instant pang of guilt for comparing her two friends. They had both been good to her; they couldn't be compared. She removed her gaze from his and stared at the billowy white material draped above them, shielding them from the elements.

"Yeah, sorry," she responded. "Just thinking about stuff."

The left side of his mouth pulled into a crooked half grin. "What *stuff*?" He emphasized the word, trying to mimic her.

She knew the word wasn't one they used in Terrish, so he was teasing her about how ridiculous it sounded to him. She tossed a pillow at him. He caught it easily in his left hand and tossed it back.

"How are you feeling about tomorrow?" she whispered.

"All right, I suppose," he responded coolly, resting his hands behind his head.

"All right?"

He glanced at her. "Fine. I am nervous. Mostly just about making sure you get out of there."

"I can take care of myself, you know."

He grinned. "Oh, I know. But it is also my job. And there will be swarms of guards there. We will have to be extremely careful."

She sighed. "Yeah . . . I really hope I do this right. I don't want to let anyone down."

"You won't," he reassured.

"I just—" She paused suddenly as a young woman approached. The girl looked vaguely familiar, but she didn't know her name. Pax opened her mouth to greet her as she neared their cots, but instead of stopping, the girl simply walked past. Pax noticed the small flutter of a slip of paper falling to the ground at the foot of her bed, but the girl didn't stop to pick it up. She kept moving, not even turning around to acknowledge them before she disappeared out of sight. Pax sat up and casually grabbed the slip of paper from the floor without appearing conspicuous. She unfolded it and read the tiny script scrawled across the front: "Meet me at Merchant's Street at sunrise. Last tent on the left. –D"

"That's Dinah," Ari said from over her shoulder in a voice barely loud enough for her to hear.

"So, I guess we're starting bright and early then?"

"Well, the celebration is at noon in the square."

Pax's heart felt like it had been filled with cement and sank into her stomach. "That's so soon. I—I don't even really know what I'm doing yet."

Ari sat beside her on the bed and placed a hand over hers. "You have nothing to worry about. They keep us in the dark until we are needed in order to keep us safe. If the plan slips into the wrong ears, it is all over. They will tell you when it is time."

She breathed a heavy sigh. "Okay."

Ari placed a finger beneath Pax's chin and lifted it until her eyes were level with his. "You should rest, *mon almea*."

Pax didn't know what the last word meant, but the way he said it made her stomach twist and her face grow hot. She turned away from his gaze to hide the redness in her cheeks.

"Yeah," she replied, lamely.

He must have seen her blush because she swore she saw him smirk to himself as he returned to his cot.

Horrified, Pax pulled the covers over her head and stared

blankly at the thin white fabric. If she hadn't made an oath to the Watch, she would have disappeared right then and there.

CHAPTER 20

T he next morning, as Pax and Ari arrived on Merchant's Street, Dinah fluttered out of the last tent in a huff and squared her small frame as she came to stand in front of them.

"You are late!" she scolded, smacking Ari's arm.

"Ow. Good morning to you too," he said, rubbing his arm.

She rolled her eyes. "Come!" She walked quickly behind a table filled with turquoise jewelry and guided them into a curtained area in the back of the tent.

Pax shuffled in behind her, rubbing the sleep out of her red-rimmed eyes. She had lain awake in the darkness for hours after her moment with Ari, just listening to the sound of strangers rustling in their sleep. She had drifted for what felt like only a blink, when the sun came peeking out over the horizon, urging her to wake up and face the day.

"We don't have as much time as I would like, but I will make it work." Dinah huffed as she yanked Pax into a seated position on a stool in the corner of the room.

Pax looked around the small space. A clothing rack stood in the opposite corner holding modest embroidered pieces and a single cloth garment bag. On the other side of the room was a table that held a little vanity mirror and a spread of makeup in striking vivid hues that made Pax feel even more uneasy. "So, what do I need to do?" she asked nervously.

"You? You do nothing. You sit still, stay quiet, and for the love of the Holy Mother, do not touch anything."

Pax nodded as Dinah suddenly shoved a warm bowl into her hands. "Eat this while I start on this mess." Then Dinah separated Pax's hair into sections.

"So," Ari interrupted from the corner. "What do I do?"

"You sit outside and sell jewelry until I tell you to come in," Dinah said without turning around.

"What? But I don't—"

"You don't what? Nothing! You ask what is your job, and this is your job. My friend offered us her tent on the condition that we sell to customers and don't get caught. Now go!" She shook her head and cursed under her breath in Terrish.

Ari stood for a moment as if debating on whether he should fire back. But he seemed to have thought better of it because he simply sighed in exasperation and trudged his way back through the curtain.

Pax firmly set her jaw to keep from crying out as Dinah ran a comb through her tangled hair. She couldn't remember the last time someone else had done her hair nicely, or her makeup. It had probably been Ayana before some party or dance. Tears formed in the corner of her eyes, and she wasn't sure if it was from missing her friend or the sharp pull of her hair from her scalp by Dinah's rough hands.

"How are you feeling about today?" she asked Pax.

The question took her off guard. She hadn't expected Dinah to actually talk to her. She seemed so stressed about the tangled web of knots on the back of Pax's head. "I'm okay, I think."

"Scared?" she asked. "I would be if it were me."

Pax chuckled a little. "I don't know. You don't seem like you would be scared of anything."

"You don't know me. I am scared of many things."

Pax sat quietly for a moment until she finally responded, "Yes. I am scared."

Dinah nodded. "You will do it, though."

"How do you know?"

"Because they need you to, and because you are brave," she said matter-of-factly.

"You don't know me either." Pax laughed.

"Yes, I do. I took care of you and watched you fight for yourself every day until you recovered. You stood up to your papa. You left everything behind and started a new life here. Even though you didn't have to, you joined the Watch and risked your life. I know you, but if you think you are not brave, then maybe you don't know yourself."

Pax felt the weight of Dinah's words sink into her skin like a salve. Dinah said those words as if she had just stated that two plus two was four. It wasn't up to debate for her—there was no question, no emotion behind it at all. Pax was brave. It was just a fact. The power of that assurance spread across her body and dissolved into wounds that had festered for years. Years of being abandoned and abused had left thousands of tiny pinpricks into her confidence, leaving her feeling raw and exposed. But as she let herself acknowledge the truth in Dinah's words, it felt as if those little holes were closing. Instead of feeling raw, she felt powerful. Instead of feeling exposed, she felt strong. She would do this, even if it terrified her, for herself and for the people she cared about.

She couldn't explain in words what she was thinking or how she felt at that moment, so she simply responded, "You're right."

"Of course I am." Dinah smiled.

Hours had passed, and Pax's face ached from being pinched and plucked and having her hair pulled back so tight she could nearly feel her blood pulsing through her scalp. She scratched the side of her head, which was warm and itchy under the pink bobbed wig Dinah had glued to her hairline.

Dinah's hand swatted at her fingertips as she shouted, "Don't touch!" before returning to painting an angular design on her eyelids with a shocking electric-blue liner. Pax sulked down in her chair, tired of being poked and prodded at, but was firmly instructed to sit up straight again.

When Dinah finally finished Pax's face and hair, she didn't bother to let her look at the finished product before she stood her up and grabbed the garment bag from the clothing rack. She untied the bag and revealed a bold pink strapless dress. Pax's eyes widened at the ensemble as Dinah stripped her down to her underwear.

"I had to guess your size, so I hope it fits." Dinah helped her step into the structured hoop sewn into the lining of the dress.

The zipper closed with no issue, and when she was fully clothed and strapped into the matching chunky pink heels, Dinah held up a small mirror for Pax to see the finished product.

"What do you think?" she asked expectantly.

Pax squinted at her reflection, taking in the woman in front of her. Dinah's goal was to make her look unrecognizable, and she certainly had accomplished that.

Pax remembered looking at pictures of celebrities in a magazine who had gotten dressed up for the Met Gala in New York. They were donned in over-the-top couture with dozens of layers and colors and fabrics all meshing together in a way that was so unharmonious, yet it somehow still looked amazing. That was what this dress felt like.

She ran her fingers across the pink silk fabric at the top, stitched with dramatic, angular pleats around her bustline. Her skirt cinched at the small of her waist and then dramatically exploded into bustles of pink fabric cascading down to the middle of her thigh. The top layer was embroidered with hundreds of little flowers and pearls. She looked almost inhuman, but just like the Met Gala gowns, it worked.

"You look ridiculous," said Ari from behind her. She turned to see him leaning against the tent post, smirking as his eyes traveled down her body, taking in her full ensemble.

Dinah scoffed. "What do you know? Here." She crossed the room to force another garment bag into his hands. "Go put this on."

He rolled his eyes. "Pax, you have a visitor." He fluffed her skirt playfully as he passed, and she smacked his arm in false warning.

She turned to see Zohn and Felyine standing in front of the open curtain. Zohn was smiling at her through tired eyes. "You certainly look like a Traveler now. Well done, Dinah," he praised, patting her hand as he slowly made his way to Pax.

"You look lovely," Felyine offered kindly as she entered the room.

Dinah smiled warmly and excused herself from the tent.

"Now, my dear, how are you feeling?" Zohn asked.

"A little uncomfortable, but . . . okay, I think."

He smirked. "I have something for you." He reached into the pocket of his trousers and pulled out a small black sachet. He gingerly placed it into the center of her palm.

"What is this?" she asked, fingering the delicate fabric.

"This is the package you will deliver," said Felyine.

"Well, actually, the package is inside," Zohn explained. He opened the little pouch, retrieved a small, rectangular device, and handed it to Pax.

She eyed it carefully and her brows furrowed in confusion. "Is this a . . . flash drive?" she asked, inspecting it closely.

Zohn nodded. "Well, yes. How else were we to store the video?"

"Video?"

"Each year, the Travelers' festivities kick off with a video acknowledging the accomplishments of Terra's elite. This year we will replace it." He took the drive from her hand and held it up to her.

The plans were becoming clearer to Pax now. "So, I have to get this to someone before the celebration starts at noon?"

"Yes," Felyine said. "Alaric. He's our man on the inside. He works in tech, mostly monitoring information and reporting back, but today he is putting himself at great risk to switch out the videos. It will most certainly be traced back to him."

"Wow." Pax's heart sank, thinking about what that might mean for this man . . . and possibly for her.

"Do not worry, child." Zohn grabbed her hands. "You will be protected."

She smiled tentatively at Zohn, then turned her head at the sound of rustling from behind them. Ari was standing awkwardly in a crisp, form-fitting navy suit. His curls were slicked back and fastened to his head at the back.

"You look nice," Pax said.

He scoffed. "You would think with all their money and inventions, they would have found a way to make their clothes less hot . . . and itchy." He scratched behind the collar at his neck for emphasis.

Zohn chuckled at Ari's discomfort. "They certainly prefer fashion over function here."

"So, we're set then?" Ari looked to Felyine.

"Almost. We just have to take care of the trackers," she started, hesitantly.

"And it's going to hurt, isn't it?" Pax asked, though she already knew the answer.

"I'll be quick," Felyine assured her. She motioned for Pax's hand. Pax obeyed and placed her palm upward into Felyine's hand.

"Normally, I would give you tonic for something like this, but you must have a clear head for today." She looked apologetic.

Pax sighed. "Just do it." She turned her head and tensed her body as Felyine reached for what looked like a scalpel and a little gripping tool. She prodded around Pax's palm with her fingers until she located the injection site. Ari's warm, familiar hand grabbed hers, and she squeezed it tightly.

"We can't arouse suspicion, so please try not to scream," Felyine instructed.

That made her heart sputter wildly in her chest. She opened her eyes to find Zohn was also looking away. She made eye contact with Ari, who appeared to be nervous but was trying to mask it with assurance. He nodded at her in solidarity as she felt the cold tip of the scalpel touch her skin, then pain. Searing, ripping pain as the skin in her hand split open as easily as soft butter.

She bit down so hard, her jaw twitched. Ari flexed his hand against her tight grip, but she didn't care. She leaned her head against his arm and strained against her own will to cry out as Felyine grabbed the tiny tracker that had latched onto her muscular tissue and ripped it out in a quick motion. Pax inhaled sharply in surprise and released her grip on Ari so she could slap her hand over her mouth to muffle her cry. Tears formed in her eyes, and she breathed heavily as Felyine applied a numbing salve and a translucent-looking bandage across her hand. Pax watched as the bandage began to dissolve and seal the skin together until the small, ragged wound was nothing but a puckering pink scar atop her hand. She looked at Felyine in shock.

"One of the capitol's latest accomplishments. They are not all useless, it would seem." Felyine chuckled.

Pax nodded in shock.

Then it was Ari's turn. He, however, could not muffle the sound of his pain. When Felyine ripped the tracker from his hand, before he could stop himself, his eyes flung wide and he let out a short, pained scream.

Dinah peeked her head into the tent and yelled a feigned curse. "I told you to be careful with that merchandise, you stupid boy! Now pick that up!" Her scold was very convincing and allowed Felyine enough time to finish the job.

Once he was sufficiently recovered, Pax looked at Ari, amusement playing on her lips. "Wow, that must've really hurt."

"You will never allow me to forget this, will you?"

"Nor will I!" Dinah called from the other side of the curtain.

Zohn chuckled at their teasing. Then his smile faded to a grave expression, and he lowered his voice. "Now, it is very important to remember that when you step out of this tent, you two are no longer friends or equals. You are an employer and an employee. Arivhan, you must never look Pax, or any other Traveler, directly in the eyes. Keep your head down and speak only when spoken to. Pax, you must try to keep yourself a few paces ahead of him, and carry your head high, like you know you are supposed to be there. If you get stopped, keep your answers short and vague, and excuse yourself as quickly as possible without looking too obvious. Do you think you both can manage?"

"I think so," she responded.

Ari nodded.

"Me too." Zohn's smile returned. He retrieved a small piece of paper from his back pocket and unfolded it.

Pax studied the series of sharp lines and angles that were labeled in Zohn's hurried handwriting.

"This is a map of the square. This is where we are now."

He pointed to a section labeled "Merchant's Street," which was located behind the square. "Your goal is to get from where we are to the volunteer's tent just behind the stage before noon. But the streets are crowded already, so you must go soon. Alaric will be waiting at the opening of the tent wearing a black tunic with a small sun emblem sewn to it, like this one." Zohn adjusted his bag from his shoulder to reveal a small patchwork sun sewn to the inner collar of his tunic. A pattern alternating from deep crimson to marigold spiraled outward from the center, bursting into jagged rays. "It is the emblem of the Watch. We use them to identify each other when needed. This one's for you." He handed Pax a small matching patch attached to a woven thread.

Pax's heart warmed. She tied it around her neck and looked down at the little emblem now resting on her chest. She couldn't explain why the simple patchwork sun filled her with a sense of belonging. "Thank you," she said.

"Of course."

"It is time. Are you two ready?" Felyine prompted.

Pax hesitated. "Wait."

"What?" Ari asked.

She scurried to the garment rack, grabbed a copper hanger, and broke it in half. She wrapped half of the hanger around the flash drive until it resembled a pendant.

"I'm afraid if I have to hold it, I might drop it or something," she explained as she inspected the piece. It wasn't her best work, considering it was rushed, but it was interesting and certainly looked like something that might be sported by a woman in the capitol. She looked at Ari. "Clasp this around my neck, will you?"

"Impressive," he grinned and carefully secured the new piece of art at the base of her neck so that it rested on top of the small patchwork sun necklace, obscuring it from view.

She smiled, thankful her little hobby found some use in this new world. Once it was secured around her neck, she exchanged a glance with Ari for a moment. Then she nodded. "Okay, we're ready."

Zohn grabbed their hands and led them to the entrance. As they stood there, Pax swore she could see tears forming at the edges of his clouded eye. "The Mother be with you, my friends."

"And with you both," Ari replied to Zohn and Felyine, bowing his head slightly.

"Now go!" Zohn whispered.

As they exited the tent, a large crowd surrounded the merchants' tables. Mostly Terrans, but a few Travelers were scattered about, inspecting the goods as if they were exotic relics from another land. A few heads turned to face them as they walked past the table of turquoise jewelry where Dinah was seated next to the woman who must have been the owner. She did not make eye contact with them. She simply said, "Did not find what you were looking for in the back, miss?"

A moment of silence passed between them until Pax realized she was talking to her. She squared her shoulders and turned her head, then spoke with a clear, confident voice, "No, I did not."

"Sorry for the inconvenience. Good day to you, miss." Dinah bowed her head slightly as they passed.

"Good day," Pax called in return. She felt like an alien walking around in a body that didn't belong to her, the body of a more respectable person. Men and women of all ages smiled and bowed to her, and asked her how her day was. It felt strange and slightly uncomfortable, but she maintained her composure as she trudged past the merchants and onto a darker, emptier street that would lead them into the city square. She turned to find Ari walking a few paces behind with his hands behind his back.

He looked around for a moment, then whispered, "What is it?" He read the discomfort in her expression.

She hesitated. "We can do this, right?" She looked into his eyes, searching for reassurance.

He met her gaze with resolve. "Yes. You can."

Pax was reminded of the conversation she'd had with Dinah this morning. The words she had spoken rang in her mind again, and confidence blazed down her spine. She grabbed Ari's hand and squeezed it tight.

"Ouch!" He jumped.

Pax wrenched her hand free. "Oh, sorry. I forgot about the hand."

He rubbed his scar and shook his head. Then he smirked as he reached out and firmly wrapped his hand around hers.

She smiled. "Okay. I'm ready." They proceeded up the dark cobblestone street hand in hand.

As they reached the mouth of the alleyway, Ari tugged at her. "Pax," he whispered.

She turned to face him. "Yeah?"

"I almost forgot." He took the paper map from her hand and opened it in front of her. "We are going here." He pointed to the square labeled "Volunteer Tent." "But if you want to meet your mother, the workers' housing is just past here." He dragged his finger slightly to the left and pointed to an unmarked street. "So, are we going to find your mom today?"

Silence passed between them as she met his expectant gaze once again. "I . . . I don't know. I forgot my paper, and—"

"I have it." He retrieved a folded piece of paper from his jacket pocket.

"You do?"

"I grabbed it from your bag this morning before we left. I was going to talk to you about it when we got to the tent, but Dinah had other plans."

"Oh." Seconds passed. Pax's breathing quickened. Finding her mother was all she'd been able to think about since she learned of her connection to this place. But now that she faced the possibility of seeing her again, it almost felt like too much.

"Pax," Ari said softly. "You can do this."

She looked at him and smiled. "Okay. Let's find my mom."

He returned her smile. "Once we drop off the package, don't stop. Just keep walking. I'll be behind you the whole time. I'll tell you which way to go."

Ari gave her an encouraging nod, then slowed his stride and begrudgingly released his hold on her hand so he could follow behind. Pax slipped both pieces of paper into the bust of her dress, then straightened her shoulders and strode into the busy square. She was surrounded by women who were dressed in colorful garb, clinging to the arms of men in tuxedos. Some were accompanied by manservants in blue suits, like Ari, who followed dutifully behind their employers. Guilt twisted in Pax's stomach, aware of Ari's presence behind her. She hated to think of him as a servant, least of all, *her* servant. It made her ill to think of his proud, confident expression fixed on the ground so as not to make eye contact with Travelers. She pulled the slip of paper from the bust of her dress and unfolded it. She looked past the swarm of people and the mountains of pristine white buildings and shopping centers, but she couldn't locate what she was looking for. There were people crowded at every corner, looking at booths that boasted "festival specials" and one-of-a-kind items for purchase. Small drones were flying about, taking drink orders and giving directions. One flew right over her. It paused in mid-flight, projected a soft light her way, then returned in her direction.

"Is there anything I can help you with, General?"

She sighed. Not this again. She wasn't sure who, or what, this thing thought she was, but it was in her way. Then she realized that while she wasn't the "General," today she was a citizen of New America. She could use this to her advantage. "Yes, actually. Can you help me find the volunteer booth by the main stage?"

The little disk flashed a series of blinking lights as if it were thinking. "The volunteer tent, an orange clearance area, off-limits to pedestrians. General Dickinson, red clearance citizen, you may proceed. This way." It whirred overhead, leaving Pax running to keep up. She wrinkled her brow at the name the drone had called her. Did it really think she was the leader of New America? *Wait*, she thought. That was *Commander* Dickinson. Who was the general?

The burning pain of her shoe straps cutting into her heels interrupted her thoughts. She tried to ignore it and focus her energy on getting to that tent.

"Pax, it is almost time," Ari mumbled from behind.

Pax nodded and picked up the pace as she spotted the drone overhead. A bead of sweat formed on her forehead from her rapid pace, but she didn't break stride. She looked up at the clock tower above her and walked even faster. She only had ten minutes. She turned behind her to make sure Ari was still following her. He gave a slight nod to signal he was fine, and she turned to find herself almost face-to-face with a guard. She tried to shift direction, but a child ran past, shoving her out of the way as he went, and she collided with the guard and fell to the pavement.

"I'm so sorry, miss!" the guard said.

Pax's legs were shaking beneath her dress, but she tried to remain composed. "Oh, no. It's all right." Ari rushed to her side and extended an arm.

"No, boy. I will help her," the guard said firmly, blocking Ari with this arm. Ari gritted his teeth and stepped backward.

The guard extended both hands and lifted Pax up with ease, but as her feet met the ground, the map and the note she'd placed in her bust fluttered to the ground. She prayed he didn't notice, but to her chagrin, he turned his head and watched the pieces land gently on the pavement. "Here you are, miss!" He stooped down to retrieve her paper. Then, just as he went to extend the sheets, a breeze blew the folded map slightly open. "What is this?" he said, opening the sheet to inspect.

"I—I am going to meet a friend, and I did not want to get lost."

"Are you not from the city then?" He looked at her quizzically. She knew the question was loaded. If she said no, he would know she was not a Traveler. If she said yes, he would know she was lying. Sweat pooled above her brow, and she glanced up at the clock that was ticking closer and closer.

Suddenly, the little silver drone whizzed between them. "Are you all right, General Dickinson?"

The guard looked at her, then back at the drone. "This is not . . ." Then his eyes fixed on her in a way that was predatory. Pax knew they had been caught.

She looked at the man for a brief second and, without warning, snatched the sheets of paper from his open hands and bolted into the crowd. She prayed Ari had followed her lead.

"Right behind you!" he called.

"Are you all right, General Dickinson?" the drone asked again, whirring right by her ear.

"Go away!" she shouted.

"Of course, General," it replied in monotone before gliding in a different direction.

She breathed a quick sigh of relief as she forced her way through the crowd, pushing innocent bystanders from their path. She slipped a glance over her shoulder and saw the large guard gaining ground behind them. Her ankles threatened to give under the weight of her chunky heels, but she kept pushing through, coming closer to the tent that was now in sight.

A tall, thin man dressed in black stood at the head of the tent. She squinted but couldn't see a sun patch. She was too far. And the guard was now only ten, maybe twenty, feet behind. His voice boomed over the crowd, warning her to stop. Heads turned all around her in confusion, but she didn't care. She had to finish this. Her chest was burning as she sprinted closer.

The man at the tent leaned forward, squinting dubiously in her direction. She frantically pulled the flash drive from around her neck and gripped it in her hands, then pointed toward her sun emblem. She desperately hoped he was the person she was looking for. The man paused, then revealed a sun emblem from beneath his shirt and extended his hand. Without stopping, she tossed the flash drive into his palm. He gave her a single nod and disappeared behind the booth.

Pax glanced behind her to see Ari breathlessly running to catch up and the guard bursting toward them at full speed. Her heart shattered in her chest at the realization that this was the end. She would not reach the house just a few streets down. She would not find her mom. She probably wouldn't even make it out of the city today. Then she heard Ari calling from behind her.

"Pax! Listen. I've got this, okay? I'll distract him, but you cannot wait for me. You have to run."

"I'm not leaving you!"

"Yes, you are. You have to."

"No, I won't leave without you."

"Pax . . . go," he pleaded. Then he turned to face the guard, who was advancing toward them. Ari bolted, closing the space between them, and lunged for the guard's gun. But he came up short, so he punched the guard as hard as he could in the vulnerable space between his headgear and his neck. The guard gasped, trying to catch his breath, and then, to Pax's horror, another guard ran past her and wrestled Ari to the ground, wrenching his hands behind his back as he did.

Pax wanted to scream or find some way to distract the guards so Ari could get away, but before she could even think, a pair of hands grabbed her wrists and yanked them behind her back. She pulled hard against them and screamed. She tried to kick and bite, but to no avail. People were staring, but their attention was quickly diverted as the line of screens in the city square flared to life. The guard pulled her away as the massive crowd turned their attention to the stage.

The little man from yesterday walked on stage, followed by Commander Dickinson and people who Pax assumed must have been other members of the Fellowship. The little man called everyone to attention. "Welcome to the hundredth annual Founder's Festival!"

The crowd cheered wildly, allowing Pax enough distraction to slip away again, but her efforts were for naught. The guard's grip tightened and yanked her farther away from the crowd as the man rambled about what a great year it had been. The guard signaled toward the volunteer tent, and every head turned at the sound of screams coming through the speakers, echoing off the white stone buildings. The guard continued to pull her away. She fought him with every step, but soon he stopped dragging her, but still held tightly to her wrist as his eyes, too, were fixed on the screen.

Pax looked up to see an old blurry video of guards bursting down the door of a village home, the sound of gunshots exploding across the city square.

The crowd gasped in unison at the gruesome sight of a mother and her young children being gunned down by the guard. The sound of their screams washed a wave of nausea over Pax, and tears filled her eyes. She knew she should run, but all she could do was stare, entranced as violent scenes played out in front of the crowd.

Old news clippings flashed across the screen, detailing the story of the guards kidnapping young girls and women and selling them to other guards and wealthy Travelers. There were clips of factory workers passing out from exhaustion and being dragged off the floor by armed guards. There were wide shots of living conditions of Terrans inside the capitol walls, children emaciated from starvation, families being torn apart as guards separated mothers from babies. Shot after shot of the devastation caused at the hands of New America. Everything the Fellowship had worked so hard to keep hidden was laid bare for all the city to see. Pax scanned the crowd and saw Traveler women crying and covering their mouths in horror. A murmur sounded through the crowd, and she knew that no matter what followed, the Watch had succeeded today. The Travelers knew the truth about their utopia, and now they would have to face it.

Suddenly, hordes of Watch members emerged from the shadows and moved through the crowd, holding signs and chanting, "*Na estras aqival!* We are here!"

The Travelers shrank back as the crowd moved through the streets, chanting in unison. A chill rolled down Pax's spine as the sheer electricity of their powerful dissent filled the air. *We are still here.* She knew exactly what they meant, and so did the Fellowship: no matter how hard they tried to push them out, lock them up, or kill them off, they were still here, and they would always be here. She watched with pride as men and women of all ages filled the streets, demanding to be heard.

Commander Dickinson stood on the stage in the center of the square, his jaw set tight, his lips in a straight line as he overlooked the pandemonium. Suddenly, a guard in the center of the square raised his gun and fired two shots into the air. Screams peeled across the expanse. People ran through the streets, trampling over others. Chaos filled the square.

Pax was still being firmly held by the guard, who clearly didn't know how to proceed. She looked down at the guard's feet. He was wearing black steel-toed boots, similar to the ones her father wore. If she was going to get away, this was her shot. With a hard thrust, she kicked her foot back until it made contact with the space that converged between his legs. The guard crumpled to the ground, groaning in pain, but Pax did not turn around. Instead, she sprinted off, following the flow of the crowd. She located the alleyway she and Ari had used earlier to enter the square. But just as she had found a clear path, a hand yanked her backward by the back of her neck.

"Where do you think you are going?" the guard growled into her ear.

Pax cried out in pain as she was hoisted over the man's shoulder and dragged through the square. Sobs rose in her chest. She knew very well that this could be the end.

CHAPTER 21

P ax wrapped her arms across her shoulders, trying to shrink herself as small as possible. They had shoved her into the back of a holding van with twenty or thirty Watch members. Her heart pounded in her ears, her chest rising and falling as the vehicle rumbled down the road. No one looked up, no one said a word. Someone tapped her shoulder and she turned to find it was Kitara.

Tears filled her eyes as she met his weary gaze. "Kitara," she whispered. A few heads turned to watch the reunion.

"So, you made it." He smiled. His lip was cut, and a bead of blood streamed down his face, but he still seemed like himself.

"I'm so happy you're okay. Where are they taking us?"

"To the Fellowship's headquarters." He clenched his jaw. "Have you seen Ari?"

Her chest tightened again, and she shook her head. "We got separated."

"He must have escaped," he reassured.

The van rolled to a stop. Footsteps approached the vehicle, and then the back doors flung open, assaulting them with harsh sunlight and the shouts of more than a dozen guards demanding them to get in line. As they stood in a line, their wrists were cuffed one by one, and they were guided into a massive stone building. The front step was lined with columns. The stone engraving on the front read: "Justice Will Prevail." Under different circumstances, Pax might have found the irony in that statement humorous. There were groups of prisoners filtering out of other vehicles and being assembled into a line on the building's steps like lambs to the slaughter. Behind her, someone cleared their throat. When she turned around, her chest heaved a sigh of relief when she saw Ari. They exchanged glances for a moment, and he nodded at her. It was a gesture of reassurance, though he had none to give.

They were ushered in rows into the back of the building. The guards pushed them and shouted curses as they walked down a narrow hallway. Soon, they were lined outside the doorway of what appeared to be a booking room. Beyond the desk, past a sealed office area, was a line of holding cells. Pax stood in wait with the rest of the prisoners as the guards paced back and forth, glaring at them.

Just then, a woman turned the corner, and a guard ran to meet her. "General Dickinson!" he shouted.

Pax perked up at the sound of the familiar name. She craned her head, trying to see the interaction. Was this the woman the drones confused her with? The woman's face was blocked by the towering guard who was speaking to her, and she returned his speech with hushed tones. Pax tried to make out the gist of the conversation. She only briefly heard the woman say, "We will just have to pack as many as we can into the cells and figure out what to do after questioning."

Pax's stomach twisted at the thought of being questioned by these people.

The woman turned to face them for only the briefest moment, and in that fraction of a second, a pair of cool, gray eyes met Pax's gaze. Her heart sputtered frantically, and her body grew warm.

"General Dickinson," she whispered. A sudden realization struck her like lightning. The woman had sleek black hair, olive skin, and those stark gray eyes. Eyes that held the memories of another lifetime. Eyes that looked just like her own.

Suddenly, it made sense. The reason the bots were confusing her with someone else, the reason she felt she was meant to be here. She didn't know what she was doing, but it was as if she was possessed by another person when her feet forced her toward the woman, and her mouth opened without her permission and shouted, "General Dickinson!"

The woman's sleek black bob flipped over her shoulder as she turned to face Pax. When their eyes met again, Pax was more certain than anything that this was the woman from her memories. Her chest felt tight, and her mouth went dry. Pax spent the past ten years dreaming about the day she would see her mother again. Playing out every scenario in her mind. She thought about what she would say, what she would do. But now that they were face-to-face, she was frozen. It wasn't supposed to happen like this. Part of Pax wanted to shrink back, but as she felt the guard pulling her back to the line, she knew she couldn't let herself come this close just to lose her mom again.

She fought against the hands of the guard. She needed to find a way to communicate who she was without fully giving herself away. She didn't want to risk revealing herself as the intruder from beyond the wall and getting shot where she stood.

Suddenly, she heard Ari's voice from behind her. "Pax," he whispered. "You need to get back."

"Listen to your friend, girl," the guard warned as General Dickinson turned again to leave.

Pax's brain scrambled before remembering the note. She elbowed the guard in the stomach. He immediately released her, and she ran forward as the woman opened a door behind the holding area. "I have your Ohio State sweatshirt!" Pax shouted.

The woman paused and turned to her again. Their eyes met for one excruciatingly long moment before she finally said, "I don't know what you mean."

Pax's face fell and grew hot as she allowed the guard to pull her away. Ari had followed at her heels, and the guard pulled him back as well.

"Take them to block E," the woman commanded the guard.

The guard dragged Pax and Ari away from the crowd that the guards were now filing like animals into the line of holding cells. Pax was terrified and exhausted, but mostly she was crushed. She had been so sure that woman was her mother.

Two guards led them down a dimly lit stone hallway that vaguely reminded Pax of the shelter back in the village, but instead of being warm and peaceful, this long corridor was cold, musty, and threatening. When they reached a hall labeled with a steel sign engraved with the letter *E*, the guard unlocked a door and shoved her and Ari into a room with only a table and four chairs.

Pax steadied herself against the table, still wobbly from the force of the guard's strength. She unbuckled the straps of her heels, which had cut into her ankles, making them bleed.

"Pax," Ari said. "What were you thinking?"

She faced him, placing the pink wig on the table next to her jewelry. She ran a hand through her hair as it fell down her shoulders. "I don't know. I just . . . I was so sure." Her voice wavered and she crossed her arms over her chest.

Ari gathered her into an embrace. "I'm sorry she was not who you thought she was."

Pax buried her head into his arm and wept heavy sobs. "What are they going to do?"

"I don't know, but I swear I'll get you out."

She shook her head. "You can't. There's nowhere for me to go."

He sighed, resigned for now, and sank further into their embrace.

Suddenly, the door burst open and they jumped. General Dickinson stood in front of them, cool and collected. She smoothed a hand over her blunted bob, then turned to the guards and assured them, "Just stand outside. They are children." She chuckled. "I think I can manage."

The guard nodded and stepped out the door. The general locked the door behind him, then calmly crossed the room and flipped off the switch on a camera mounted in the corner of the room. Pax's stomach sank. She wasn't sure how she had missed the only camera in the room, or what was going to happen now that there was no one else to watch.

The general turned to her, and her cool, serene expression faded. Her eyes went wild, and she stormed toward Pax. "What were you thinking?"

Pax stepped backward until she pressed against the table. She wasn't sure what the woman meant, so she just opened her mouth and stuttered, "I . . ."

"What are you doing here, Paxton?" General Dickinson demanded.

Paxton. Pax's eyes widened and her mouth dropped. "Oh my God. You're my mother."

The general looked at her, emotionless. "And *you* are not supposed to be here."

Pax took in the woman in front of her. She was as beautiful as ever, but her eyes held none of the warmth and compassion of the woman from Pax's memories. This woman was cold, severe, intense, and seemed to have no soft spot for her daughter. Pax's eyes watered, and she looked down at the floor.

"You should not have come back after the warnings went out about you."

Pax looked up at her mother again. "You mean you knew it was me this whole time?" her voice quivered.

"Of course I did! You think I wouldn't recognize my own daughter?"

"You knew I was here, and you didn't say anything or try to find me?"

"No, I didn't. Because you are not supposed to be here. You are supposed to be in Ohio with your father living a normal life."

The tears flowed freely now as her last sliver of hope was dashed. "So, all this time, you mean you really just didn't . . . want me?"

General Dickinson stepped forward, tentatively extending a hand toward her, but then lowered it back to her side and clenched it into a fist. "It's not that I didn't want you." Her voice softened slightly. "It's just that my life is complicated, and I cannot be a mother to you here. And if my father had ever learned that you existed . . . I don't know what he would have done. So, I did what I thought I had to do. I kept you where you would be safe."

Pax laughed humorlessly. "Safe? You thought I would be safe with an abusive alcoholic?" her voice raised.

General Dickinson's eyes softened. "Abusive? I . . . the Victor I knew was a good man. He had a house, a job. I thought he could give you a stable life."

"Well, I guess he's not what you thought."

"Paxton, I had no idea. When I left New America, I was pregnant and terrified, and Vick was kind, and he lived with his mother, and I thought when the time was right, she could take care of you."

"Well, Grandma died right after you left, so it was just me and Dad." Pax trailed off mid-sentence, her brain finally catching up to what her mother had just said. "Wait . . . you said you left New America *pregnant*?"

Her mother shook her head and squeezed the space between her eyebrows. "Yes. I was pregnant with you before I left. Victor is not your father. He only thinks he is."

Pax's gaze flickered to the corner of the room where Ari stood taking in the information. His shocked expression mirrored her own. She turned to her mother, speechless. "So, you mean my real dad is—"

"He was from Terra. His name was Torian, and he was from one of the Nomadesales villages. He worked for our family, and he and I fell in love. I knew if anyone found out we were together, he would face serious consequences because I was the commander's daughter. So, we ran away together and tried to live on our own, but we were young and naive. When the commander found me and your father, he ordered him to be killed on sight. He demanded that I come home, but instead I traveled to Ohio. I fled to keep you alive, so I will not apologize for what I did or how I did it. Not to you," she said fiercely.

Pax was trying to wrap her head around the flood of new information. "So, I'm . . ."

"You are half-Traveler, half-Terran."

Pax's body was shaking. She thought about her dreams for the first time in months. How her body was fighting against itself every moment she was on Earth. Of course it was, because she was not meant to be there. Before she ever knew it, her very consciousness was trying to tell her that Terra was her home.

"And now you must go."

Pax knitted her brows together. "You mean you are letting us go free?"

Her mother looked at her as if she had said something ridiculous. She spoke slowly, "I am telling you to go back to Earth."

Pax shook her head. "*No.* I'm not going back. I can't go back there."

"And why not?"

"Because when I left, Vick was going to send me away. When I refused, he snapped. He *hurt* me. And now you're telling me he's not even really my father? That I don't even belong there? I'm not going back."

She thought for a moment. "I don't think you understand what I am telling you. Your grandfather, the commander . . . he murdered your father right in front of me. If you think for even a second that he wouldn't kill you, too, if he knew about you, you are mistaken. I know your situation with Victor is not ideal, but perhaps you could live with a friend—"

"It's not that simple," Pax cut her off.

"Enough!" She pounded her fist against the table. "You were smart enough to sneak through Terra unseen for weeks. You are smart enough to take care of yourself."

"*I'm not going.*" Suddenly, this scene felt all too familiar. She thought about the last exchange she had with her father— Victor. The look in her mother's eyes was almost the same.

Her mother exhaled loudly. The calm expression she had worn when they first met returned, and it chilled Pax to the bone. "Let me make this clear. You will leave or I will take you myself."

Pax's mouth dropped. "You can do that?"

"It seems you don't know much about the gift. Good. Keep it that way. You won't be needing it."

"No, I'm not going. I don't care what I have to do. You can take me, but I'll just keep coming back."

Her mother cleared her throat. "Perhaps I'm not making myself clear. If you stay here, you will be tried as a criminal. You and your friend here ripped out your trackers and played accomplice to an act of treason. Commander Dickinson will have you tortured until you name every name and betray every person you love in that damned village, then he will have you thrown in prison for the rest of your life."

"I thought the Travelers were supposed to be peaceful. What happened to that?" Pax asked disdainfully.

"Do you know how you keep peace? You eliminate threats. That is my job, and the commander will expect me to carry out my job regardless of who you are to me. If you will not go to save yourself, then go to save him." She pointed a slender hand at Ari.

Pax's eyes widened in terror. "What?"

"Every major player in this stunt is being considered a threat to our national security, which means they will be prosecuted to the greatest extent of our laws. He will most likely be killed."

Pax returned her mother's gaze with fire. "You disgust me."

"I do not operate under my own power. This is what happens to those who threaten the capitol," she said, emotionless.

"If I go, what will happen to Ari?"

"He will be questioned, and since I can tell he is most likely not the brains behind this little spectacle, I will make sure he is released to live out his life under the close monitor of the guard, as will the rest of the villagers who participated."

Pax looked at Ari, and his golden eyes met hers. "Pax," he breathed. "It's okay. I said you would get out, and this is your way out," he reassured.

Her eyes filled with tears. "I'm so sorry."

He shook his head. "Do not be sorry. Just . . . find a way to be happy. You know, in Ohio."

She laughed through her tears, then turned back to her mother. "The only thing I'm taking comfort in right now is that I will never have to see your face again."

Her mother blinked, unmoved by the insult. "If you want me to make good on my promise, I have one more thing to ask."

"What else could you possibly want?"

"You were given what seems to be a very important role in this little display. It must have been assigned to you by a very important person, was it not?"

Pax crossed her arms and said nothing as her mother inched closer.

"We have been monitoring the rise of the Watch for some time now. We know it operates out of Rehama. We just have not been able to trace it back to a specific person, and the people we have questioned are not connected enough to know who it is."

Pax's stomach sank.

"Now, much to my disappointment, you have decided to run with a very dangerous crowd here."

"You don't know the first thing about them," Pax spat.

"That is true," her mother admitted. "But you do. And you will tell me."

Pax glared at her. "I'd rather die here."

"Well, that won't be happening, as you and I already have an arrangement. But if you can't come up with a name, I might just forget to hold up my end." She gestured to the guards that were still holding Ari by the arms, the one to his left raised the barrel of his gun to Ari's temple once more. "After all, the Rehamans are such violent people. And your friend here, Ari, right? Well, he's such an impulsive little thing, isn't he? Whose to say he didn't lash out at me first?"

Pax looked over at Ari. His eyes were cast to the floor and

his shoulders sagged. She felt as helpless as he looked. This was too much. She was only sixteen. She should be back on Earth, worrying about things like what college to go to and whether or not Zeke was going to ask her to prom. She didn't deserve this . . . but neither did Ari. Neither did any of the kids in Terra who were forced to grow up too fast, and fight the battles of adults too soon.

"How can I even be sure you'll make good on your promise if I go?" she muttered quietly.

"Pax, no. Please don't do this," Ari said.

"You can't. But I can tell you for certain that if you don't help me, he will be tortured, and he will die here in a cell before the week's end." She summoned the guards into the room. "Take the boy."

Tears spilled down Pax's face, and Ari cried out as a guard wrenched his arms behind his back, while another guard forced him to his knees and pointed the barrel of a gun at the base of his skull. Pax remembered the oath she took, the oath she swore to uphold or else risk exile. If she gave this information, she wasn't just betraying the Watch, she was ensuring that she could never return.

"Pax, just go! Don't tell them anything. Just leave and don't look back!" Ari shouted.

She stood frozen, tears flooding her vision.

"Pax!" he shouted. "Please go!"

"I can't! I can't do this to you."

"Yes, you can. You have to, you made an oath! For the Watch! Just go, please!" he begged through tears as a guard pointed the barrel of his gun to Ari's temple. Fear burned in his golden eyes. His body shook, and his teeth were clattering.

Pax knew what she had to do. She looked over at her mother and nodded.

A bone-chilling smile curled at the corners of her mother's lips. She motioned toward the guards.

Ari's mouth dropped. "Pax!" He shouted after her, his voice breaking as the guards dragged him out of the room and back toward the cell block.

Pax's lip quivered. The sound of his voice, his broken-hearted betrayal, echoed in her ears as she closed her eyes and called forth images of home. She could do this. She could leave. It would be hell, but she could do this. She had to save him, even if it meant betraying the Watch.

As she felt her body begin to dissipate, she called to her mother: "Felyine. The leader's name is Felyine."

"New America thanks you for your loyalty, Pax," the general said.

Pax looked into her mother's slate-gray eyes one more time. "I hope I never see you again."

"Yes, me too," her mother replied. Pax could swear there was a hint of sadness in her voice.

Pax's heart felt as if it had crashed down through her toes and shattered around her, but she couldn't stay to see the wreckage.

Her body gave way to nothingness, and she succumbed to the void.

ACKNOWLEDGMENTS

I want to thank my family. Joshua, your belief in me has carried me through this process. Your support and the sacrifices you have made to help make my dream possible is beyond comprehension. Hazel and Phoenix, you are the light of my life and everything I do is for you. I love you all so much.

To my brother, Regan Adcock. You were my beta reader, my sounding board, and the very best support system through this twelve-year process. Thank you for championing my dreams and being one of my all-time favorite people.

Dr. Rose DePaula-Cox, when we were in high school, you read every short story, every poem, and every manuscript I pushed your way. Your encouragement and support pushed me to believe in myself. If it weren't for you, I would have never started this book that day in English class. Thank you for sparking this dream in me.

To the group of powerhouse women lovingly known as "the liberal heathens." I never could have imagined that a group message formed at the height of the pandemic would become a consistent source of strength, encouragement, and support. Watching you all pursue your dreams inspired me to do the same. Thank you for your enthusiasm of this project and all the conversations that inspired the themes in this book.

To my editor, Andrea Vande Vorde, thank you for putting up with an endless parade of comma splices and grammatical errors, and doing it all with grace and compassion. Your expert eye is exactly what I needed, and I am so thankful for your work on this project.

A special thanks to Terri Leidich and everyone on the Boutique of Quality Books team. Your efforts through every step of this process are so greatly appreciated, and your wisdom and experience have been truly invaluable. Thank you for taking a chance on me.

ABOUT THE AUTHOR

Melissa Day is a debut novelist from Baton Rouge, Louisiana. She is married to her best friend and is the mother of two very active toddlers. As a Louisiana native, her true passion is great food, great parties, and good people. Her love for writing was inspired by all of the strong female characters she read in YA books as a teenager. She hopes to write characters and stories that well represent women, the LGBTQ+ community, and diverse cultures, because she believes every young reader deserves to see themselves in the stories they read.